Praise for Michael Chabon's
The Mysteries of Pittsburgh

"There's a lot of talk about this novel. It's almost as if there's going to be a great big literary bash. The guys who will be on the guest list are a cinch. Tom Sawyer and Huck Finn and Holden Caulfield . . . and now, from *The Mysteries of Pittsburgh*, Art Bechstein."

—*Washington Post Book World*

"The quiet lushness of both the concept and the language are typical of Chabon's fresh, convincing style. What makes the novel extraordinary, however, is the exactness and care with which he manipulates such images and patterns of imagery. . . . Making a reader experience again a sense of endless possibility is one of the most satisfying and quintessentially American things an American bildungsroman can do. Chabon's *The Mysteries of Pittsburgh* adds to the canon one of the rare novels actually able to do it."

—*Village Voice*

"Remarkable. . . . What makes this book—and Chabon—worth our attention is [that] Chabon has chosen not merely to record all the ills of an oversexed, overindulged generation with nowhere to go but to bed or to a bar; he has chosen to explore, to enter this world and try to find what makes it work, why love and friendship choose to visit some, deny others."

—*Los Angeles Times*

T·H·E

MYSTERIES OF

PITTSBURGH

◆

MICHAEL CHABON

HARPER **PERENNIAL**

HARPER ● PERENNIAL

Grateful acknowledgment is made for permission to use the following:

"Goody Two Shoes," by A. Ant and M. Pirroni. Copyright © 1982 by EMI Music Publishing, Ltd. All rights for the U.S. and Canada controlled by Colgems—EMI Music, Inc.

"Oh What a Beautiful Morning," by Richard Rodgers and Oscar Hammerstein II. Copyright © 1943 by Williamson Music Co., copyright renewed. All rights administered by Chappell & Co., Inc. International copyright secured. All rights reserved. Used by permission.

"Three Airs," by Frank O'Hara. From *The Collected Poems of Frank O'Hara,* edited by Donald Allen. Copyright © 1971. Reprinted with permission of Alfred A. Knopf, Inc.

A hardcover edition of this book was published in 1988 by William Morrow and Company, Inc.

P.S.™ is a trademark of HarperCollins Publishers.

HarperCollins books may be purchased for educational, business, or sales promotional use. For information please write: Special Markets Department, HarperCollins Publishers, 10 East 53rd Street, New York, NY 10022.

First Perennial edition published 1989.

Reissued in Perennial 2000.

First Harper Perennial edition published 2005.

Library of Congress Cataloging-in-Publication Data is available upon request.

ISBN-10: 0-06-079059-8

ISBN-13: 978-0-06-079059-2

08 09 OFF/RRD 20 19 18 17 16

To Lollie

We have shared out like thieves
the amazing treasure of nights and days

—J. L. BORGES

THE
MYSTERIES OF
PITTSBURGH

1

ELEVATOR GOING UP

♦   ♦   ♦

At the beginning of the summer I had lunch with my father, the gangster, who was in town for the weekend to transact some of his vague business. We'd just come to the end of a period of silence and ill will—a year I'd spent in love with and in the same apartment as an odd, fragile girl whom he had loathed, on sight, with a frankness and a fury that were not at all like him. But Claire had moved out the month before. Neither my father nor I knew what to do with our new freedom.

"I saw Lenny Stern this morning," he said. "He asked after you. You remember your Uncle Lenny."

"Sure," I said, and I thought for a second about Uncle Lenny, juggling three sandwich halves in the back room of his five-and-dime in the Hill District a million years ago.

I was nervous and drank more than I ate; my father carefully dispatched his steak. Then he asked me what my plans were for the summer, and in the flush of some strong emotion or other I said, more or less: It's the beginning of the summer and I'm standing in the lobby of a thousand-story grand hotel, where a bank of elevators a mile long and an endless red row of monkey attendants in gold braid wait

9

to carry me up, up, up through the suites of moguls, of spies, and of starlets, to rush me straight to the zeppelin mooring at the art deco summit, where they keep the huge dirigible of August tied up and bobbing in the high winds. On the way to the shining needle at the top I will wear a lot of neckties, I will buy five or six works of genius on 45 rpm, and perhaps too many times I will find myself looking at the snapped spine of a lemon wedge at the bottom of a drink. I said, "I anticipate a coming season of dilated time and of women all in disarray."

My father told me that I was overwrought and that Claire had had an unfortunate influence on my speech, but something in his face said that he understood. That night he flew back to Washington, and the next day, for the first time in years, I looked in the newspaper for some lurid record of the effect of his visit, but of course there was none. He wasn't that kind of gangster.

Claire had moved out on the thirtieth of April, taking with her all of the Joni Mitchell and the complete soundtrack recording of the dialogue from Zeffirelli's *Romeo and Juliet*, a four-record set, which she knew by heart. At some point toward the sexless and conversationless finale of *Art and Claire*, I had informed her that my father said she suffered from dementia praecox. My father's influence upon me was strong, and I believed this. I later told people that I had lived with a crazy woman, and also that I had had enough of *Romeo and Juliet*.

The last term in my last year of college sputtered out in a week-long fusillade of examinations and sentimental alcoholic conferences with professors whom I knew I would not really miss, even as I shook their hands and bought them beers. There was, however, a last paper on Freud's letters to Wilhelm Fliess, for which I realized I would have to make one exasperating last visit to the library, the dead core of my education, the white, silent kernel of every empty Sunday I had spent trying to ravish the faint charms of the study of economics, my sad and cynical major.

So one day at the beginning of June I came around the concrete corner that gave way to the marbleized steps of the library. Walking the length of brown ground-floor windows, I looked into them, at the reflection of my walk, my loafers, my mess of hair. Then I felt guilty, because at our lunch my father, the amateur psychologist, had called me a "devout narcissist" and had said he worried that I might be "doomed to terminal adolescence." I looked away.

There were very few students using the building this late in the term, which was officially over. A few pink-eyed and unshaven pages loitered behind the big checkout counter, staring out at the brown sun through the huge tinted windows. I clicked loudly in my loafers across the tile floor. As I called for the elevator to the Freud section, a girl looked up. She was in a window; there was an aqua ribbon in her hair. The window was a kind of grille, as in a bank, at the far end of the corridor in which I stood waiting for the elevator, and the girl in the window held a book in one hand and a thin strip of wire in the other. We looked at each other for perhaps three seconds, then I turned back to face the suddenly illuminated red Up arrow, the muscles in my neck warming and tightening. As I stepped into the car

I heard her say four distinct and strange words to someone with her, there behind the bars, whom I hadn't seen.

"That was him, Sandy," she said.

I was sure of it.

Freud's letters to Fliess make much of the near-cosmic interaction of the human nose with matters of sexual health. Work on my paper, therefore, proved to be relatively entertaining, and I wrote for a long time, stopping rarely to drink from the humming fountain or even simply to look up from my hilarious scholarship. Late in the long afternoon I saw a young man looking at me from behind his book. Its title was in Spanish and on its cover there was a bloody painting of a knife, a woman in a mantilla, and a half-undressed brown strongman. I smiled at him and lifted an eyebrow in skeptical salute to what must be a pretty racy book. It looked as though he might keep his eyes on me awhile longer, but I told myself that one of those kinds of exchanges a day, and that with a woman, was excitement enough, and I dropped back to the nose, nexus of all human desire.

When I put down my pencil it was almost eight o'clock. I stood up with a habitual silent "Oy" and went over to one of the tall, narrow windows that looked out over the plaza below. The sky was whitish brown in the twilight through the smoked glass. Small groups of kids called and ran on the concrete down below, obviously heading somewhere, in a way that made me think of getting something to eat. At the far left, toward the front of the building, I saw a flashing light. I gathered up my books and papers and noticed that the Spanish Potboiler Guy had left. Where he'd been sitting there were a small empty can of pineapple juice and a little scrap of origami that was like a dog or a saxophone.

Going down in the elevator, I thought about the Girl Behind Bars, but at the ground floor everything was closed up, and an articulated wooden shutter had been pulled down behind the grille. There was one disheveled dramat type slumped behind the checkout counter now, and as I went clicking through the theft detectors he waved me away without looking up.

I stood feeling the air and smoking a nice cigarette for a little while, then heard the loud crack of police voices on radio and saw again that flashing light, off to the left. Little bunches of people were there, balanced between walking and sticking around. I walked over and came through the outer ring of people.

In the center of everything stood a young woman, her head slightly bowed, whispering. To her left a fallen cop with a cut on his face pulled himself to his knees and then tried to stand, gesturing with unconvincing menace toward a huge boy. To the girl's right, across the impromptu arena we formed, stood another cop, his arms struggling to enlace those of another huge boy, who swore at the policemen, at the girl, at his enraged twin who faced him, and at all of us who watched.

"Let me go, you fucker," he said. "You bitch, you fucker, you assholes, I'll kill you! Let me go!"

He was tremendous and fit, and he tore away from his captor with a short backward wrench that dropped the tiny blue cop to the concrete. The two boys came closer to each other, until they both stood within arm's length of the woman. I looked at her again. She was slender and blond, with a green-eyed, small-nosed, nondescript kind of hill-billy face and a flowery skirt. She looked down, at the sidewalk, at nothing. Her thin ankles wobbled on four-inch spikes and her lips moved soundlessly. The two cops were both on their feet now, billy clubs drawn. There was a strange momentary lull in the action, as though the police and the giants were waiting for some soft command from the dazed woman before grabbing for the various difficult things they had assembled to grab. It was suddenly cool and almost night. A new siren threatened and grew from the distance. The girl looked up, listening, and then turned toward the boy who had just freed himself. She pushed against his great chest and clung.

"Larry," she said.

The other boy undid his fists and looked at the two of them, then turned toward us, with tears in his eyes and an uncomprehending look on his face.

"Too bad, man," someone said. "She picked Larry."

"Good going, Larry," said another.

It was done; people clapped. The battered policemen rushed over, the reinforcements squealed up, Larry kissed his girl.

"One more Pittsburgh heartbreak," said a voice right beside me. It was Spanish Potboiler.

"Hey," I said. "Yes. Right. There's one for every kielbasa on Forbes Avenue."

We moved off together in the general chattering retreat of those who weren't interested in seeing the actual arrests.

"When did you come in?" he asked. There certainly was

sarcasm in his tone, yet at the same time I thought it seemed as though he'd been impressed or even shaken by what he'd seen. He had short, white-blond hair, pale eyes, and a day's growth of beard, which lent his boyish face a kind of grown-up decadence.

"At the good part," I said.

He laughed, one perfect ha.

"It was crazy," I continued. "I mean, did you see that? I never understand how people can be perfectly frank all over the sidewalk like that, in public."

"Some people," he said, "really know how to have a good time."

Even the first time that I heard Arthur Lecomte employ this phrase, I already had the faint impression that it functioned for him as a slogan. There was a radio-announcer reverb to his voice as he pronounced it.

We exchanged names and shook hands over the fact that we were both named Arthur; meeting a namesake is one of the most delicate and most brief of surprises.

"But they call me Art," I said.

"*They* call me Arthur," he said.

At Forbes Avenue, Arthur started left, his head half turned to the right, toward me, his right shoulder lingering slightly behind him, as though it waited for me to catch up, or was reaching back to hook me and carry me along. He wore a white evening shirt, still brilliant despite the weakening daylight, of an extravagant, baggy, vintage cut, which billowed out over the top of his blue jeans. He stopped, and seemed on the petulant point of tapping his foot impatiently.

I hadn't a doubt that he was gay, that he was taking advantage of our having crossed paths to make good his short initial attempt in the library, and that he probably supposed that I was as homosexual as he. People made this mistake.

"Which way were you going, anyway, before you ran into Jules and Jim back there?" he said.

"Jules and Larry," I said. "Um, I have to have dinner with a friend—my old girlfriend." I bit it off hard at the "girl" and spat it at him.

He came back to me, extending his hand, and we shook for the second time.

"Well," he said. "I work in the library. Acquisitions. I'd be glad if you'd stop by." He spoke stiffly, with an odd courtesy.

"Sure," I said. I thought momentarily of Claire, and the dinner she might be preparing for me, if only I hadn't invented it, and if only the mere sight of me didn't make her stomach collapse in distress.

"What time are you supposed to be at your friend's?" Arthur asked, as though we had not shaken hands at all and I were not yet free.

"Eight-thirty," I lied.

"Does she live very far from here?"

"Near Carnegie-Mellon."

"Ah, well, it's hardly eight o'clock. Why don't we have a beer? She won't care. She's your old girlfriend, anyway." His emphasis lay on the syllable before "girl."

I had to choose between drinking with a fag and saying something inexpert, such as "Uh—I mean eight-fifteen" or

"Well, gee, I dunno." He made me afraid of seeming clumsy or dull. It was not as though I had any firm or fearful objection to homosexuals; in certain books by gay writers I thought I had appreciated the weight and secret tremble of their thoughts; and I admired their fine clothes and shrill hard wit, their weapon. It was only that I felt keen to avoid, as they say, a misunderstanding. And yet just that morning, while watching a procession of scar-faced, big-breasted, red-wrapped laughing African girls tap-dance down Ward Street, hadn't I for the fiftieth time berated myself for my failure to encounter, to risk, to land myself in novel and incomprehensible situations—to misunderstand, in fact? And so, with a fatalistic shrug, I went to drink one beer.

2

A Free Atom

◆　　　　　　　◆　　　　　　　◆

My father, solid, pink, handsome, used to say that he was a professional golfer and an amateur painter. His actual career was knowledge I was not fully permitted until the age of thirteen, when it was conferred on me along with the right to read from the Torah. I had always liked his watercolors, orange, pale, reminiscent of Arizona, but not as much as I liked the cartoons he could draw—never if one asked or begged him to, not even if one cried, but when he was suddenly seized, magically, perversely, with the urge to draw a picture of a top-hatted clown on one's bedroom chalkboard, in seven colors.

His comings and goings inside the house, accompanied always by the stink of cigars and the creaking of whatever piece of furniture he had chosen to receive the weight of his gangster body, were a great source of mystery and specula- tion for me on those nights when we'd both be up with insomnia, the family disease; I resented the fact that be- cause he was old, he could roam around, painting, reading books, watching television, while I had to stay in bed, try- ing brutally to make myself fall asleep. Some Sunday morn- ings I would come downstairs, very early, to find him, having already surmounted the titanic Sunday *Post*, doing his sit-ups on the back porch, awake for the twenty-ninth or thirtieth straight hour.

Before the day of my bar mitzvah I was certain that, with his incredible but rarely displayed powers of mind and body, my father had a secret identity. I realized that the secret identity would have to *be* my father. Hundreds of times I looked in his closets, in the basement, under furniture, in the trunk of the car, on a fruitless hunt for his multicolored superhero (or supervillain) costume. He suspected my suspicions, I think, and every couple of months would encourage them, by demonstrating that he could drive our car without touching the steering wheel, or by unerringly trapping, with three fingers, flies and even bumblebees in midflight, or by hammering nails into a wall with his bare fist.

He'd been on the point of telling me the truth about his work, he said much later, on the day of my mother's funeral, six months shy of my thirteenth birthday. But his half-brother, my Uncle Sammy "Red" Weiner, made him stick to his original plan to wait until I put on a tallis for the first time. So instead of telling me the truth about his job on that bright, empty Saturday morning, as we sat at the kitchen table with the sugar bowl between us, he told me, softly, that she had died in an automobile accident. I remember staring at the purple flowers painted on the sugar bowl. The funeral I hardly recall. The next morning, when I asked my father, as usual, for the funny papers and the sports page, an odd look crossed his face, and he looked away. "The paper didn't come today," he said. During the night Marty had moved in. He had often come to stay with us in the past, and I liked him—he knew a poem about Christy Mathewson, which he would recite as often as I asked, and once, for an instant, I had seen the gun he wore inside his jacket, under his left arm. He was a thin little man who always wore a tie and a hat.

Marty never moved out. He would drive me to school in the morning, or sometimes take me on sudden vacations to Ocean City, and I did not have to go to school at all. It would be a long time before I knew the circumstances of the abrupt removal from the world of my singing mother, but I must have sensed that I had been lied to, because I never asked about her, or hardly even mentioned her, ever again.

When, on the afternoon of my bar mitzvah, my father first revealed to me his true profession, I enthusiastically declared that I wanted to follow in his glamorous footsteps. This made him frown. He had long ago resolved to buy me college and "unsoiled hands." He had been the first Bechstein to get a degree, but had been drawn into the Family (the Maggios of Baltimore) by the death of a crucial uncle, and by the possibilities that had just begun to open up for a man with a business degree and a C.P.A. He lectured me sternly—almost angrily. I had, after years of searching, finally discovered the nature of my father's work, and he forbade me to admire him for it. I saw that it inspired in him an angry shame, so I came to associate it with shame, and with the advent of manhood, which seemed to separate me, in two different ways, from both my parents. I never afterward had the slightest desire to tell his secret to any of my friends; indeed, I ardently concealed it.

My first thirteen years, years of ecstatic, uncomfortable, and speechless curiosity, followed by six months of disaster and disappointment, convinced me somehow that every new friend came equipped with a terrific secret, which one day, deliberately, he would reveal; I need only maintain a discreet, adoring, and fearful silence.

When I met Arthur Lecomte, I immediately settled in to await his revelation. I formulated a hundred questions about homosexuality, which I didn't ask. I wanted to know how he'd decided that he was gay, and if he ever felt that his decision was a mistake. I would very much have liked to know this. Instead I drank beers, quite a few of them, and I began my patient vigil.

Perhaps five seconds after I realized that we were standing on a loud street corner, surrounded by Mohawks and black men with frankfurters, and were no longer in the bar with a strangling ashtray and a voided pitcher between us, a green Audi convertible with an Arab in it pulled up and honked at us.

"Mohammad, right?"

"Hey, Mohammad!" Arthur shouted, running around to the passenger's seat and diving into the red splash of interior.

"Hey, Mohammad," I said. I still stood on the sidewalk. I had drunk very much very quickly and wasn't following the action of the film too well. Everything seemed impossibly fast and lit and noisy.

"Come on!" shouted the blond head and the black head. I remembered that we were going to a party.

"Go on, asshole," someone behind me said.

"Arthur!" I said. "Did I have a backpack at some earlier point this evening?"

"What?" he shouted.

"My backpack!" I was already on my way back into the bar. Everything was darker, quieter; glancing at the Pirates game flashing silently, in awful color, over the bald head of the bartender, I ran to our booth and grabbed my sack. It was better, there in the ill light, and I stopped; I felt as though I had forgotten to breathe for several minutes.

"My backpack," I said to the ganged-up waitresses who chewed gum and drank coffee at a table by the dead jukebox.

"Uh huh," they said. "Ha ha." In Pittsburgh, perhaps more than anywhere else in our languid nation, a barmaid does not care.

On the way out again, I suddenly saw everything clearly: Sigmund Freud painting cocaine onto his septum, the rising uproar of the past hour and a half, the idling Audi full of rash behavior that lay ahead, the detonating summer; and because it was a drunken perception, it was perfect, entire, and lasted about half a second.

I walked out to the car. They said to get in, get in. Between the backs of the bucket seats and the top of the trunk was a space the size of a toaster.

"Go and fit yourself there," said Mohammad, craning around to shine his brown movie-star face into my eyes. "Tell him, make the boot a seat, Arthur." He spoke with a French accent.

"The boot?" I threw in my backpack. "Now there's no room for me," I said.

"The trunk. He calls it the boot," said Arthur, smiling. Lecomte had a hard, sarcastic smile, which made only rare appearances, chiefly when he meant to persuade or to ridicule, or both. Sometimes it surfaced only to give a kind of cruel warning, come far too late, of the plans that he had made for you, a genuine smile of false reassurance, the smile Montresor cast at Fortunato, hand on the trowel in his pocket. "You have to sit on the edge of the trunk, where the roof folds up."

And this, though I have always been easily terrified, I did.

We pulled into the heavy Saturday-night traffic on Forbes Avenue, and perhaps because of the incident I'd witnessed earlier, the welter of taillights around me—so near and red!—reminded me of police sirens.

"Is this legal, what I'm doing?" I yelled into the overwhelming slipstream.

Arthur turned around. His hair blew across his face, and the cigarette he had lit threw bright ash, like a sparkler.

"No!" he shouted. "So don't fall out! Mohammad has a lot of tickets already!"

The people in the cars that managed to pull alongside the Audi gave me the same shake of the head and roll of the eyes that I myself had often given other young drunks in fast cars. I decided not to think about them, which proved to be a simple thing, and stared into the wind, and into the steady flow of streetlights. Gradually, lathed and smoothed by my five hasty drinks, I recognized only the speed Mohammad expertly gathered, and the whine of the tires on the blacktop, so fragrant and near my head. Then the wind died as we fell into a red light at Craig and stopped.

I took out my cigarettes and lit one in the momentary stillness. Arthur turned again, looking slightly surprised not to find me livid, sick, or half-unconscious.

"Hey, Arthur," I said.

"Hey what?"

"You work in the library, right?"

"Yes."

"Who's the Girl Behind Bars?"

"Who?"

"By the elevators on the ground floor. A window. Bars. There's a girl in there."

"You must mean Phlox."

"Phlox? Her name is Phlox? There are girls named Phlox?"

"She is nuts," said Arthur, with mingled scorn and enthusiasm. Then his eyes widened, as though something had occurred to him. "A punk," he said slowly. "They call her Mau Mau."

"Mau Mau," I repeated.

When the light changed, Mohammad pulled left quickly, only signaling for the turn after he was halfway into it.

"What are you doing, Momo?" said Arthur.

"Momo?" I asked.

"Ahshit! We go to Riri's!" said Mohammad. He seemed to have just recalled that we had an actual destination.

"Momo," I said again. "Riri's."

"You should have kept going up Forbes, Momo," said Arthur, laughing at me. "Riri's house is straight up Forbes Avenue."

"Okay, yes, I know, shut up," shouted Mohammad. He made a U in the fortunately bare middle of Craig Street, and pulled, with a loud rumor of tires, back out onto the avenue. Despite the sixty-mile-an-hour wind, his black hair lay fat and shiny and motionless on his head, like ersatz hair of papier-mâché and varnish. Another happy cloud of dullness bloomed and settled over my senses. I tossed away my cigarette and took up my position once more, clenching the chrome luggage rack behind me and taking great swallows of air, like a jet engine.

Riri's house was a Tudor hugeness off the campus of Chatham College, where her widowed father, Arthur told me as we climbed the driveway to the front door, taught Farsi, and from which he took many sabbaticals, as he now had; his house poured light all over its immense lawn, and the neighborhood rang with loud music.

"You are now glad that you came," Mohammad said to me, rather irrelevantly shaking my hand. Then he barged into the pounding foyer.

"Gee, thanks," I said.

"It's nice that your old girlfriend was so understanding," Arthur said, nearly smiling.

I'd faked an apologetic telephone call to Claire, explaining to the dial tone that something had come up, I wouldn't be able to make dinner, and that I was sorry she had gone to so much trouble for me for nothing, which last, I'd reminded myself, was certainly true.

"Ha. Yes. Where is Momo from?"

"Lebanon," said Arthur, and then a lovely brown

woman in a sarong approached, with a delighted look and arms spread, preparing a brace of wide hugs.

"Momo! Arthur!" she cried. Her eyes were large and brown, made up with gold flecks and three mingled eye shadows, and her hair was shot through with colorful objects, lacquered chopsticks, and bits of feather and crepe. I stood by the open door, watching the traded embraces, keeping a patient, big, phony smile on my face. Momo cried out, cursed in French, and ran deep into the house, with a grim, insane look on his face, as if in pursuit of some prey he'd finally cornered after a million-year hunt. Our greeter, whom I took to be Riri, had splendid shoulders, which fell, smoothly and unhindered by clothing, to the bouncing top of her flowered wrapper. Like many Persian women, she had an eagling kind of beauty, hooked and dark, and mean about the eyes. After she had kissed her two boys, she turned to me and held out a hostesslike cute hand.

"Riri, this is my friend, Art," said Arthur.

"Delighted," I said.

"Oh, delighted!" said Riri. "So polite! All your friends are so polite, Arthur! Come in! Everyone is here! Everyone is drunk—but politely! You'll feel quite at home! Come into the parlor!"

She turned and walked into the parlor, a large, red-curtained room, which deserved its antique name. It was filled with vases, people drinking, and a grand piano.

"Is it really that obvious?" I whispered, close to Arthur's ear but not too close.

"You mean that you're polite?" He laughed. "Yes, it's embarrassingly obvious—you're making a well-mannered fool of yourself."

"Well, let's get rude, then," I said. "Is there a bar?"

"Wait," he said, grabbing me by the elbow. "I want you to meet someone."

"Who?"

He led me through a web of kids, most of whom seemed to be foreign, holding a drink, and smoking a cigarette of one kind or another. Some halted their loud conversations and turned to greet Arthur, who gave all an able, curt, and rather arrogant "Hi." He seemed to be well-liked, or at least to command respect. Many of the small bundles of people tried to enclose him in their conversations as he passed.

"Where are you taking me?" I said. I tried to sound apprehensive.

"To meet Jane."

"Oh, good. Who is she?"

"Cleveland's girlfriend. I think she's here—just a second. Stay here for a second, okay? I'm sorry. Be right back. I'm sorry about this, but I see someone, um—" said Arthur, and he unhooked me and vanished.

I stayed, and surveyed, and wondered at all the handsome women of many lands. He had deposited me in a corner of the parlor with a towering piece of furniture, which I leaned upon and cooled my cheek against. Many of those I saw had brown skins, every lovely grade of brown: Iranians, Saudis, Peruvians, Kuwaitis, Guatemalans, Indians, North Africans, Kurds—who knew? Caucasian women were draped about like bits of pale lace; and there were boys with interesting headgear and Lacoste shirts, or ill-fitting gabardine suits, laughing and eyeing the women. Arthur studied in that department of the university to which rich or very aggressively lucky foreign children are sent, to learn to administer great sums of international money and the ills of their homelands. Diplomacy, he'd said, when I'd asked him where his future lay.

"I go to these parties to practice," he'd said. "There are factions, alliances, secrets, debts, and a lot of messing around—I mean, of course, sexual messing around. And they all see themselves as Iranians, Brazilians, whatever, but I—I don't see myself as an American: I'm an atom, I bounce all over the place, like a mercenary. No, not a mercenary, a free agent—a free atom—isn't that something in chemistry? I'm always at the outside orbit of all the other, um, molecules?"

"I don't think that's it," I'd said. "I forget what a free atom is. I think you've made it up."

The parlor was noisy, smoky, jammed, and gorgeous. At the shah's fall, Riri's father had smuggled out a modest planeload of carpets and statuary, and these rather grimly gay furnishings made his daughter's party seem dark, ornate, and somehow villainous. I looked into the glass panels of the cabinet that held me up; it was filled with daggers and eggs. The eggs were large enough to have been laid by emus, and jeweled, painted. Delicate hinged doors, cut from the shells, opened onto miniature scenes of courtly, contortionist Persian love in 3-D. The artist had paid more attention to the figurines' limbs and genitalia than to their faces; the little twisted lovers wore that cowlike expression you see in Asian erotic art, which contrasts so oddly with the agonized knot of bodies. The daggers displayed their hilts but hid their blades in fantastic sheaths of blue velvet

and dyed leathers. Scattered here and there on the glass
shelves of the cabinet were cunning, unidentifiable implements of silver.

"What do you think?" It was Arthur. Though his tone
was light, he looked angry, or preoccupied, anyway.

"I think Riri's father is a white slaver. Say, this is some
party." I tried to get that tone of slogan in my voice. Then
I chanced a slight indiscretion. "Did you find 'someone
um'?"

He evaded the question, physically. He averted his
eyes, and blushed, like a maiden, like Fanny Price in *Mans-
field Park*. All at once I liked him, his firm grace with others, his unlikely modesty, the exotic parties he attended.
The desire to befriend him came over me suddenly and certainly, and, as I debated and decided not to shake his hand
yet again, I thought how suddenness and certainty had
attended all my childhood friendships, until that long, miserable moment of puberty during which I'd been afraid to
befriend boys and seemingly unable to befriend girls.

"No," he said at last. "'Someone um' has already been
found and disposed of." He looked off into the blare.

"I'm sorry," I said.

"Forget it. Let us find the lovely Jane."

3

SOME PEOPLE REALLY KNOW HOW TO HAVE A GOOD TIME

◆   ◆   ◆

To find Jane Bellwether, who acquired a last name and a few vague features during our search, we passed out of the jumping seraglio and through a long series of quieter, darker rooms, until we came to the kitchen, which was white. All the lights shone from overhead, and, as is sometimes the case with kitchens at large parties, an unwholesome-looking group, all the heavy drinkers and eaters, had convened in the fluorescence. Its members all looked at us as we entered the kitchen, and I had the distinct impression that a word had not been said in there for several minutes prior to our arrival.

"Say! Hi, Takeshi," Arthur said to one of two blenched Japanese who stood near the refrigerator.

"Arthur Lecomte!" he yelled. He was well more than half in the bag. "This is my friend Ichizo. He goes to C-MU."

"Hi, Ichizo. Glad to meet you."

"My friend," Takeshi continued, his voice rising, "is very horny. My friend say that if I were a girl, he would fuck me."

I laughed, but Arthur stood straight, looked deeply, beautifully sympathetic for perhaps a tenth of a second, and nodded, with that fine, empty courtesy he seemed to show everyone. He had an effortless genius for manners; remarkable, perhaps, just because it was unique among people his age. It seemed to me that Arthur, with his old, strange courtliness, would triumph over any scene he chose to make; that in a world made miserable by frankness, his handsome condescension, his elitism, and his perfect lack of candor were fatal gifts, and I wanted to serve in his corps and to be socially graceful.

"Does any of you know Jane Bellwether?" said Arthur.

The louts, so morose, so overfed and overliquored, said no. None looked at us, and it seemed to me, in the exaggerating way that things seemed to me that exaggerated evening, as though they could not stand the sight of Arthur, or of me in his magic company, in our Technicolor health and high spirits, in our pursuit of the purportedly splendid Jane Bellwether.

"Try on the patio," one, some kind of Arab, finally said, through a white mouthful of shrimp. "There are many people sporting out there."

We came out into the yellow light of the back porch, that estival old yellow of Bug Lite, which had illuminated the backyards and soft moth bodies of so many summers past. It was untrue; there were not many people sporting on the murky lawn, though a large group had gathered with their drinks and their light sweaters. Only one young woman sported, and the rest watched her.

"That's Jane," Arthur said.

She stood alone in the dim center of the huge yard, driving imperceptible balls all across the neighborhood. As we clunked down the wooden steps to the quiet crunch of the grass, I watched her stroke. It was my father's ideal: a slight, philosophical tilt to her neck, her backswing a tacit threat, her rigid, exultant follow-through held for one aristocratic fraction of a second too long. She looked tall, thin, and, in the bad light, rather gray in her white golf skirt and shirt. Her face was blank with concentration. *Thik!* and she smiled, shaking out her yellow hair, and we clapped. She fished in her pocket for a ball and teed it.

"She's plastered," a girl said, as though that were all the explanation we might require.

"She's beautiful," I heard myself say. Some of the spectators turned toward me. "I mean, her stroke is absolutely perfect. Look at that."

She smashed another one, and a few moments later I heard the distant sound of the ball striking metal.

"Jane!" Arthur shouted. She turned and lowered her shining club, and the yellow light caught her full in the face and fell across the flawless front of her short skirt. She put a hand to her forehead to try to make out the caller among us shadows on the patio.

"Arthur, hi," she said. She smiled, and stepped through the grass to him.

"Arthur, she's whose girlfriend?"

Half a dozen people answered me.

"Cleveland's," they said.

A few moments later, in one of the less noisy rooms off the parlor, we were three in a row on what could only be called a settee. Jane smelled interestingly of light exertion, beer, perfume, and cut grass. Arthur had presented me as a new friend, and I'd watched Jane's face for a trace of a knowing leer, but there'd been none. I began to wonder if I'd made a mistake about Arthur's intentions toward me, and to reproach myself for mistrusting what might have been his mere friendliness. After Jane and I had exchanged our academic pursuits—hers was art history—and agreed that neither of us could explain why we had chosen to pursue them, but that we were glad to be through, we turned to talking of plans for the coming summer.

I knew better than to state my true intentions, which were vague, and base enough that they could easily have included the pursuit of herself and of the ultimate source of all her exciting fragrance, in spite of this Cleveland, whoever he might be.

"I'm going to turn this town upside down," I said. "Then in the fall I have to become a responsible adult. You know, have a career. My father claims to have something lined up."

"What does your father do?" said Jane.

He manipulates Swiss bank accounts with money that comes from numbers, whores, protection, loan sharks, and cigarette smuggling.

"He's in finance," I said.

"Jane's going to New Mexico," said Arthur.

"Really? When?"

"Tomorrow," Jane said.

"Jesus! Tomorrow. Gee, that's too bad."

Arthur laughed, rapidly reading, I suppose, the thrust of my head and the proximity of my denim thigh to her shaven one.

"Too bad?" Jane had a southern accent, and "Too bad" fell out in three droll syllables. "It isn't bad! I can't wait— my mother and father and I have wanted to go forever! My mother has been taking Spanish lessons for fourteen years! And I want to go because—"

"Jane wants to go," Arthur said, "because she wants to have carnal knowledge of a Zuni."

She blushed, or rather flushed; her next words were only slightly angry, as though he often pestered her about Zuni love.

"I don't want to have 'carnal knowledge' with any old Zuni, asshole."

"Wow," I said. "Asshole." From the way she seemed to relish the word as it unwound from her lips, I guessed that she rarely used it. It sounded like a mark of esteem, a sign of her intimacy with Arthur, and I was momentarily very jealous of him. I wondered what it might take to get Jane to call me an asshole too.

"But I'm *intrigued* by the Native Americans, you know? That's all. And by Georgia O'Keeffe. I want to see that church in Taos that she painted."

Someone began to play the piano in the other room, a Chopin mazurka that mixed very uncomfortably for a few measures with the thump music that came from the half-dozen speakers scattered around the house, until someone else attacked the pianist with a squeal and a silk cushion. We laughed.

"Some people really know how to have a good time," Jane said, confirming that it was indeed a motto of theirs, and I was suddenly mad for the opportunity to employ it myself.

"Yes," said Arthur, and he told her about the scene at which we had stopped, and met, so many hours before.

"But I saw you in the library," I said. "What was that Spanish potboiler you were reading, anyway?"

"*La muerte de un maricón*," he said, with a humorous flourish.

"Oh. What's that mean?" I said.

"Ask Jane's mother, the hispanophone."

"You can't just stop right now about my mother," she said. "You can just shut your trap." Drunk, Jane spoke as though she were Nancy Drew. I was a fool for a girl with a dainty lexicon. "My mother didn't get to spend a year cutting up in Mexico and getting hepatitis like you did, Arthur."

"Well, and thank goodness," said Arthur.

"Oh, no! You didn't really . . . cut up, did you?" I said.

"Like the big time," he said.

"And what will you do this summer, Arthur?"

"I'm going to live at Jane's and watch the dog. You'll have to come visit me. It's going to be a fun place after the Bellwethers leave."

Arthur and Jane had just gotten to the part where the blind truck-stop waitress, feeling with her spotted, overjoyed hands Cleveland's nose and forehead, accuses him of being Octavian, the shining man from another planet who had loved her many years ago, but had then returned to his own world, leaving her sightless, and with a brilliant, freakishly formed child—"the kind of thing," Arthur said, "that is always happening to Cleveland"—when Mohammad fell into the dark room, shouting: "The Count! The Count!"

"The Count," Arthur said, frowning slightly.

"My friend," Momo said, almost as though he meant it, "my friend, my tremendous friend Arthur the Count! Tell me, what may I do for you? What would there be that I would not do it for you, my friend?"

He teetered, wore a bib of spilled whiskey, and the wide things he said, I felt, would be discounted as the typical CinemaScope friendliness of a sot. But Lecomte looked at him without answering, looked into his fat eyes while an obviously well-considered reply fought to free itself from his shut mouth.

"Arthur? Only to say it. Only! Anything in the world."

"You could," said Lecomte, "keep the fuck away from Richard."

There was only the din of the party, and it was as nothing. The obscenity flared and then collapsed into itself in the dazzling white half of a second. It was like the echo of an ax blow filling the air between him and Momo. He immediately blushed and looked ashamed at having said too much.

Mohammad's hand, which he had intended to give to Arthur to be shaken, hung from his wrist as though un-muscled. He fought down his astonishment, with the aid of his alcoholic heart, and smiled at me, and then at Jane.

"Jane," he said, "you will tell him I am quite okay for Richard and everything is okay and he has not the claim to everyone like he think he has and you will now tell him this."

"Let's go outside," Jane said to me. "I know how to get the neighborhood dogs to bark all at once."

"Hey, yes, fine," said Mohammad, "then it is enough for now. I will be back later." He headed for the large, dark parlor and disappeared into the large, dark music there.

"Arthur, was Richard—" I said.

"Let's not talk about it," he said.

Jane put her moist pout just by my ear and whispered, raising the hairs all down me.

"Richard is Cleveland's cousin," she said.

"Ah, Cleveland!" I said. I wondered at the Eiffel mesh of liaisons rising up and up around me. Were all of them related? Were Arthur and Richard an item? I looked at him. He stared down into his cool, yellow-foaming plastic cup of regret. His hair fell over his rather flat profile and hid the eye.

"The subject," Jane murmured into my ear again, undoing a giant zipper within me.

I grabbed her hard hand. "What subject?"

"Change it." Three syllables.

"So, Arthur, you didn't tell me," I said, "about the waitress's baby. Was it his? Did it have Cleveland's good looks and fabulous sense of humor?"

And the thought of Cleveland lifted him, and threw

him, and within a few minutes I listened as a hitchhiking Cleveland made his way headlong through the Black Hills toward Mount Rushmore, with an AWOL army demolition man in a pickup full of trinitrotoluene and plastique, and tears appeared at the corners of Arthur's eyes, he laughed so.

Later, long into the ever dimmer and louder evening, I looked around me, as though for the first time in hours.

"Cleveland," I said.

My vision and hence recent memory had smeared completely at the edges, and the edges had contracted with each drink, until two faces, Jane's and Arthur's, bewilderingly alike, filled the unbearably focused, narrow center of everything, and babbled. I wanted Jane, I wanted quiet, I wanted just to stop; so I stood up, a feat, and went out of doors to slap my face three times.

Cleveland, Cleveland, Cleveland! They had spoken of nearly nothing but his exploits. Cleveland riding a horse into a swimming pool; coauthoring a book on baseball at the age of thirteen; picking up a prostitute, only to take her to the church wedding of a cousin; living in a Philadelphia garret and returning to Pittsburgh six months later, after having hardly communicated with any of his friends, with a pair of dirty tattoos and a scholarly, hilarious, twenty-thousand-word essay on the cockroaches with which he'd shared his room.

I had the impression that as far as Arthur and Jane were concerned, Cleveland flew, or had flown, as far above their twin blond heads as I saw them flying above me—but he had fallen, or was falling, or they were all on their way down. They hadn't said it, but I saw that in their fancies, the great epoch, the time when Cleveland and Arthur had been two and angelic and fast, was long gone. Here I am, I thought, for I felt shitty and sour and wry, at the start of the first summer of my new life, and they tell me I've come in late and missed everything.

Though I'd intended to step out into the yellow comfort of the back porch again, my condition, and my un-familiarity with the house, led me through the wrong series of rooms, and I found myself verging on another part of the immense lawn, a part completely illuminated, in green shock. A pair of swimmers was talking quietly in the water, a boy still softly trying to convince a girl to do that thing whose moment had probably come and gone much earlier in the evening. I couldn't hear the words, but the urgency in the refusal of the young woman was clear and familiar. There would be denial, then silence, and then the rapid beat of water.

Someone touched my elbow, and I turned.

"Hi," said Arthur.

"I'm just getting a little air," I said. "I guess I've been sitting too long. Drinking too long."

"Do you like to dance? Would you like to go dancing?"

I wondered what he meant. I didn't really want to go dancing, mostly because I never had "gone dancing" (Claire did not dance), but also because something in his tone, and the whole idea of a discotheque, frightened me.

"Sure," I said. "Sure I like to dance."

"Well. There's a club in East Liberty. Not far."

"Okay."

"Well. It's a gay club."

"Oh."

There had been a time in high school, see, when I wrestled with the possibility that I might be gay, a torturous six-month culmination of years of unpopularity and girllessness. At night I lay in bed and coolly informed myself that I was gay and that I had better get used to it. The locker room became a place of torment, full of exposed male genitalia that seemed to taunt me with my failure to avoid glancing at them, for a fraction of a second that might have seemed accidental but was, I recognized, a bitter symptom of my perversion. Bursting with typical fourteen-year-old desire, I attempted to focus it in succession on the thought of every boy I knew, hoping to find some outlet for my horniness, even if it had to be perverted, secret, and doomed to disappointment. Without exception these attempts failed to produce anything but bemusement, if not actual disgust.

This crisis of self-esteem had been abruptly dispelled by the advent of Julie Lefkowitz, followed swiftly by her sister Robin, and then Sharon Horne and little Rose Fagan and Jennifer Schaeffer; but I never forgot my period of profound sexual doubt. Once in a while I would meet an enthralling man who shook, dimly but perceptibly, the foundations laid by Julie Lefkowitz, and I would wonder, just for a moment, by what whim of fate I had decided that I was not a homosexual.

I looked at Arthur. There was a faint golden stubble on his cheek and a flush at the pink skin of his throat. His eyes were clear and pale, as though he had not been drinking. I felt something. It flew around my chest like a black bat that has got into the house, terrified me for an alien moment, and then vanished.

"I don't think so. I'm straight, Arthur. I like girls."

He smiled his politic smile.

"That's what they all say." He reached up and almost touched my hair. I shrank from his hand. "Okay, you're straight." It was as though I had passed or failed some test.

"But we can be friends, can't we?"

"You'll see," he said, and he turned on his heel and went back into the house.

Objects changed during the long run of Riri's party: A girl's frail satin handbag became the spoils, torn in half, of a battle between two briefly furious boys; a lamp became a pile of shards to be cursed, swept up, and hastily thrown away; and the swimming pool, which had probably started the evening as everyone's notion of beautiful wealthy blue fun, was now garish and green and almost empty. I'd spent my whole evening, however, in sweet, subtle darkness, in the company of fun, and I had my shirt half off by the time I reached poolside.

4

THE CLOUD FACTORY

◆ ◆ ◆

My worst nightmare was a boring nightmare, the dream of visiting an empty place where nothing happened, with awful slowness. I would awake tired, with a few unremarkable traces that never seemed to do justice to the dull fear I had felt while still asleep: the memory of the low hum of an electric clock, of an aimless albino hound, of a voice incessantly announcing departure times over a public address system; and that summer, my job was a dream of this sort. I'd wanted to work in a true, old-fashioned bookshop, crammed with the mingled smells of literature and Pittsburgh blowing in through the open door. Instead I'd got myself hired by Boardwalk Books.

Boardwalk, a chain, sold books at low prices, in huge, fluorescent, supermarket style, a style pervaded by glumness and by an uncomprehending distaste for its low-profit merchandise. The store, with its long white aisles and megalithic piles of discount thrillers and exercise guides, was organized as though the management had hoped to sell luncheon meat or lawn-care products but had somehow been tricked by an unscrupulous wholesaler—I imagined the disappointed "What the hell are we going to do with all these damn books?" of the owners, who had started in postcards and seaside souvenirs on the Jersey shore. As far as they were concerned, a good book was still a plump little paperback that knew how to sit in a beach bag and keep its dirty mouth shut.

Literature was squeezed into a miniature and otherwise useless alcove between War and Home Improvement, and of all the employees, several of whom were fat and wanted to be paramedics, I was the only one who found irregularity in the fact that Boardwalk sold the Monarch notes to works, such as *Tristram Shandy*, that it did not actually stock. I was to spend the daytime summer stunned by air-conditioning, almost without a thought in my head, waiting for the engagement of evening. Summer would happen after dinner. The job had no claim upon me.

Early one evening at the beginning of June, a few days after the party at Riri's, my lease on the "Claire apartment" had at last come up. I locked the glass door of Boardwalk behind me, said good-bye to Gil Frick, flinched at the slam of sudden heat outside, and, with the very last of the furnishings from the old place in a grocery bag on my lap, rode the bus to my new house, on the Terrace.

The Terrace had been, many years ago, a fashionable place to live. A horseshoe of large, identical brick houses enclosing a long incline of grass, it still retained some of the genteel quality of an enclave that had once attracted families with servants and livery. I knew this last from the fact that I was moving into what had been a kind of coach house or chauffeur's quarters, small rooms over the garages behind the Terrace proper. None of my new neighbors seemed to bear any resemblance to me: an old man, babies, parents.

After setting the brown bag down among the scattered cartons of my life from the old place, I went outside to rest and smoke at the top of the twenty-six fissured concrete steps that drew up to my door. To the left, the Terrace, the kids and happy schnauzers running there; to the right and all before me, the maze of tumbling stables and garages, some doorless, most sheltering skis or autos. Along the tops of all the garages ran apartments like mine, spindly creepers in their windows, various musics from radios coming through their wire screens. The late sun was still the major fact of the day, setting the parked cars around me to creak, heating the metal banister against my bare neck. A warm breeze carried dinner smells and birdsong across the neighborhood, ran lightly over my sweaty face, and stirred the hair on my arms. I had an erection, laughed at it, and patiently pushed it down. Four years of familiarity and unconcern with Pittsburgh turned suddenly to arousal and love, and I hugged myself.

The next day was my day off, and I had plans. I walked into Hillman Library, sleeveless and sunglassy and ready for lunch with Arthur. The summer term had started (but not for me!), and the library was relatively crowded with students in shorts, struggling to remain seated and docile and scholarly. Arthur typed book acquisition forms in a room off the same hallway as the Girl Behind Bars, and to get to him I had to pass those bars, behind which she sat again today. I approached slowly, glad to be wearing sneakers and not my noisy shoes, because she was intent on fooling with her piles of books and did not glance up, and I got a good look at her.

She wore, today, several layers of red and white, T-shirts mostly, with a skirt here or there, and many different kerchiefs and bracelets. Her red-brown hair, cut in a neat, heavy-banged, lopsided forties style, left her bowed profile only partly visible, but she seemed to have a look of deep concentration on her face and did not hear me as I slipped past and headed down the hallway to Arthur's section. I remembered he'd said that she was punk, but her demeanor and her neatness were not, and she clearly placed an un-punklike emphasis on looking somewhat traditionally femi-nine, pink fingernails and ribbons. I wondered what she was, if not a punk.

Arthur had his lunch bag ready and quickly slipped a bookmark into what he was copying as I came in.

"Hi," he said. "Are you ready? Did you see Phlox?"

"Hi. Yes, I saw her. Phlox, ha ha. What a great name."

"Well, she certainly likes you, boy. You'd better watch it."

"What do you mean? How do you know? What did she say?"

"Come on, let's eat. I'll tell you on the way out. Good-bye, Evelyn—oh, I'm terribly sorry, Evelyn. This is my friend Art Bechstein. Art, this is Evelyn Masciarelli."

Evelyn was one of his co-workers, his superior, nomi-nally. She was a tiny old thing who had trembled away her life in Hillman Library, and, as Arthur later told me, was "in a therm" over him. I walked over and shook hands with her, very conscious of, and somehow more comfortable with, the formality with which Arthur had made the introductions. It allowed me to choose to be for her whoever I wanted to be, and I chose to be bright and young, fresh from the sun of the outer world and free to return to it, as she was not. After I had briefly held her small, wet hand, showing Evelyn all my charming teeth, we made a courteous farewell and left.

On the way out, of course, we came upon Phlox, drinking from the fountain in the hall. She had to place a protective hand above her breast to keep all the gear she wore around her neck from getting into the stream of water when she bent over.

"Phlox," said Arthur, a slightly mocking tone in his voice, "I have somebody I'd like you to meet."

She straightened and turned to face us. Her eyes, in the middle of all that hair and scarf, were the bluest I had ever seen, and they widened at the sight of me. I felt exposed by the bareness of my shoulders. Her face was long, her skin smooth, she had a broad, unflawed forehead; she was unquestionably beautiful, and yet there was something odd, wrong, about her looks, her clothing: something a little *too*, from her too blue eyes in their too direct stare to the too red stockings she wore. It was as though she had studied American notions of beauty from some great distance and had come all this way only to find she had overdone the details: a debutante from another planet.

"Art Bechstein, I'd like you to meet Phlox," Arthur continued. "Phlox, I'm sorry, I don't know your last name, but this is my friend Art. He's a wonderful person," he finished, somewhat strangely, and suddenly, under the weight of her regard and of Arthur's overintroduction, I felt compelled to impress but no longer wanted to—I wanted to back up the hallway, put on a pair of black horn-rims and a heavy coat, and come out again, this time farting and seized by grotesque tics.

Phlox had not yet spoken. She stood there, her hands poised at her sides, wrists bent upward, fingers slightly splayed: a really classic pose that cried out for a sentimental, string-heavy sound track, that rush of Borodin to mark the Moment Every Girl Dreams About. She looked at me for a long second or two.

"Hello, Art," she said finally. "I can't believe you know each other—I mean, I can't believe that Arthur knows both of us. How are you?"

"Quite well, thanks. How are you?"

"Fine. I'm— Arthur says you're not from Pittsburgh."

"He does?" I looked at Arthur, who was looking at his hands. "No. Washington. No, well, I'm almost from Pittsburgh. My mother's family lives in Newcastle," I said.

"She's dead." Sympathetic smile.

I looked at Arthur again. His fine hands obsessed him.

"Uh, yes. A long time. Are you from here?"

"I," she said, "am a very important part of Pittsburgh," and she fixed me with her twin blues. There was a lull in the action.

"All right," said Arthur, "that's enough." He took my elbow.

"Um, will you, um, will you be visiting the library—visiting Arthur—are you having lunch together?"

Arthur, adopting a sort of medical voice, explained the nature of our rendezvous, my liberty from my job that day, his unfortunate lack of lunchtime, and pulled me away, promising Phlox for me that she would see me again. Then we walked out into the blinding noon.

"Whew," I said, "that is one bizarre girl. What did you say they call her?"

"Mau Mau. Only that was when she was punk. I understand now that she's a Christian."

"I knew it had to be something. What will she be next?"

"Joan Crawford," he said.

No one ever satisfactorily explained to me the enormous hole, bridged in three separate places by long iron spans, that makes the whole southeastern end of the Oakland section of Pittsburgh into a precipice. Between the arrogant stupid prow of Carnegie-Mellon University and the ugly back end of the Carnegie Institute, between the little shrines to Mary in the front yards along Parkview and the park itself, lies the wide, dry ravine that contains, essentially, four things: the Lost Neighborhood, the Cloud Factory, train tracks, and a tremendous amount of garbage.

It was from a semisecret luncheon belvedere, the top step of a high concrete staircase that rose at least ten landings from the floor of the big hole, that I got my first long look at the Lost Neighborhood: the mysterious couple of streets and row or two of houses—a diorama, which one sees only from above, if one ever even notices it. I had probably seen it once or twice during my four years in Pittsburgh, but had never known of the half-dozen ancient staircases scattered throughout south Oakland that led down to it, nor realized that there were people really living in it. There were even a school and a baseball field; you could see the tiny shapes of children running bases down there at the bottom of Pittsburgh.

Arthur had chosen this uppermost step, where the sun warmed our backs and wilted the lettuce of our sandwiches. And sitting very close beside him there, behind the Fine Arts Building, at the grassy bottom of one of Oakland's hundred abrupt endings, I felt uncomfortable, extremely conscious of the seclusion and intimacy of our perch and of the distinct possibility that he had brought me here to broach again, as he might say, a delicate subject. I decided to reiterate my position at some point during lunch; unfortunately, my position was that I was crazy about him. I wanted to be like Arthur Lecomte, to drink, take, deny, dominate; and, with the wild friendship of Cleveland, to hold aloft the enchanted flag of summertime.

"What a weird place to live," I said, gesturing with my ham-and-cheese to the Lost Neighborhood.

"Have you ever been down there?"

"Nuh uh. You?"

"Yes, sure. Cleveland and I used to go down there all the time. We used to cut school"—here he gestured back over his shoulder toward, presumably, Central Catholic High School—"and come down that way"—tracing the route with his blue-and-white-striped arm—"behind the museum, past the Cloud Factory, and down along the junkyard. There used to be marijuana growing up through the trash and old tires and stuff."

"The Cloud Factory?"

He laughed, looked down at his hands, then looked back up again, avoiding my eyes, as usual, and blushing slightly. I'd never met a man who blushed so frequently, although he was to begin with a rather pink person.

"Yes, the Cloud Factory. Haven't you ever noticed it? When you walk across the Schenley Park bridge, there, from the park into Oakland, you pass above the Cloud Factory. What does it do? we used to wonder. Why do these great clouds, perfectly white and clean, white as new baseballs, come out of that building by the tracks? Cleveland and I would be all stoned and out of school and we'd loosen our neckties, and there would be the Cloud Factory, turning out a fresh batch of these virgin clouds."

I'd seen the building a million times, I realized, and it was indeed a cloud factory, nothing else. I said that, and then thought about Catholic school, how typical it was for Arthur to have gone in an altar boy and come out a catamite.

"Is Cleveland Catholic?" I asked.

"No, he's nothing," said Arthur. "He's an alcholic. Do you want some pear?"

I thanked him and took a warm, grainy slice. The reiteration of my straightness began to retreat from its urgent position on the tip of my tongue, and I found myself unwilling to derange the smooth rhythm of our conversation, full of leisurely pauses and the sound of chewing.

"When can I meet Cleveland?"

"Yes, he wants to meet you too; I've told him about you. Well, this weekend I'm having a little party out at the Bellwethers'—and hey, you haven't come out to visit me yet, Bechstein. You should come out and spend the night."

"Oh," I said.

"Mohammad has. We've broken the rules. We've profaned Nettie and Al's bedclothes."

"Oh!" I said. "That's against the rules?"

"Are you kidding? You should see! There's a twelve-page list of things I'm supposed and not supposed to do. Their bed is off limits."

This casual revelation of his having slept with Mohammad after the incident at the party was so complex, so wondrous, that it left me simultaneously relieved, curious, confused, nauseated, and admiring. I formulated and rejected eight or nine incoherent questions before realizing that they all boiled down to something along the lines of "You slept with Momo?" Instead I said, "I'll come out for the party, I guess, this weekend. Cleveland'll be there?"

"Well, he's on the list too."

"Supposed or—"

"Forbidden. Absolutely. But we'll see."

"Why is he forbidden to come over?"

"Because," Arthur said, "he is feared and despised wherever he goes. He is, my mother avers, Evil Incarnate."

"I see," I said, laughing.

He stood up, lit a cigarette, and jerked his head toward the library.

"I have to get back," he said.

I shook his hand and left him at the main doors, thanking him for another fine half hour, and, silently, for not having ruined everything with a furtive caress. When he went back to work, I later learned, he invited Phlox to the party and told her that I planned to attend only to dance with her.

I smoked and looked down at the bottom of Pittsburgh for a little while, watching the kids playing tiny baseball, the distant figures of dogs snatching at a little passing car, a miniature housewife on her back porch shaking out a snippet of red rug, and I made a sudden, frightened vow never to become that small, and to devote myself to getting bigger and bigger and bigger.

5

INVADERS

◆　　　　　　◆　　　　　　◆

At six-thirty in the morning of a wet June Tuesday that promised only the dry revelations of another day at Boardwalk Books, I showered (radio loud on the toilet in the steam), took my orange juice, chewed a hard brown heel of bread whitened with margarine, and clunked around the apartment—still half in cartons—trying on and abandoning a long series of shirts, at the same time rooting about, with no particular intent, for a photograph I had of the egg from which Godzilla hatched.

I'd slept badly, wakened too early; but it is good for a habitual late sleeper to waken early once in a while and have nothing to do. I drank instant coffee and looked through the water drops on the wire screen, at the rain quietly running down the gutters, at the dwarf loading the morning papers with an alarming clank into the yellow steel vendor chained to the lamppost on the corner of Forbes and Wightman, at my next-door neighbor the psychiatric nurse, coming home from the graveyard shift at Western Psych, swinging her umbrella and shaking her long blond hair out of the bun into which she had bound it. Being up this early made me feel as though I'd been taken to a new part of town, or like a hardened New Yorker who, finally standing atop the Statue of Liberty, cannot spot the water tank on the roof of his building and realizes with a strange delight how big and beyond him his city is.

I found and threw out the badly packed, crumpled photograph (minute figures on a wan beach ring the monster in his dappled shell). Since the rain had stopped and there was still time before Boardwalk expected me and my bad attitude to show up for work, I decided to skip the bus and to walk into Oakland.

The morning was warm; vapor drifted and curled along the fragrant asphalt and covered the golf course as I approached. A bit of antique ribbon rose from the cotton wool of mist around the clubhouse flagpole. As I reached the gates of Schenley Park, the grounds keepers climbed onto their green lawn mowers and filled the air with the utmost sound of a wet summer morning. Hopping the low white rail, I checked as always for the little tangle of graffiti I'd scrawled on it one laughing, runny-nosed night with Claire two winters before. I trod across the long, flawless way of grass, until the scruples drummed into me after years of golfing with my father overcame me, and I stepped off the inviolate links and into a stand of oak that bordered the clubhouse and the eighteenth green.

Running my fingers along the half-tumbled wire-and-picket fence, picking up silvery drops of old rain on the tips of my shoes, I felt a momentary pang for my father, and then, as I pronounced the soft word "Dad" and inhaled the turfy air, I remembered that he was flying into Pittsburgh again tomorrow; we'd have lunch, and I would shout, "Ele-

vator—going up!" and he'd shake his big head, pay the
check, and tell me for the tenth time about the Weitzman
girl, on a full fellowship at Brandeis, and perfectly lovely,
and remarkably intelligent.

The golf course eventually gave way to the parklike skirt
of Carnegie-Mellon University, and then the park gave way
to the bridge, the ravine, and Oakland. Nothing doing at
the Cloud Factory; they weren't making any today. A block
of white brick, two beige stacks, an enigmatic series of catwalks and closed doors, the Cloud Factory sat on the other
side of the bridge, down the hill from the Carnegie Museum, along the railroad tracks that ran beneath the bridge.
The steel confusion of scaffolding and cable around the
building seemed to connect it both to the museum above,
filled with geodes and dinosaurs, and to the automobile-
laden trains that passed alongside it in the night.

As I approached, I looked far below me, into the ravine, and tried to imagine two cravatted schoolboys, kicking through the sand and Coke cans down there, discussing
the primes of their lives as though they were yet far off, and
not already upon them. Since I had no idea of how
Cleveland looked, however, the image was unclear, and
anyway, I thought, they would probably have been stoned,
just talking about trigonometry, John Lennon, and fathers.

When I reached the end of the bridge, I ducked right,
on an impulse, and down a set of concrete stairs I'd never
before noticed, which ended in the chain-link and iron
grating of a padlocked entrance to the Cloud Factory. From
there, steps of wood led down to the sandy floor of the
ravine, and I took them, checking my watch; I had a half

hour or so. When I hit bottom I looked up at the corroded red bridge stretched over my head, reverberating with each passing car. I came around the Cloud Factory a bit, trying to look through its opaque white windows.

Arthur, I suppose, was content to think it a cloud factory; but I had to know its real purpose before proceeding to *pretend* I was equally content. I couldn't decide whether the place had to do with the museum or with the rails, however, and after a brief, fruitless examination of some rusted signs lying bent and nearly illegible in the dirt around the building, I turned to climb the steps.

Inside the building something engaged, and a low rumble grew quickly to a whine and a tattoo. I took my steps in time with the metallic tapping of the Cloud Factory, jolted out of my rainy-Tuesday sleepiness. Looking backward at it as I climbed, I had nearly gained the summit when a dense white billow blew from a giant valve, and then spread and rose into the air until a model cloud hung above my head, a textbook cloud, like a sheep, like cotton and all the cloud clichés. At the same time, Phlox rather prissily crossed the bridge on her bicycle, trailing thin scarves, posture perfect, sunglassed face forward and intent, probably, on the waiting white library in the distance. She seemed to be beautifully dressed. I stood still, half hidden against a cold red pile of the bridge, until the cloud began to break apart and she vanished into traffic. I'd spied on Phlox again. Something about her frightened me, though at the time I hadn't the word for it.

As I walked into Boardwalk I caught the unmistakable signs of "it" being "whooped up" in the back room. Gil

Frick, ex-Yeshiva, weekend marksman, and a deadly boring
shrimp of an engineering student, had been left to attend the
front cash register, a rare procedure, the management generally reserving for Gil the tasks it considered too menial or
benumbing even for me and my malcontent ilk, such as
peeling the price stickers from huge cairns of unsold paper-
backs or burying the dead remaindered autobiographies of
noncelebrities in the remote and freezing basement. In addition, the fifteen or so customers around the wrestling and
men's magazines and the Sports section of the store had their
heads turned attentively toward the workroom at the back;
some of them seemed to be laughing in deep appreciation of
whatever fun was being had back there: shouts, hysterical
feminine laughter, someone singing.

"Hey, Gil," I said. "Well! It sounds as though someone
is enjoying himself in the rear office." Following Arthur's
example, I'd begun to affect an overgrammatical, precious
manner toward people like Gil Frick, to keep them, as I
imagined Arthur saw it, from wanting to talk to me.

"Yeah, someone," he said. I noticed he sported a small
set of facial bruises, and a fresh glum chunk of electrician's
tape on his eyeglasses.

"Were you involved in some kind of scuffle or fracas,
Gil?"

"No," he said, coloring.

I didn't press it. Crossing the gum-blackened white tile
floor from the front of the shop to the bins chock-full of
abysmal children's books (this week: *Tuffy the Egg* and *A
Zillion and One Really Funny Jokes to Tell and Color*) by the
back room, I decided that the current festivities must be the
result either of liquor, despite the early hour, or, more

likely, of five or six dozen doughnuts, both of which seeds of brute merriment were sometimes introduced, with pathetically good results, into the usually sere Boardwalk moonscape.

Actually, there were both whiskey and doughnuts, but the laughter was due not to these but to Ed Lavella, three hundred pounds, and his brother Joey, two hundred and seventy-nine pounds, who had on dresses, high heels, and makeup, and in their costumes were demonstrating cardiopulmonary resuscitation.

"Bechstein!" they shouted as I entered the room. "How about a date, you big fag?"

I winced inwardly, though Ed and Joey always called me this; for the first time I took it half-seriously, as though my friendship with Arthur made me gay by association. Of course, I reminded myself, they didn't mean homosexual, exactly; what they meant was: you thin, weak kid whom we could completely crush under our tremendous butts or dismember with very little exertion. I laughed.

"Ha ha," I said. "What is this? *Some Like It Fat?*"

"Ha ha," said everyone in the room. These included, in addition to the pair of giant future paramedics: three chain-smoking, bulimic young women who occupied various higher levels in the byzantine Boardwalk management hierarchy; Rodney, a tall, quiet black man who had gone to jail for evading the Vietnam draft, and who was now in the process of converting to Catholicism, with the eventual aspiration of becoming a Trappist monk, "like Thomas Merton," who, as Rodney often told me, died in a terrible and ridiculous fashion; and Calvin, another budding paramedic, a fan of knives and small firearms, and Gil Frick's only friend at work—one friend more than I had myself. These people sold books in the shadow of the University of Pittsburgh.

"Skit Night at the station tonight," said Ed, lurching to his feet. Joey remained flat on his back, his upper body a mess of décolletage, the tangled gray straps of his bra, and wadded Kleenex. "Just trying out the costumes on you'ns."

"Great costumes, fellas," I said. "Terrifying. Um—it's not ten yet, is it? I have time? Excuse me. I have to make a phone call."

I walked back out into the store, hands shaking, and up to the telephone at the front.

The phone was busy at the Bellwethers'. I tried to determine whether this was fear I felt, or anxiety. What, I asked myself, what is the big deal? They were still laughing in the back room; two customers stood nearly on the threshold, probably eyeing the doughnuts. Who was he talking to? What would I say if he answered?

Despite the several girls I had loved and made love to since my last year of high school, my childhood weakness and sexual uncertainty, all my suffering as a "fag" under the insults and heavy forearms of stronger boys, and what amounted to my infatuation with Arthur had made me an easy victim to this unintentional surprise attack by the two cross-dressed fatsos. I asked myself, in that matter-of-fact, soldierly way one asks oneself this sort of question, standing with the still-chirruping telephone in my hand, if I felt like having sex with Arthur.

"Art!" shouted Valerie, the smartest, most important, and most alarmingly thin of the women at Boardwalk. "You were just about to hang up!" She looked at me sternly; Valerie considered sternness to be the most effective managerial technique, and could deploy a tremendous battery of stern expressions, made even more effective by her long, heavy eyebrows and Afghan hound's face.

"Why, yes, Valerie, I was. Gee!" I said, quickly hanging up. "How'd you know?"

"Home Improvement," said Valeri, "now. It looks like they've been playing jai alai in it."

"Right." I grabbed a feather duster from Gil and headed back to the Home Improvement section, to make order and glittering shelves; to push around the dust until my head was thoroughly ringed with little clouds of motes and murk.

All day, as every day, I wove past customers with my arms full of books, repeating the words "Excuse me" so many times without getting a response that I began to feel genuinely inexcusable. Like the mounting evidence of a subtly evil betrayal of daily life (dead birds and telephones, the roisterous sheriff's sudden sobriety, the neighborhood children chanting in mesmeric circles in the desert schoolyard) in a movie about invasion from outer space, it seemed that every ten minutes a new reminder of homosexuality intruded into the usually eventless world of Boardwalk Books—a handsome couple of men, a copy of *Our Lady of the Flowers* that I'd never noticed before, a worn naked-man magazine that fell like a severed limb from inside a book on wiring and fuses. It all culminated with a little boy who came and stood beside me.

"Um, mister?" he said.

"May I help you?"

"Yeah," he said. "I'm looking for a book about makeup."

"Makeup?" I said. "As in, say, cosmetics? Health and Beauty books? You mean *makeup?*"

"No way!" he nearly screamed, stopping the assault, saving the earth at the last moment from complete alien domination. That wasn't what he meant at all. He meant werewolf makeup and exploding-forehead makeup. I could have fallen to my knees in thanks.

I wasn't, I insist, stupid enough to imagine that the mere fact that I had a gay friend—though I'd never, to my knowledge, had one before—meant that I was myself, somehow, a homosexual. I was, however, insecure (and stupid) enough to imagine that the only reason Arthur had befriended me was to seduce me, that he found nothing in me to admire, as I found in his manners, his intelligence, his clothing, his ease with others; in short, that he didn't really like me. If any of the attempts I made that day to telephone Arthur had succeeded, I would have asked him nothing. I would only have listened to the way in which he spoke to me, listened for accents of friendship: the banality, relaxation, and lack of style that characterize a conversation between two friends.

After their morning fun, the day, for the others, dissolved into utter antihilarity and six or seven reputedly atrocious late-afternoon hangovers. I was watching the clock slowly fold up my last ten minutes like the pleats of a fan, when an enormous BMW motorcycle, 1500cc, jumped

the curb outside the store and made the plate glass shake.
The rider, wearing black leather chaps, black jacket, and
an impenetrable black visor, dismounted without cutting
the engine. The bike was so loud that Valerie and Ed and
Joey came running up from the back, Valerie pressing at the
headache in her temples.

He wasn't big, the biker, not tall at any rate, but he had
a gut, and his boots thudded as he tore open the front door.
Why couldn't you have waited eight and a half minutes? I
thought. Usually the bikers went right over to the magazines, to *Easyriders*, and giggled at the Biker Chick of the
Month for a while in the air-conditioning before stealing
Hustler and swaggering out; *usually* they turned off their motorcycles and left their helmets hung over the sissy bar, or
whatever, and did not loom at the front counter like sym-
bols of Twentieth-Century Leather Death. I looked at Valerie, who was trying to prepare a stern look, and then
turned to face the biker, who had pushed up his face shield.
He wore glasses, Clark Kents.

"May I help you?" I said.

"Yes," said the biker, but he just stood and examined
my face without speaking. His gaze drifted up to my hair,
which seemed to check with something in his mind, and
then back.

"You forgot to turn off your motorcycle, mister," I said.

"Goodness me," he said.

"May I help you?"

"I'm looking for *Son of a Gangster*, by Art Bechstein,"
he said. He smiled, big teeth.

For a moment my mind was perfectly blank; all mental

activity ceased. Then I felt afraid, and in my bewilderment I opened the cash register, then closed it. I looked at the clock and was unable to interpret its message. And yet I was not at all *surprised* by the arrival of the Fell Biker. It was as though I'd finally been caught at a crime I had long been committing, and I thought: So.

I was being called to account for my father's sins; old scores were being settled. I decided to do whatever he said. I didn't see a gun, but I didn't have time to give the setup much careful consideration. I simply surrendered.

"Just kidnap me, okay?" I said. "It'll work. I know how my father thinks."

"Let's go," he said. He seemed reasonable. He smiled again. His front tooth was chipped.

"What is this, Art?" said Valerie.

"It's Gangland," said the biker.

"I might need a few days off," I said.

He pulled me from the register stand and dragged me out to the sidewalk. I looked back into the store and saw Valerie going to the telephone. Ed and Joey lumbered out behind us and hesitated for a moment.

"It's okay," I said. "Don't make trouble. Punch my card for me."

"Who is that guy?" said Joey. He looked more interested than ready to roll.

"I'm Death," said the biker.

"Come on, man," I said. "Let's go. I can walk."

"I can walk," he said in a squeaky voice.

Climbing onto the gigantic black saddle, I began to tremble, and clutched the hot bar behind me. I imagined being taken to some Bloomfield garage and thrown up against the grimy wall and shot. They would have to drag the Monongahela to find my riddled corpse. My father would get on the phone and plead with his bosses for an eye for an eye. My cousin Debbie would play the guitar and sing "Blackbird" or "Moonshadow" at my funeral.

We pulled out onto Forbes Avenue, and when we finally hit a red light he reached his right hand around behind him and held it out for me to shake. I shook.

"Art Bechstein," said my potential executioner, "how the hell are you?" He laughed, the light turned green, we headed toward Highland Park, he didn't stop laughing: He actually went "Hee hee."

"Cleveland," I shouted.

6

OBEDIENCE

◆ ◆ ◆

Arthur had told me the story of Happy, the most beautiful dog in the world, and of her ruin by Mrs. Bellwether, who was insane.

One day several years ago, Happy had appeared at Jane's feet, collarless, playful; a large puppy, perhaps ten or eleven months old, almost completely white, housebroken, well-behaved, and breathtakingly lovely. The family made no effort to discover who had lovingly trained then lost her, and adopted her immediately into its tortured bosom, giving her her tragic and idiotic name. Wrapped in her extravagant fur, with her long, noble face and elegant walk, Happy was, in every way, the Anna Karenina of dogs, even expressing, Jane claimed, a distinct mixture of fear of and fascination with the trains they would have to stop for in the course of the marathon walks they took together. When Jane took Happy out, people slowed their cars to watch the dog's perfect gait, her leash superfluous, slack, vulgar.

Jane loved the dog and had cared for her well, letting her take the firm white remainders of strawberries from between Jane's own lips, unleashing her for three-hour chases across the Highland Park cemetery (since, she said, dogs love graveyards), and painting pink the collie's black toenails; unfortunately, however, Happy spent most of her days with Jane's mother, so, in time, the dog developed both colitis and a skittish fear of women, even of the sound of their footsteps, and her coat began to turn the tan that now, years later, had become a fragile, shifting brown.

Thus the dog became a genuine Bellwether, visiting Dr. Link, the veterinarian, as often as migrainous Mrs. Bellwether visited Dr. Arbutus, her internist; as eczematous Dr. (of Philosophy) Bellwether consulted Dr. Niyogi, his dermatologist; as imprisoned, fearful Jane went to weep before Dr. Feld, her psychotherapist. Though it may seem a silly conceit to view Happy's consignment to a doctor's care as an inevitable result of her adoption into the Bellwether family, it may seem less so when one learns that Jane one day descended into the basement to rummage among her father's abandoned five irons and woods, and found her mother administering blows to Happy's unbearably beautiful head with a ball-peen hammer, because the dog had managed to void her agonized bowels onto the basement floor.

Well, unhappy families may each be unhappy after their own fashion, but their houses are always alike, at least in my experience. The Bellwethers lived in the only ordinary-looking house in a wooded, wealthy section of Highland Park that was otherwise filled with period pieces, stylistic excess, and eccentric ornamentation. Peaked roof, red brick with white siding, white "lace" curtains blowing out through the open windows of the kitchen, azalea bushes, concrete driveway, a French horn of garden hose in the front yard. Nothing I'd heard about the Bellwethers prepared me for the discovery that the house in which Jane had grown up looked exactly like my grandparents'. Cleveland parked the bike in the street, and as I swung off the seat and did a couple of stiff deep-knee bends, I sequentially settled on each of the neighboring houses as being the probable residence of the crazy Bellwethers, before Cleveland, with some amusement, grabbed me by the elbow again, as though we were still playing Crime, and tugged me onto the slate path of stepping-stones that made its typical way to the Bellwethers' front door.

"It's this one; this is the nice normal house where Arthur is living for the Bellwethers while they're 'on holiday.'"

I took my first good look at him. He did not at all have the face I'd expected. Wrongly but quite naturally, I'd assumed that he would look just like Arthur, blond and rosy. Not at all. He had, to a degree, the head of a biker: uncombed, red-skinned, heavy, with the chipped incisor. But his hauteur and his Clark Kents threw everything off; they made him peculiar.

"Cleveland," I said, as we walked up to the front door, "how did you know about my father?"

He turned his head toward me for an instant, and his eye was bright and crafty.

"Everyone knows," he said. "Don't they?"

"Nobody knows," I said, grabbing hold of his leather sleeve. "Absolutely no one."

He turned toward me and threw off my hand, so hard that it slapped against my hip.

"Your cousin David Stern knows."

"He isn't my cousin," I said. "We used to play G.I. Joe together. A long time ago."

"Well, he grew up into a real asshole."

"He has a big mouth." I thought for an instant, then said, "How do you know Dave Stern? You work for his father?"

"I don't work for anybody. The Sterns are simply associates of mine."

"It's nothing to brag about."

"I get to make my own hours," Cleveland said. He dashed up the steps, then whirled to face me. "And"—he gave me a menacing, humorous look—"'Nobody knows. Absolutely no one.'" He rattled the aluminum screen door like a maniac, and it came off in his hand. "Whoops," he said.

"Jesus," I said. "You're a monster."

"I'm walking destruction," he sang. "I'm a demolition man."

We went inside, where it looked nothing like my grandparents' house, and I relaxed. The most immediately memorable feature of the decor was the carpeting. A "soothing," embarrassingly synthetic flavor of sky blue, it illuminated the whole floor of the place, like a lit ceiling; and so from my first minute in Jane's house I felt subliminally but undeniably upside down. The furniture had been accumulated, rather than chosen. An empty wicker birdcage hung in the corner of the living room, its bottom still lined with newspaper and its water bottle a quarter full. They had partitioned the dining room from the living room with an ugly brown stack of metal shelves that held Jane's many golf tro-

phies and pictures of Jane and her dad, who looked like a
frail Alec Guinness. I liked seeing the photographs of Jane,
with her strawberry of a face and her remarkably fine posture.

"Hey!" said Arthur, coming from the kitchen in nothing but boxer shorts. Wiping his floury hands on his bare,
sunburned legs, he held out the right one for Cleveland and
me to shake. "Cleveland!" He wore the only unfeigned
look of surprise I was ever to see on him. "What the hell is
going on?"

"What do you mean?" I said. "Didn't you send him to
get me?"

"Hell, no," said Cleveland. "I thunk it up myself.
Arthur was telling me about his new friend"—here
Cleveland gave me a very complex sort of false leer, as
though to say, "I know you two aren't making it, but then
again maybe I don't know"—"Art Bechstein, who works at
that shitty little Boardwalk Books on Atwood, which doesn't
have a single book by Brautigan or Charles Bukowski, and I
said to myself, 'Well, Art Bechstein; I know who that is!
And I'll bet that at this very moment that late-afternoon
emptiness of the spirit is stealing over him like a shadow.
Like a shadow.'" He shook his long black hair.

"You two know each other?" said Arthur. He was edg-
ing his way toward the blue staircase, and it occurred to me
that there was someone upstairs.

"Only by reputation," said Cleveland. "Who do you
have upstairs, Artie?"

"Someone. I was making our dinner. You don't know
him."

"Cleveland kidnapped me," I said.

"I'd imagine so," said Arthur. "Look, could you fellas come back in about a half hour?"

"No!" said Cleveland. They played a game, fell into it instantly, sharpening on each other their abilities—Cleveland's verbose and graceless, Arthur's cool and mannered—to manipulate situations, to see the motives behind motives, to note and expose the telltale flicker of a glance. They could, finally, put two and two together; most people cannot. "You'll just make him go out the back door feeling all sticky and naked and unloved. Why not get him down here? Who is it? Cousin Richard? No—no, I'll bet it's Mohammad. I'll bet you two were making up again. He has some paper about Andrew Jackson he needs you to write for him, and so he came over here with a pound of swordfish and made a big charming kissy-face, and now everything is jake."

Arthur laughed and looked delighted. "Mohammad!" he shouted. "Come downstairs!"

"Where's the dog?" said Cleveland.

"Downstairs trembling, as usual. I think she's in heat." He turned to me. "Scary, isn't he? Actually, it was the Emancipation Proclamation and veal scallops. I'm making veal marsala."

Our stomachs were full of veal and asparagus and we had been drinking for a long time; the sun set and the neighborhood grew still. In between songs on the radio, I could hear a lawn mower off in the distance, a dog barking. The Bellwethers had no screens on their windows, and a cloud of gnats hung over the center of the living room.

Arthur laid great significance on the fact that Momo
was full Maronite Christian. This lent him a special charm.
He had the thin veneer of civilized French manners and
sullenness over the dark, hirsute heart of the Levantine
(Arthur liked them swarthy); he was the dazzling Beirut
hotel harboring an unexploded bomb. Their very casual affair had been going on for a long time and had fallen into a
comfortable pattern. "Every week," said Arthur, "we have
knock-down-drag-out sex and then a tender and passionate
fight." Momo had sat chewing and scowling all through
dinner, and left immediately afterward, telling us that he
was "a fucky one," because he had forgotten that his cousin
depended on him for a ride home from her music class and
would be waiting for him on the sidewalk outside the Y
with a few choice phrases of French.

Arthur, after Cleveland had called him on the hidden
boy in the bedroom, showed not a trace of embarrassment.
Something changed in his behavior because Cleveland was
there; he withdrew from his usual position at the center of
attention and just laughed, in his underwear and shirttails.
Cleveland drank and drank. My involvement with Phlox
seemed already to be a foregone conclusion, despite the fact
that I had barely spoken to her, and they subjected me to
several minutes of intensive teasing. Cleveland said he had
slept with her, embarrassed me with the strange details,
gave me a few "pointers"—and then said that it had perhaps been with a girl named Floss and not Phlox that he
had dressed as Batman and she as Robin and then rolled
around on the floor of a dark garage. I changed the subject
and asked about Jane.

"I'm in the Out column of the Bellwether Fashion

Forecast," Cleveland told me, crushing another empty can and flinging himself out of the paisley recliner out of which—it was on page eight of the list—Dr. Bellwether had forbidden anyone to fling himself. As he catapulted his big self toward the refrigerator, the La-Z-Boy produced exactly the metallic groan I supposed Dr. Bellwether most dreaded.

"Does that include Jane too?" I said, trying not to sound hopeful. I didn't, truly, entertain any hopes about Jane; some questions just have a dangerous tone built in.

"Sometimes it does and sometimes it doesn't," Arthur said. "Jane and Cleveland have been in love for about three of the six years they've been in love." He grinned—another first. "Bring me a beer, Cleveland?"

"The problem," said Cleveland, tossing an emerald can of Rolling Rock right at the nook between Arthur's stretched-out feet, where it lodged perfectly, and then grinding back in the unfortunate chair, "is her parents. In their opinion, of course, the problem is me."

"Evil Incarnate," I said.

"Oh, yeah; I'm the problem in Arthur's mother's opinion too. In fact, however, I am *not* a problem."

"Only a little socially disturbed," said Arthur.

"I am only in love with Jane Bellwether," Cleveland said, and then said it twice again. "This is a reality that Nettie and Al will just have to accept. However unpleasant. I wish they would just die. I hate both them and their guts."

"When are they coming home from New Mexico?" I said.

"Soon," said Arthur. "And I'll have to move."

One of the big songs that summer came on the radio.

Don't drink, don't smoke, what do you do?
Don't drink, don't smoke, what do you do?
Subtle innuendos follow:
"Must be something inside."

Before the next song there was a short silence and we could hear some shouting—not angry shouting, more like a cry of "Telephone!"—from inside the next house.

"The kid next door is really kind of unusual," said Cleveland. "He keeps pit bulls. Of course Nettie and Al hate him because of the dogs, which, as you've probably seen on TV, will eat helpless infants and the elderly. And Jane claims that Teddy is violent, and—what does she say?—lewd. I've known about him for a long time, but you know, I've never met him. Currently he's nothing but a joke. A Figure of Fun. In fact," he said, and he got up and went over to the open window and shouted, "Teddeeee!" and from inside the other house someone said, "What?" and we laughed. "Let's go out back," said Cleveland. "Fuck the fucking Bellwethers." Arthur went to put on his pants.

The two backyards were separated by some half-dead shrubs and that was all. They formed one big lawn, filled with fireflies.

"Hey, Teddy!" said Cleveland.

Teddy came out onto the grass with the dogs, three of them, at his heels, in a very obedient kind of arrangement, like a squadron of navy show jets. We waved.

"Hello, Teddy," said Arthur, his tone cool and condescending again.

"We think he's retarded," Cleveland said to me, sotto voce. I made an inquiring face. "Well, because Jane always refers to him as 'poor Teddy,' you know? See—his hair is cut too short, the way retarded kids' hair is, like no one asks him how he wants it, and he can't sit still for very long, so they just lop the hell out of it one two three." He lopped the air with two scissoring fingers. "Big shoes. Hey, Teddy, can we see your dogs?"

"Wait," I said. "Stop. You aren't going to torment a retarded kid and his pets."

"Wait," said Cleveland.

"No, I'm not ready for ugliness from you guys. Sordidness, maybe, but not something brutal, or cruel, okay? I don't know you well enough."

"Wait. Everything will be jake."

Teddy and the pit bulls came snapping through the hedge and crossed over to us.

"Where are the Bellwethers?" he said. "What have you done with them?" He smiled. It was immediately clear that he was not retarded. He was probably eighteen and bright, but his terrible haircut, his small nose and eyes, and his fat cheeks made him look younger and more stupid. Arthur asked him if he would care for a beer and then went back into the house to get him one.

"Terrific dogs," said Cleveland.

"I trained them myself," said Teddy. "They're perfectly trained."

They sat in a row, panting almost in unison, three

tough little good-natured knots of dog muscle that attended every movement of Teddy's hands. He commanded them to stop panting, and blip! their tongues shot back into their mouths.

"Amazing," said Cleveland. He knelt down and patted the series of heads. Then he grinned a sinister grin. "Well," he said, "what *should* we have done with the Bellwethers?"

"Talked them into moving away."

Arthur came out with Teddy's beer.

"Say, Artie," said Cleveland. "Didn't you mention something about Happy being in heat?"

"Aw, no," I said. "Aw, no. Come on. Don't do it."

"It's one of the items on the list," said Arthur, looking up as he tried to remember the wording. "Somewhere toward the end: 'Do not . . . do not be alarmed if Happy seems to behave strangely, as she is in estrus right now.' Good Queen Estrus. As if the dog could get any stranger than it is. Why?"

"Well, just look at these fellows," said Cleveland. "I imagine they're dying for some high-class tail. And they have a right to it. Isn't that so, guys?" he asked the dogs, speaking now almost as though he were their attorney. "They've probably had three little pit-bull crushes on Happy for years and years, sending her flowers and gifts and love letters that Nettie always intercepts and throws away. Think how many times these guys have had their hearts broken."

7

THE CHECKPOINT

♦   ♦   ♦

So Cleveland could not be stopped from bringing Happy up from one of her basement hiding places and mating her to Teddy's three pit bulls, which, when introduced to Happy in the Bellwethers' dining room, showed a great deal of alacrity in mounting to the distant heights of her vagina.

Initially Happy froze, stood rigidly with her tail down and her ears collapsed against her long head, eyes half-closed, in that distinctive near-catatonic state which Cleveland called a ball-peen trance. Manny (the dogs were named for the Pep Boys), her first consort, tupped a trembling, unresponsive statue of a dog, but by her second partner, Moe (who scramblingly presented himself half an hour later, as it took Manny rather a long time to extract himself from Happy's tightly clenched depths), she began to loosen up, and even appeared to be enjoying herself. When Jack's turn came (in the interval Cleveland went out and came roaring back with more beers), Happy sniffed at him as much as he sniffed at her, and even crouched a little, to make his ascent easier. We yelled and cheered the boys on, and kept drinking.

And then we hit the Checkpoint, as Cleveland called

it—the bane of his career as one who always tried to push things; and at that inevitable one-way Checkpoint of Too Much Fun, our papers were found in order and we crossed into the invisible country of Bad Luck. Teddy's mother— whoops, Teddy was only fifteen years old, after all—came looking for her son and found Mr. Genteel, Evil Incarnate, her unretarded, badly coiffed boy, and myself lying on the floor of the Bellwethers' salon, surrounded by empty green cans of Rolling Rock and four exhausted dogs, two of which were still linked in the midst of a painful-looking dance of extraction. The livid (bluish-white) woman grabbed her son, inhumanely commanded him to liberate Jack, and, after having terrorized Arthur into giving her the name of the Bellwethers' motel in Albuquerque, started home, trailing her woozy son and Manny, Moe, and Jack, a flawless triangle of dog.

The Bellwethers, however, were no longer at the Casa del Highway on Route 16 in Albuquerque; they were in the driveway. They had barely unbuckled their seat belts before Mrs. Teddy's Mom set upon them with a furious and fairly accurate account of our bad behavior; we could hear every word. Arthur jumped up and began quickly to collect the wreckage of twisted green aluminum that covered the furniture and the shimmering blue carpet.

"Get out, Cleveland!" he said. "Run out the back!"

"Why?" said Cleveland. He went to the refrigerator and got another beer.

At the time I thought this foolish, an overly cinematic gesture. I was wrong. In my innocent cynicism I didn't see that Cleveland was not trying to look tough; he just didn't care. Which is to say, he knew what he was, and was, if not content with, at least resigned to knowing that he was an alcoholic. And an alcoholic is nothing if not sensitive to the proper time and place for his next drink; his death is one of the most carefully planned and prepared for events in the world. Cleveland simply foresaw his imminent need of another beer. An era of covert hatred and distance-keeping between him and the Bellwethers was ending, in what would probably be an unpleasant fashion, and he wanted it to end; but he would need help.

He had just popped the tab with the fingers of one hand when an elephantine, pink version of Jane Bellwether, in a big flowered dress, filled the front doorway. Mrs. Bellwether stared for an unusually long time at the severed screen door that leaned against the front of her house, as though this were all the damage she was, for the moment, capable of understanding. Dr. Bellwether's head and left arm appeared in the shadows behind her, a garment bag slung over the arm. He spoke to us across his tremendous wife.

"We are going to prosecute," he said, very softly, with an English accent.

Mrs. Bellwether entered her house and attempted to sink to her knees before Happy; but the dog, relaxed and regal and leisurely only moments before, shrank from her mistress's touch and slunk off down the hall.

"What have you done to our dog?" said Mrs. Bellwether—to Cleveland, I decided.

Arthur started to say "Nothing," but Cleveland interrupted him.

"We bashed her head with a ball-peen hammer," he said.

Dr. Bellwether, who had stepped into the house, glanced quickly at his wife, who blushed.

"You were forbidden to enter this house," he said, or rather I afterward realized that this is what he must have said. Each of his words was a softly falling little dollop of English mashed potatoes. This speech, the last I ever heard him utter, was apparently hard on him; he sat down on a hassock and let his wife do the rest of the talking.

"Where is Jane?" said Cleveland.

"Get out," said Mrs. Bellwether.

Cleveland pushed past her; she fell against the fortunately empty birdcage. He ran out the front door.

"Who are you?" Mrs. Bellwether asked me.

"Art Bechstein."

She frowned. "Arthur," she said, "if you get out of my house right now—and take your young Hebrew friend with you—we will keep our two hundred and fifty dollars and will not call the police. That is only fair, considering the harm you have done to our house and our pet. Cleveland we will not forgive. Cleveland will pay for this."

"Where is Jane?" Arthur said. He had drawn himself erect, in the way a drunken person will when alcohol cowardly flees in the face of whatever trouble it has caused, and he tucked in his shirt as though ready for business.

"She stayed on. She'll be back in a few days. But not for Cleveland, she won't."

Cleveland came back into the house, beer in hand, wearing an ornate black felt sombrero, embroidered in silver thread, that he must have found in the Bellwethers' car.

"Where is she?"

Mrs. Bellwether's face lit up, and she said that Jane was

dead. "It was awful, wasn't it, Albert?" Mr. Bellwether
shook his head and said something. "And here we come
home in our grief, we want only to remember Jane in the
peace of our own home, and what do we find? Depravity!
Cruelty to animals! And you!"

Arthur started to speak, after Jane's mother said that
she had died—to deny, I suppose, the most ridiculous lie I
had ever heard in my entire life, a lie made with such wild
disregard for probability of success that I saw then how
crazed she really was, and I saw that telling a good, simple
lie was a sign of sanity; but Cleveland smirked, very briefly,
and Arthur said nothing.

"Dead! No, it can't be!" said Cleveland. "Not Jane!
Oh, God, no! How—how did it happen?" He started to
cry; it was beautifully done.

"Dysentery," she said, less harshly, perhaps brought up
short by the effect her lie was having on Cleveland.

"And this hat . . ." He was overcome, and could not
speak for just the right amount of moments. "This hat is all
that's left of her isn't it?"

"Yes. We had to burn her clothes."

"Look, Nettie, in a minute I'll walk out your front door,
never to darken your welcome mat again. That's a promise.
I know that you hate me, and I certainly always hated
you—until now—but I loved your daughter, passionately. I
know you know that. And so—may I keep this sombrero?"

Here Dr. Bellwether raised a pale hand and started to
speak again, but his wife overrode him and said that
Cleveland might keep it.

"Thank you," said Cleveland, and stepped over to her,

and kissed her fat cheek with the reverence of a son. He put the hat on his head, then doffed it, bowed, gracefully swept the floor with the tacky thing, and split. He had won something: Now that Jane was dead at her mother's hand, she was someone else, she was a girl without parents, which is the dream of every young man like Cleveland, if not every young man, period.

Mrs. Bellwether went over to the La-Z-Boy and fell into it. She had won something too, but it was something made up and pretty stupid.

"He believed you," said Arthur in a suitably awed tone. "He's probably wild with grief."

"I hope he doesn't try something foolish," I said.

"Let him jump off a bridge," said Mrs. Bellwether. "And good riddance." A sudden pragmatic thought seemed to invade her perfectly factless mind. "You'll tell him. I shouldn't have told you. You'll tell him she's alive!"

"Gee, I just might, Mrs. B.," said Arthur. He had sat back down in his chair and was lacing up his sneakers.

"Don't tell him. Please. Let him think she's dead."

"But what if they end up on the same bus someday? Or at adjoining tables in the Dirty O?"

"I'll send her away. I'll send her down to my mother's farm in Virginia. She'll be safe there. Don't tell him!"

Arthur sat up and gave the demented woman the relentless, clear stare that was going to make his career at the State Department.

"Two hundred and fifty dollars," he said.

While Mrs. Bellwether, looking pleased with herself,

made out the check to Arthur on the kitchen table, I carried his suitcase out of the house.

"Nice meeting you, Mrs. Bellwether," I called. "Shalom!"

We walked all the way back to my house. For some reason I felt depressed, and we didn't laugh. Arthur smoked cigarette after cigarette; when I gave him an account of my abduction by Cleveland he only sighed; he cursed the humid weather.

"Do you feel bad because you failed in your responsibility to the Bellwethers, or something ridiculous like that?" I said.

"No."

We reached the corner of Forbes and Wightman, wide, empty, and phony-looking in the light of the halogen lamps. Chained to one of the lampposts was the vending machine, now empty, that I had watched the dwarf fill with newspapers that morning. The sky to the south, over the steel mills, looked evil and orange and miasmic. We came to the Terrace and walked up through the maze of garages to my apartment, and I fumbled with the house key. I was still very drunk.

As I pushed open the door, Arthur put his hand on my shoulder, and I turned to face him.

"Art," he said. He touched my face. His beard was too heavy, there was a puffiness under his eyes, and he seemed almost to waver on his feet, as though he might fall over at any moment. There was something so drunken and ugly about him that I flinched.

"No," I said. "You're tired. You're just tired. Come on."

And then, as the song says, he kissed me, or rather pressed his lips against the upper part of my chin. I stepped back, into my apartment, and he fell forward, catching himself as his knees hit the floor.

"Oh, God, I'm sorry," I said.

"What an asshole I am, huh?" he said, standing carefully. "I'm just tired."

"I know," I said. "It's all right."

He apologized, said again that he was an asshole, and I said again that it was all right. I loved him and I wished he would leave. He slept on my floor among the boxes, while I trembled in bed under my cool, damp comforter. When I woke up the next morning, he had gone. He had ripped open his pack of Kools and folded it into the shape of a dog, or a saxophone, and left it on the pillow beside my head.

8

THE MAU MAU CATALOGUE

◆　　　　　　　◆　　　　　　　◆

Work the next day was not the circus I had expected. People are always ready to hear that something disturbing was after all only a prank—and that includes the police, who had come shortly after my abrupt departure. I called and explained to them, and to my fellow employees, that the Black Rider was a Pi Kappa Delta brother, upset over the fact that I had been seen dancing with his girlfriend, but essentially a nice guy who had only wanted to put a little of the fear of God into me. This story went over big, and even earned me some points, in the strange estimation of the apprentice paramedics and the Pittsburgh police, for having had the balls to dance with the girlfriend of a Pike, notoriously large fellows. By eleven o'clock I was able to go about my work as though I had never been torn from the register stand, manhandled, and driven away on the back of a gigantic motorcycle, and the momentary vortex I had created in the usually calm surface of Boardwalk Books closed over me.

After work I stepped outside, weakened by air-conditioning, and tugged out the last cigarette in the pack. Arthur and Phlox, side by side, approached from the direction of the library. Phlox wore pearls, a strapless white dress patterned with blue flowers, and a pair of high-heeled white sandals; Arthur, light-gray trousers and a powder-blue blazer, with a tie, and oxfords without socks, like Prince Philip. They were still far from me, and I watched as those they passed turned admiring heads; they drew near like an advertisement for summer and beauty and healthy American sex. The sun was in their faces, but they neither squinted nor averted their eyes; the light fell across Phlox's necklace and Arthur's hair and the hint of silver wristwatch at his cuff. I felt another of those sudden onslaughts of love, the desire to run to them and embrace them both, to be seen in their company, to live my life among men and women who dressed up like this and then went down the sidewalk like cinema kings.

"Hi, Art Bechstein," said Arthur, when they'd reached me. I had about half a cigarette left.

"Hi, Art Bechstein," said Phlox.

"Hello, Phlox; hello, Arthur. Wow."

The two of them panted after their brisk walk through sunlight, admiring stares, and the posh resorts and spas of my imagination. Thin strands of perspiration hung across their foreheads.

"Did you go to work like this?" I asked.

"Sure," said Arthur. "It seemed like a good day to do it."

"Arthur and I had the same idea today. Telepathically. Come into the old library all dressed up. We created a sensation. Telepathically. For your pleasure." She was plainly excited, by my undisguised astonishment at her lovely big

face and by the handsome man standing beside her, his fingertips nearly—bewilderingly—brushing her wrist.

"Well, I'm very pleased," I said.

"I could care less," said Arthur, "about your pleasure."

"Thank heavens," I said.

We looked at each other oddly, as though we neither of
us knew what exactly we were talking about.

"Ha," I said.

"Let's drink something cool and refreshing," Phlox said,
bobbing her head, widening then narrowing her eyes like
some lustful and wily biblical queen.

"Beer," said Arthur and I.

"Jane is dead," Arthur was saying. "And everything is
fine. That's all." He was drunk.

"But what did you do?" Phlox asked. She'd already
asked him five or six times, and each time he'd blushed,
looked down, and refused to explain.

"Do you want to know?"

"Ah," she said, perhaps imprudently, "you're finally
drunk enough to confess."

"No!" he said, lurching slightly into Phlox, who sat beside him in the booth, and spilling his fine hair across her
bare shoulder. "I'm not going to tell you."

"Watch it," she said, not taking her eyes from me as she
delicately shoved Arthur back over to his corner. Each cool
and refreshing sip she took seemed to increase the pressure
of her unsandaled silken foot against my sockless ankle. In
my drunkenness I'd lost any trace of the caution that had
propelled me only the day before into the brambles along

the Schenley Park bridge. I wondered suddenly (as suddenly as my eyes falling for the hundredth time upon her blue-flowered breasts) whether or not she wore a bra.

"Phlox," I said, before I could reconsider, "are you wearing a brassiere?"

"Never," she said. "Never in high June." She spoke without coyness, without shock or outrage at my impertinence.

"Hey, Blanche DuBois!" said Arthur. "'Never in high June.'"

She continued to look at me levelly and nearly without blinking. I began to get an unmistakable impression that this girl wanted me in a matter-of-fact, practical, and serious way. Arthur, I think, got the same impression. He stood up and excused himself, blushing again, but with a slightly businesslike tone, as though he had a job to do and were doing it.

"No, no," I called after him. "Don't leave me alone with this woman."

I have a photograph of Phlox here before me; the only one in which she wears no makeup. Her forehead appears, quite frankly, tremendous. She has adopted a disheveled, Thursday-night-at-home-with-my-boyfriend pose, ripped sweatshirt collar dipped over one round olive shoulder, face uncharacteristically Levantine (her father was related to the great Pittsburgh Tambellinis), saintly. A faint something, a hint of redness in the eyes, suggests that she's been crying; the lower lids seem slightly puffy. Of course she's been crying. Her nose, as ever, looks big and straight and radiant. A few limp curls drape the vaulting eyebrows and silver screen of a forehead. And the eyes, the legendary blue eyes of Death Itself. Yes.

Arthur returned from the rest room, looking pale but considerably more rational. He watched with great interest as I hastily undid my fingertips from Phlox's own, lavender-nailed.

"Arthur Bechstein likes you, Phlox Lombardi," he said.

"Oh, do you really think so, Arthur LeComte?" said Phlox. Her bosom heaved measurably.

Arthur slid in beside me, without stirring the foam on the beers. His face had changed; he was feeling, clearly if unusually, a strong feeling about something or other. He spoke into his collar, his beer, the beery tabletop, his lap, eyes downcast and invisible.

"I hate you, Phlox Lombardi," he said.

I laughed. Arthur looked up and smiled, radium white, an elegant, old-fashioned, moneyed, sad kind of smile, like a relic of that remote age when radium was still our friend. He unleashed this smile on Phlox, right in front of me; I was sitting there, confronted, I imagined, by the unimaginable, dizzying nastiness of homosexuality thwarted.

"Excuse me," I said. Arthur rose to let me out.

This bar was esteemed for the quality or at least the profusion of the graffiti in both its gentlemen's and ladies' rooms, which were rarely washed or repainted. I read this exchange:

WHAT'S SO GREAT ABOUT WOMEN, ANYWAY?

And, lower:

HEY, EVERY WOMAN, PAL, IS A VOLUME OF STORIES A CATALOGUE OF MOVEMENTS A SPECTACULAR ARRAY OF IMAGES

Then:

PLUS THERE'S THE MYSTERY OF LEARNING ABOUT HER CHILDHOOD

A fourth man had concluded:

AND OF EVERYTHING THAT'S CONCEALED UNDER HER CLOTHES

When I returned to our table, Arthur was in the middle of his story, now apparently master of his earlier and revelatory outburst.

"Every so often, Cleveland yelled, 'Teddeeee,' and inside the house someone next door said, 'What?' and we would laugh."

"Just tell me what you did," said Phlox. "Enough."

"No, let him keep you in suspense, why don't you?" I said. "This is good."

"Oh, but I hate suspense, Arthur. Arthurs. Arthurs, ha ha. No, but really, what did you guys do?"

"We drank," said Arthur.

"Well, that can hardly have shocked the Bellwethers."

I sat down across from Phlox and slipped off my shoes. Arthur told her that Teddy's control over the dogs was amazing, and at this point in Arthur's confession, just at the word "amazing," Phlox and I began in earnest a delicate, grueling, almost motionless game of footsie, a classic in excruciation, both of us playing to win, employing every one of the considerable mudras for lust or for a pledge of which the foot is capable. At no point did we take our eyes off Arthur; I was only marginally aware of the rapt attention Phlox expertly appeared to pay to him. She'd withdrawn both feet from her limp sandals. In similar circumstances, that is, drunk as I was, I would probably have done this with any attractive woman who happened to be sitting across from me with her feet bared and her cheeks flushed, but not with the same overwhelming awareness of technique, the same impulse toward skill, that Phlox inspired in me. Neither of us heard much of Arthur's account, delivered as it was by a drunken man in a jukebox-dominated bar to two people whose already beer-impaired attention was largely directed to the slow, feathery wrestling match taking place beneath the wet surface of the table. I later had to run through the whole story with her all over again.

"I'm ashamed of myself," Arthur finished. "I haven't felt so chastised in ages."

"Ah, that's why you got all dressed up today," I said. Phlox snorted.

"I can't believe it," she said. Abruptly she took her feet from mine, leaving them cold and interrupted, and I was momentarily seized by intense loneliness. "What won't you guys do when you're drunk? It's no wonder her parents were furious—a fifteen-year-old boy, my God."

"It wasn't that, Phlox. They don't give a damn about Teddy. Two facts: the fact that I let the Evil Cleveland in the house, and the fact that I let three Stanley Kowalski dogs take advantage of their delicate darling; that's it."

"Well, they have every right to be angry."

"You women always stick together," I said, which wasn't a particularly funny thing to say, but I was having difficulty thinking, and I wanted back the nylon feel of her toes.

"So what are you going to do, Arthur?"

"I think there's another couple who want me to house-sit for them. And they haven't a dog."

That summer's Stevie Wonder song came on the jukebox. I gathered that it was about a kiss like a water-melon or a chocolate chip.

"Will you dance with me, Art?" said Phlox.

"No," I said, and I ran the nail of my big toe down the length of the top of her foot, hard; but I didn't mean it.

The bar was built around a small central courtyard. When the management turned up the volume on the jukebox, people danced among the white iron tables and tame trees strung with lights, under the open sky. There were too many couples dancing; Phlox and I found our-selves backed into a corner, surrounded by people neither of us knew, who paid us no attention, and our strange but unsurprising conversation had all the exciting flavor of complete isolation. Unseen, unattended, we grew intimate, talkative, drunk, aroused. I kept my feet bare and tickled them against the Astroturf surface of the courtyard.

Phlox had covered herself in pearls that day, at the ear-lobes, the throat, the wrist. As she moved her hands and head in the still-light evening, talking about herself, the pearls seemed to string and restring themselves on the invis-ible thread of her gestures. This shifting nebula about her head and bust, like a sudden attack of phosphenes, first fas-cinated, then distracted, and ended by annoying the hell out of me. I had the constant sensation of having stood up too quickly, of seeing stars, which should at the very least have led me to drink fewer gin and tonics, two of which I had had the dubious foresight to carry out into the court and to set down on a little table beside us. A gin and tonic under its tiny canopy of lime, I said, elevates character and makes for enlightened conversation.

We danced; Phlox was trying to speak to me in French. She said amorous things. I answered promptly in English, mentioning also that I'd read that it was nowadays considered in poor taste to talk of love in French. "Don't be mean to me," she said, laughing. I laughed. She wriggled, minutely, in her strapless dress. I looked more closely at her makeup, and could see, as she glanced suddenly over her shoulder, that she had indeed been a punk sometime in the recent past; her eye shadow and blush defied her looks, rather than enhancing them, her ears had been pierced many times, and there was even, I thought, a dimpled trace of the piercing of her nose.

"Look," she said, "look up there. There's some kind of gallery up there. You can see things hanging on the walls. Look, Art, you can see art on the walls. There are African masks."

"Speaking of Africa, Phlox," I said.

She'd been expecting this, I suppose, or something like it, and was instantly outraged, stopped moving. "No. No, no way. If you ever call me Mau Mau, it will be the last thing you say to me."

"But why?" I said. "Why do they call you that?"

"Nobody calls me that. Don't you call me that."

"Never," I said. "Never will I call you that name."

"*Merci.*" She reached up and pulled tentatively on a lock of my hair. "*Que tu es beau, Arthur,*" she said.

"Don't call me that. Never call me 'Artoor,'" I mimicked. "And '*que tu es beau*'—come on."

She ranged her fingertips along my arm. I couldn't stop looking at her oversophisticated, tricolor eye shadow.

"That's what Daniel says to me. *Que tu es belle, Phlox.* Tries to say. His accent's terrible."

"I see. And just who is this Daniel fellow, anyway?" The name had cropped up in Arthur's conversation, at odd intervals, without any specific virtue or stigma being attached to it, but often enough that knowing some vague person named Daniel had come to seem one of Arthur's minor traits; and it was jarring somehow to hear Phlox say the name.

"A friend. He works in the library. The three of us go drinking sometimes."

This little statement left two unmistakable impressions: that I had a rival for Phlox's affections, and that I had somehow been deceived by Arthur, who obviously knew Phlox much better than he'd led me to believe. I thought: Well, it's okay, I am a rivalrous guy, this is going to be fun. But I also felt I had, or certainly ought to have, one or two important questions for Arthur.

"Daniel says I'm beautiful in a post-Godardian way."

"That Daniel. What a charmer."

"But there's something I dislike about him. I like you much more. He's moody, he's cruel. He suffers from spleen; do you know what spleen is? He's, well, he's an artist. You know. But you're a happy person, I can tell. Smiley. Sunny. I'm going to call you Sunny," she said.

"Next!" I called, lightly shooing her away, snapping my fingers impatiently, as though she'd just blown the audition. "Stop. All right. But I'll find something else to call you,

I swear. Are you going to kiss me, Arthur Bechstein?" she said.

"Eventually, I'm sure."

"Now," she said.

"You look very beautiful, Phlox," I said, and with my ridiculous heart beating as though I were that first German laborer, ignorant of engineering and about to remove that first wooden support from that first lacy thousand-ton dome of poured concrete, I made a fractional movement toward her lips with mine; then I drew her slightly into the shadow of a little tree and kissed her; somebody coughed. I heard the scrape of her dress against the thin branches, and the faint noise of her lips, fleshy, wet, tasting of lime and gin. I opened my eyes.

"There," she said, "that's over."

We went at it.

When we got back to the booth, a tall, skinny boy dressed for basketball, with an Italian face and filterless cigarettes, was sitting with Arthur. The tall boy was lighting Arthur's cigarette and I saw that the evening's arrangements had shifted. Now we were two couples who would go our separate ways.

"Phlox, Arthur, this is Bobby."

We said hello. Phlox and I were standing very close to each other, and I couldn't tell whether Bobby's careful top-to-bottom scrutiny was of Phlox or of me. I slid into the booth, next to Arthur, but Phlox remained on her feet, eyeing her purse.

"Oh," I said, "I guess we're going."

"Yes, I guess you are," said Arthur. "Good-bye." He

looked away from us, Bobby handed Phlox her little bag, I left a few dollars on the table, and we went out.

"How strange," I said.

She took my arm, a bit brusquely.

"I think it's disgusting," she said. "I think it's terrible that poor Arthur is gay."

"Why?" I said. "It doesn't—"

"I'm sorry, I just think it's disgusting and a shame. Men who sleep with men are just big cowards." She shivered once, then redoubled her grip on my arm and turned smiling to me. "Art, let's go to my house."

I kissed her behind the ear, came away with a mouthful of hair.

"Ooh," she said. "Do you want to take the bus or walk?"

"Let's walk," I said. "It'll give me a chance to burn off some of this rampaging heterosexual energy."

"I'll bet you're just a big battery, aren't you?"

"Um, Phlox, could we do something about these endearments of yours? 'Ooh.' 'A big battery.' You sound like a starlet, like Mamie Van Doren or someone."

"I love Mamie Van Doren," Phlox said, slapping me lightly across the face. "I am a starlet."

9

THE HEARTBREAK THING

◆ ◆ ◆

I admit I have an ugly fondness for generalizations, so perhaps I may be forgiven when I declare that there is always something weird about a girl who majors in French. She has entered into her course of study, first of all, knowing full well that it can only lead to her becoming a French teacher, a very grim affair, the least of whose evils is poor pay, and the prospect of which should have been sufficient to send her straight into business or public relations. She has been betrayed into the study of French, heedless of the terrible consequences, by her enchantment with this language, which has ruined more young American women than any other foreign tongue.

Second, if her studies were confined simply to grammar and vocabulary, then perhaps the French major would develop no differently from those who study Spanish or German, but the unlucky girl who pursues her studies past the second year comes inevitably and headlong into contact with French Literature, potentially one of the most destructive forces known to mankind; and she begins to relish such previously unglamorous elements of her vocabulary as *langueur* and *funeste*, and, speaking English, inverts her adjectives, to let one know that she sometimes even thinks in French. The writers she comes to appreciate—Breton, Baudelaire, Sartre, de Sade, Cocteau—have an alienating effect, especially on her attitude toward love, and her manner of expressing her emotions becomes difficult and theatrical; while those French writers whose influence might be healthy, such as Stendhal or Flaubert, she dislikes and takes to reading in translation, where their effect on her thought and speech is negligible; or she willfully misreads *Madame Bovary* and *La Chartreuse*, making dark romances of them. I gathered that Phlox, in particular, considered herself "linked by destiny" *(liée par le destin)* both to Nadja and to O. That is how a female French major thinks.

She lived in an apartment on the second floor of an old house, in a vague, quiet area between Squirrel Hill and Shadyside. As we climbed her bright stairway, I counted steps and watched the play of flowers on her broad, rather flat derriere. I knew what was about to happen, but I did not stop to think, except to think that I knew what was about to happen.

"We can talk loudly," she said, stepping into her apartment and turning on the light. "It's only ten o'clock, and my roommate is never home, anyway."

"Good!" I shouted.

The living room was small and plain, an ordinary student's living room, with secondhand furniture that had probably looked old the day it was made, a Renoir poster on one of the long walls, and a terrible, homemade painting of a cat on the other. On the coffee table there was a porcelain statuette of a white Persian cat like a huge scoop of whipped cream, with two lifelike and grotesque blue eyes. The table was strewn with issues of *Paris-Match* and *Vogue*.

"Whose cat idol is that?" I said.

"That's my Chloe," said Phlox. She stepped over to the ugly thing and began to tickle its porcelain chin. "Chloe, Chloe, Chloe, Chloe, Chloe," she said in a doll voice. "He lives at my mother's. I'm not allowed to keep a cat here. This is my little substitute Chloe. I made him in art in high school."

"It is beautiful. Isn't Chloe a girl's name?"

"Come and see my bedroom," she said, clasping my fingers and pulling me gently into the dark of the corridor.

I found her room apt and exciting: salmon-colored, neat, draped with white lace, in one corner a partially dismembered mannequin wearing a wedding dress and a nose ring. Huge posters covered the walls, of Diana Ross and the Supremes, of Arthur Rimbaud, and of the immense gibbous face of Garbo. Across the mirror of her dressing table hung a rosary; along the dressing table's surface was a vast collection of flacons and little bottles of womanly liquids. I sat on the edge of her bed, inhaling the remnants of her cologne, while she went to the toilet. Among the few books that she kept on her slender night table, her favorites, I supposed, were *The Selfish Giant* and *The Happy Prince* by Oscar Wilde, and *The Story of O* and Mailer's *Marilyn*.

When she came back into the room, she wore nothing but a peach teddy, wide-hipped, her face coppery and new-washed, her hair pulled up by a white ribbon. She looked 1940ish, the wife of some soldier off fighting the Germans, and briefly I felt the thrill of being an intruder in the house.

"You wear Opium," I said.

She sat beside me and put her face against my neck.

"Aren't you smooth. Even know your perfumes," she said, and she bit me.

"Here we go," I said. I brought her down on the chenille spread and breathed in the soap and the Opium at the base of her jaw, where her pulse was making itself known.

While Phlox, naked, broke eggs into a white bowl for French toast, I called the Duquesne and asked for my father's room. I stood in a corner of her lovely white kitchen, lazily cradling the phone with my shoulder, looking down at the sunny backyard and smelling my fingers.

"Bechstein," said my father, sounding chipper.

"Bechstein," I said. "This is your son."

"Ah, yes. My son. How are you, son? How's your summer thus far?"

Fine, Dad. I'm calling you from this girl's kitchen and she's standing here naked, and you know, Dad, I can see that some women do indeed look a little like guitars.

"Fine."

"Am I going to buy you yet another expensive lunch downtown?"

"I have to work, Pops."

"Then I propose an extremely expensive dinner on Mount Washington."

"Great. We can ride the Incline."

"Yes, the funicular," said my father. It was one of his favorite words.

"I'll come to the hotel around six," I said, and we hung up.

"That was quick," said Phlox.

"We always have that conversation when I call him at his hotel. It's my favorite conversation in the whole world."

I sat down at the kitchen table and watched her cook. She professed to love to cook; she did a lot of authoritative drawer opening, and laid the strips of bacon in the pan as though there were some science involved, but she didn't really seem to be enjoying herself. She tormented the French toast with her spatula, peering under each slice every five seconds, and she cursed irritably when the bacon fat spat. She left the kitchen to put on a robe and a Vivaldi record, and when she came back things were burning. I said that I rarely ate breakfast anyway and only needed a cup of coffee, which annoyed her. So I ate like a pig.

"Tell me about yourself," I said, chewing.

"I was born, grew tall and fair, knew both joy and tears, grew old, and died an abbess." Phlox, recognizing early that she lacked a strong sense of humor, or rather that she lacked the ability to make up jokes, had memorized thousands of bizarre passages from books and from here and there, and had developed, in place of humor, an ability to drop these bombs into a conversation, sometimes with incongruous, killer accuracy. She had, in fact, a number of unlikely conversational skills, or rather stunts. She knew and could explain with admirable clarity the secrets of machinery, how elevators tell the third floor from the fourth, why a spot is born and quickly burns away when a television is turned off; she could mentally alphabetize a fairly long and random list of words; and, most impressively, she remembered everything anyone had ever told her about himself, trivial things—the name of a childhood pet goldfish or of a distant cousin. This last ability made her the bane of a casual liar. Deceiving her demanded a great deal of care and attention.

"I understand that you've been born again?" I said.

She banged her juice down on the table and rolled her eyes, as though she had recently run out of patience with regard to Jesus. "No, that was just a *thing*. I'm not saying that I don't believe in God, because I do believe in God, even though it's more *branché* not to. But do you know what those Christians told me? They told me I would have to learn to live without sex. I can't live without sex, Art. It's ridiculous. If Jesus really loves me, then He wants me to sleep with boys."

"Amen," I said. "So what other *things* have there been?"

"Well, let's see. I've done the punk thing, the biker's girl thing, the seamstress thing, the prep school thing, and sort of the housewife thing, although I wasn't married. I've never done the marriage thing."

"You were a seamstress?"

"I sew like an angel."

"What's next?" I said, thinking that this was a glaring straight line.

"I don't know," she said, lightly. "Probably a broken heart."

"Ha," I said.

That evening I rode downtown on an unaccountably empty bus, sitting in the last row. At the front I saw a thin cloud of smoke rising around the driver's head.

"Hey, bus driver," I said. "Can I smoke?"

"*May* I," said the bus driver.

"I love you," I said.

In the big, posh, and stale lobby of the Duquesne Hotel—in a city where some of the men, like my father, still wear felt hats—one can still get one's hair cut, one's shoes shined, and buy a racing form or a Tootsie Roll. When I was a kid, and we would come into Pittsburgh to visit with my mother's relatives, I used to think that my father, who was perhaps born forty years too late, had had the Duquesne built for him. My father believed in the sports page brought up to his room on a tray with the java in the morning, and in the cigarette girl who prowled the bar with her Luckies and Philip Morris Commanders. Although he was in many ways a man of modern tastes, for music, hats, and hotels he looked to the Depression, and loved nothing but Goodman, snap brims, and the Duquesne.

The door to his room was unlatched; I pushed against it and found him sitting in a chair by the window, talking on the telephone. I made a noise as I came in, so that he could end the call if it was something I ought not to hear, but he half-waved, puckered his lips at me, and kept on talking. From his muttered replies I tried to guess to whom he was talking.

"Fine, fine," he said. "Listen, Artie just walked in. Yeah, yeah, he looks great. I'll tell him hello, sure. Right. Thirty-seven five. Right. See you tomorrow. Good-bye."

"Uncle Lenny," I said.

"He says you should come for dinner."

"I can't stand Aunt Elaine."

"Neither can he. My God, Art, your hair—you look terrible. Do you want me to give you the money to buy a comb?"

"No, thanks, Dad. I'm going to make one at home. Out of common household items. You look great."

"Business is good."

"Oh."

We both frowned. I never knew what to say upon hearing that business was good; it was always as though my father had just gleefully told me that he'd taken out a huge life insurance policy on himself, with me as beneficiary.

Then we said we were hungry and went out, down the laborious old elevator and into the street. A thunderstorm was imminent; big dusty rings of newspapers and the straw-pierced plastic lids of paper cups blew along Smithfield Street. We walked across the Smithfield Street Bridge to the South Side, and my father reminded me of the day fifteen years before when we'd driven across this bridge and I had astonished him by spelling Monongahela, unbidden.

"You were a smart boy," he said.

"What happened?" I said, and laughed, and he laughed, and said, What indeed.

I had decided to ask him about Cleveland, though I knew that if Cleveland had not met my father, a fairly important man, it was unlikely that my father would even know of Cleveland, whom I supposed to be an errand boy for the Stern family. Rarely did I ask my father about his work, and I didn't like to do it.

"Pops," I said, trying to imply my nonchalance by dipping a morsel of French bread into my enormous bowl of lobster bisque, "do you know any of the guys who work for Uncle Lenny?"

"Know them?" he said. "I went to the weddings of half of them. Danced with their wives."

"Yes, well. I mean some of the guys in the lower echelons."

"Why, do you know one? One of the kids?" He looked annoyed. "Where are you hanging around that you're meeting that kind of kid?"

"Well, gee, at the Symphony, the Carnegie Institute, the opera, the economics department, you know. Around."

"Look," he said, the blood flowing into his ever-pink face. "You always profess such a disdain for the business of your family. And those are men who, yes, don't have the education that you and I do, but who've been working hard all their lives, who have children and wives, and who make money to give it to their children and wives. And now you, Mr. Academic, you're hanging around with punks. Greedy little morons who give their money to other greedy little morons."

"Okay, Dad, okay. I'm not hanging around with any of Uncle Lenny's apes. I just asked if you knew them."

"Happily, no," he said, in his best dry voice.

We fell silent. I looked down from our perch in the

highest and most expensive restaurant in Pittsburgh onto the lights of downtown, and the black wishbone of rivers and the stadium on the other shore, illuminated for a night game, and thought about old ball games for a minute or two.

My father was the moneyman for the Maggio family (the Bechsteins, like the Sterns and all the Jewish crime families, having long since dwindled and been absorbed), but he also served as a kind of liaison between the people in the capital and those in Pittsburgh. Coming to Pittsburgh was pleasure as much as business for my father; he had met my mother at a wedding in Squirrel Hill, and so had a lot of family here; he knew its streets and crazed beltway system and suburbs and golf courses, and was a long-standing Pirates fan. I had been to Forbes Field as a tiny boy, and to Three Rivers Stadium a thousand times. The day I kept track of an entire nine innings in my scorebook, without making a single mistake, he bought me two hundred dollars' worth of toys at Kaufmann's, far more toys than I had ever wanted.

"Pops, I met this new girl."

He drained his glass of tonic water.

"Why do you make a face?" I said.

"After Claire, why shouldn't I? I'm sorry, Art."

"Sorry what?"

"Well, I have to confess that I don't—I don't trust you anymore. Art, you've become a very strange young man."

"Dad."

"Last time we met, you spoke like an insane person.

What was all that nonsense? It was upsetting to hear you talk that way. I felt terrible. I was very shaken."

My father had a way of looking as though he were about to weep but was making a superhuman effort to contain his tears, and it never failed to destroy me. I started to cry quietly as I chewed a wet and interminable piece of bread.

"Dad."

"I don't know what to think of you. I love you, of course, but—look what you're doing this summer. What are you doing this summer? Working at that ridiculous bookstore. I can't believe you're satisfied by that kind of job."

"Dad."

Now that he really had me going, hiccuping and sniffling, so people turned around from their tables to look at this distinguished father speaking calmly to his wild-haired son in tears; now that he had reduced me to my childhood role and demonstrated to me just how far I had fallen in his esteem, he relented, tenderly, speaking as though I had just wrecked my bike or got beat up at school and he was softly applying the fragrant Band-Aid.

"Now, what about this new girl?"

"Oh, Dad," I said.

The waiter came with our dinners, and I cried a little bit longer, and we hardly said a word until he asked if I wanted to leave. Then we rode down in the rattling funicular, and I watched the lights in the office buildings downtown grow less and less spectacular as we descended, and my father put his hand briefly on my shoulder and then took it away.

"You'd probably hate her, Pops; you'd probably h
eryone I know and everything I'm doing this summ
"Yes, I probably would," said my father.
"After I leave you I'm going to go to her hou
sleep with her," I said, and then we hit bottom a
and the sudden cessation of motion made me feel sic
my father said that he was not impressed.

10

SEX AND VIOLENCE

◆ ◆ ◆

June waned; still Jane Bellwether remained in New Mexico, calling Cleveland only once, to tell him they were through ("Does that make nine times or ten?" Cleveland asked her); by the twenty-ninth of June, Phlox and I were firmly ensconced in a "thing" that she was—prematurely, I felt— calling love, although I was beginning to wonder, and listened one night to "You've Really Got a Hold on Me" thinking: Oh, Smokey.

Phlox had taken to coming over to the Terrace every night after I got off work, and we would sit on the steps smoking cigarettes, and sometimes marijuana, or would drink tequila, and just eat the limes and lick the salt from the tiny pouches of each other's hands. One night there was an enormous full moon, fat and hanging right above the horizon, as though too debauched and decrepit to rise any farther. We were stoned, and the black Romanesque steeple of the church on the corner stood silhouetted against the moon, entwined with the shapes of branches of a dead tree, like an establishing shot from a vampire film, and I said this. She pressed herself against me, her teeth chattering.

"Why are you afraid?" I said.

"I don't know. Because vampires are so beautiful," she said.

Another time she wept bitterly for an hour because Arthur had been cruel to her at work that day and told her she looked fat in her plaid dress.

"I know he's just jealous of me," she said. "Art, I know he wants you."

"Nah," I said. "He likes you."

"Art!" she shouted. "Listen to me, and don't baby me. I know he wants you, he wants to have sex with you, homosexual sex, disgusting homosexual sex with my Artichoke," which was what she called me.

"Phlox, what do you have against gays? I like all the gay guys I've met, Arthur especially, but all of his friends too. They're nice guys."

"Sure they're nice guys, they're *beautiful*, and it's a goddamn shame they're a bunch of hideous fags. Some of them are more beautiful than I am."

I denied this.

On the twenty-ninth of June, the night Phlox told me that she loved me, that Daniel was a fool and had an ugly purple penis and I need never worry about him again, she read to me from *The Story of O*, in the yellow light of my stoop. (I had read this book years before, before my mother died, finding it among her books, and I had failed to understand it. Only the scenes of more conventional sex had excited me, and the whips and owl masks and labial piercing I had found confusing, exotic, and disagreeable.) When

Phlox read to me from the book, sitting up against the bricks with her knees to her chest, in a green leather mini-skirt with no panties, I was shocked to discover what an evil book it was, although nicely written, and the thought that it was her favorite disturbed me. Nevertheless I felt the thrill of her voice and got an erection, which I could not disguise, and which, reaching over, she freed and relieved me of, and then without stopping her reading, she relieved herself.

"That was wonderful," she said when she had tired of reading.

"I want to walk you home," I said, and handed her sweater to her.

"Art, I want to stay with you."

"I'd rather walk you home."

"Arthur, I love you," she said.

"I refuse to flog you," I said.

She burst out laughing, and told me what a silly boy I was. And, as my father might have put it, indeed I was.

The next night Cleveland and Arthur and I got drunk and decided to go off to Cleveland's family's summer house in upstate New York. It would be just the three of us. At a still-sober point in the evening, Arthur began to berate Phlox, just barely. He looked terrific that evening, had been lying out in the sun, and he wore a turquoise cotton sweater that did alarming things to his blue eyes. He said that Phlox was nuts, and smiled, and that she would mess me up, and smiled again.

"You introduced me to her," I said.

"This is true," he said.

He had been reading, in Spanish, the as-yet-untranslated new book by García Márquez, and he translated for me its rather terrible epigraph, which had impressed him.

"'Love is like falconry,'" he said. "Don't you think that's true, Cleveland?"

"Never say love is like arything," said Cleveland. "It isn't."

I'd long ago noticed that it was Arthur's habit to consult his wristwatch every five minutes. There was always some plan in the back of his mind, some itinerary extending far into the evening, which he would reveal to us only one step at a time. This evening he was particularly attentive to his wrist, and Cleveland, as usual, called him on it, in a way that I supposed had been part of their game for a long time. Arthur would glance quickly at his watch, and Cleveland would say, "What time is it, Arthur?" Five minutes later, when Arthur glanced again, Cleveland again asked what time it was, making Arthur look ridiculous, and again, and again, and each time Arthur blushed more deeply, until finally he laughed and said he had to leave.

"And where are you going, Artie?" said Cleveland.

"To Mass," said Arthur.

"Oh, right," I said. "When was the last time you went to Mass?"

"Last Sunday," said Arthur. He left some money on the table, shook our hands, and went out.

Cleveland and I drank until the bar closed. It was a hot night, and the ceiling fans ruffled our hair and tore the cigarette smoke into little scraps. Each bottle of Rolling

Rock came to us pearled with condensation and trailing a streamer of cold steam. He told me stories of past years at the summer house, of the horse he'd ridden into a neighbor's swimming pool, the Good Humor lady who'd taken his virginity. Then we talked about Frank O'Hara, and how he died, struck by a dune buggy, on Fire Island; Cleveland sat back in the booth, rolled his eyes upward, and recited.

"'Oh to be an angel (if there were any!),'" he said, "'and go straight up into the sky and look around and then come down.'"

He fell silent and his eyes grew kindly and drunken.

"I like you, Bechstein," he said, which made me blush, and I felt tears come to my eyes. "For Christ's sake, don't cry, Bechstein. I don't like you that much. Let's get some pickled eggs." He ordered and proceeded to dispatch about twelve of the little beet-colored nodules, one by one. "As long as bars continue to serve pickled eggs," he said, licking his fingers, "there is reason to hope."

When the waitress called Last Call, Cleveland said that the bar was very close to his father's house, and that he would just go there to sleep tonight, instead of going all the way back to his own house.

"There are no more buses," he said, "and it'll take you almost an hour to walk home. Why don't you just sleep over. You can sleep downstairs. You'll like it; it's spooky."

Before she committed suicide, when he was seventeen, Cleveland Arning's mother, a laughing woman, taught her son to joke and to ridicule. His father, tall, thin, cut his beard in a goatee and wore great red sideburns that ran up his otherwise bald temples. His name was also Cleveland, and although he did indeed have his own grim notions of what made a joke, he laughed only rarely, generally in the privacy of his own study. In the kitchen, Cleveland and his mother would listen to the inexplicable sound of his father's laughter coming through the oaken door, and whatever story Cleveland had been telling to make her laugh would die on his lips. They would chew in silence, clatter the dishes into the sink, and go to their rooms. Cleveland senior was a psychiatrist.

Cleveland told me, I now find, very little about his childhood. He once spoke of having lived in the countryside to the northwest of Pittsburgh, saying only, naturally, that he'd very often gotten into trouble. There was a bartender in one of his usual haunts who had been a neighbor in the country years before. "This is Charlie," he said, introducing me one night. "His parents forbade me to set foot in their house ever again." Yet despite the fact that I have few details, I have a clear sense of the strangeness of the Arning household—the taciturn, warped father, who took male lovers; the nervous mother, underweight, musical, struggling with her husband's secret for as long as she could manage; Cleveland, bright, violent, already considering himself "doomed and wild" by age twelve; and his sister, Anna, the baby, her brother's target and first fan.

I visited the house only that one time, sleeping downstairs on the couch, and yet in the ten minutes I spent exploring the dim first floor at three o'clock that morning, alone, with only the sound of the toilet Cleveland had flushed somewhere in the enormous house, I felt the trouble, the tension of the place.

The furnishings were rich, antique, and cold to the touch, even in late June: huge clocks, chairs with fabulously carved arms, old, evil-looking medical paraphernalia, and rugs that would not give under my stocking feet. I entered all the rooms I could find, wincing at every creak of the floor as though I were a burglar, and as I crossed each threshold I would ask myself, Is this the room? Which room would it have been? People usually do it in the bathroom. Or the garage. Cleveland, in fact, had never told me of his mother's suicide, which happened eight, nine years before. I heard of it from Arthur, who hadn't really wanted to tell me.

In Dr. Arning's study—how my chest tightened as I fingered the heavy light switch on his paneled wall!—there was one photograph, of Cleveland's sister Anna, dressed in black, a diamond pendant, no smile. The room smelled of perfume, a man's cologne perhaps, but terribly floral and green. Dr. Arning's golden pens and marble desk implements lay in rows and columns across his enormous desk, which, in its size and in the weak lamplight, looked bare and malignant, the desk of Dr. Moreau.

I wanted to stop to examine the titles of the million books on the shelves, but something pressed me, made me feel as though I had to hurry on before I was discovered, although I knew that the house was asleep and I had, if I desired, all night to satisfy my curiosity. I shivered in my light Hawaiian shirt and flipped off the light.

After I had circled the immense domain of the ground

floor, I came once again to the long lemon sofa onto which Cleveland had thrown a fuzzy blanket and a striped silk pillow for my head. I sat down. I pulled my socks off and lay backward, leaving on the lamp, staring up into the shade at the burning bulb until it blinded me. I turned away and watched the optical blobs of color float across the immaculate walls of the living room. I felt far from falling asleep, but drunk, drunk enough to stand and to walk down the dark wooden hallway barefoot.

At the end of the hallway sat a mass of black iron grillwork with silver fittings, a cage worked with leaves and tendrils. Arthur had told me that Cleveland's father had an elevator in the house. I experienced a brief but overwhelming urge to step in and ride to the upper level, where Cleveland slept, and Dr. Arning and his "friend." The upper level! I turned around. A staircase rose on either side; I chose the left-hand set of steps and climbed, quietly, digging the joints of my toes into the soft red carpeting that led to the weird sleep of the Arning family.

There were seven brown doors, three down the corridor to my left, four down the corridor to my right, all of them closed. Cleveland's, the doctor's, a bathroom, a closet, his mother's? Anna's, two closets? two bathrooms? I went left and stopped before the door at the end of the hall. It was slightly ajar. I put my ear to the gap and listened for the breathing of a sleeper, heard nothing, put my eye to the gap and looked for the glow of a clock face or radio dial, saw nothing. I leaned a little against the door and it swung open, noiselessly.

I'd been looking into a part of the room where there was

nothing to see, a blank wall. At the other side of the room, a large, milky window threw light across an empty white bed, a girl's bed, a girl's room, soft pale draperies and cushions, girlish posters on the walls. I stepped into Anna's abandoned room and closed the door behind me. My heart pounded, and I did nothing but draw heavy breath for several moments. I felt safer and protected and yet still at risk, alone in a forbidden place. I felt ridiculous, also, as I panted and swallowed like a fugitive in a room lined with satin and photographs of infant cats, and unicorns. I laughed softly at her taste, and relaxed a little.

Anna's bed gave enormously under my weight. I leaned over to smell her pillows. I'd been expecting some kind of a girl smell, but the pillows merely smelled laundered, even faintly dusty, very cool to the tip of my nose.

When Anna was twelve and Cleveland fifteen, the family, at the brink of disaster, took their yearly trip to the summer house that Cleveland's father would buy a few months after Mrs. Arning's death.

The brother and sister pulled on their striped swimsuits and ran out into the lake, Cleveland yards ahead of Anna and heedless of her. The three years that separated them made a greater difference than they ever had before, and the quiet, angry boy wanted nothing to do with his rope-skipping sister, who adored him. He plunged into the green water and swam as fast as he could, leaving Anna to scream "Cleveland!" at the gravelly hem of the lake and to wipe the tears and snot from her face with her small hand. He surfaced some twenty yards away and trod water, the sun heating his shoulders and drops of water from his long hair

cooling them. He watched his sister dance in disappointment and rage for a moment, feeling terrible guilt, before
the feeling became too much and he grew angry instead,
furious with her for not allowing him to be alone, for being
a pest and a girl and the only person in the world who
really liked him.

In his anger he swam back to the shore and, without
surfacing, grabbed Anna by her skinny knees and with a
leap lifted her out of the water. At first Anna laughed and
began to say "Whee," but she caught sight of the look in
his eye. The next moment she was underwater, his hand
pressing down on her head, hard. He had dunked her in the
past and it always frightened her, but this time it was real
and she panicked, thinking she was about to die. When he
finally withdrew his murderous pushing hand she surfaced in
a fury, screaming, crying, confused. She called him
"fucker," took up two small handfuls of silt, and threw
them. They splattered across his chest in thin gray streaks.
"Shit," he said, and filled his own bigger fists with dirt and
pebbles and hurled them at her outraged little face, where
the smallest of small stones entered her eyes and blinded
her. She fell over shrieking into the water, slapping wildly
at her face and the air around her, while Cleveland, shouting, "Stupid! Stupid! Stupid!" stood in water up to his
knees and in three seconds thought about the awfulness of
his betrayal of his sister, and how much he hated her for
having been there to accept his rage.

Fortunately—so much more fortunately than I had any
right to expect—I woke up on Anna's bed at six-thirty the
next morning and crept downstairs, taking an early inven-

tory of my already full-blown hangover, and back onto the yellow sofa. At ten-thirty, Cleveland placed an icy Pepsi against my cheek and I woke up for the second time that day. As we walked shakily and in great thirst down to Oakland, where I had to start work at one o'clock, I asked a few innocent questions about the sister whose bed I'd slept in the night before, and he recounted the above story, albeit differently. Arthur later embellished it for me. Since Anna had recovered her sight completely after emergency surgery, Cleveland could now concentrate on the small details of being a lonely fifteen-year-old, and he made it, by dint of his genius for telling a story, a very funny story, and I laughed despite the pain in my head.

That night I took Phlox to dinner at the Elbow Room, but my stomach still felt frail and I ate only spinach leaves while I watched her put away a bowl of chowder, a heap of tortellini, and a pretty little dish of ice cream.

"We'll only be gone a few days," I said. "Absence makes the heart grow fronds, as my father says."

"But why can't I come?" said Phlox. "It's because Arthur hates me. Right?"

"No, it's because I hate you." This did not go over well. "Come on, Phlox, no one hates you."

"Do you love me?"

"Like the big time," I said. "Look, it's just me and Cleveland and Arthur. Crude jokes, poker games, sports talk, boozy sentimentality—you know, boys' stuff."

She frowned. I knew I was being too flip, but I felt lousy, and more than that, I think, I wanted to get away from her; to pause for a moment. I'd heard, somewhere in the past couple of days, the stealthy entrance of creepiness into my unsecured summer, a faint creaking of the woodwork, and I felt as though I ought to lie very still, not draw a breath, and listen for the something that might be there, for the next telltale footfall.

11

Searchlights and Giant Women

◆   ◆   ◆

Next morning before sunrise, I sat in the backseat of the old Arning Barracuda, wiping flakes of doughnut glaze from my lips and struggling to appreciate the negligible effects of a single cup of coffee. Cleveland and Arthur sang along with an old John and Yoko cassette and pointed out the windmill-shaped restaurants, the car dealerships surmounted by giant plaster statues of bears and fat men, the gunshops and gospel billboards, that were the beloved landmarks on the way to Fredonia. I sang "Hail, Freedonia," from the Marx Brothers movie. I hadn't driven a long distance since coming, with all my belongings, from Washington to Pittsburgh to start school four years before, and had forgotten how much I enjoyed lying across the backseat of a car with my hair hanging out one window and my feet out the other, watching the phone poles pass, listening to music, the engine, the wind passing over the car.

After we'd been twice through the Lennon and I'd slept, apparently, through Cleveland's other cassette, there were only the sounds of the Barracuda and of Patsy Cline

120

on the radio, coming in faintly from somewhere, and it was eight o'clock in the morning, and I watched happily the backs of my friends' heads. We pulled into a Stop & Shop for more coffee, and then I felt like talking; I asked how long, exactly, had they been friends?

"Nine years. We met in our first year at Central Catholic," said Cleveland. "We found ourselves what you might call together apart."

"He means that everyone else hated us," said Arthur.

"Speak for yourself," said Cleveland. "I simply noticed that we weren't like any of the other boys in that excellent school."

"Central always looks to me like Santa's Castle," I said.

"We weren't like any of the other elves," said Arthur.

"Arthur, here, already had, I believe, some vague notion of the perverse and sinful sexual longings that would shortly make him as un-Catholic as one might conceivably be—"

"And Cleveland was already drinking a six-pack of beer a day, and smoking cigarettes and marijuana. And reading every book on the *Index librorum prohibitorum*. And Cleveland," said Arthur, turning to look sadly at his friend, but speaking with the same sarcastic tone, "*wrote* in those days."

"Yeah. Say, isn't it too early for this discussion? Couldn't we save it for such time as I am drunk enough to ignore it and fall asleep mid-reply? That reminds me," he said, and without slowing he swerved the car off the small state highway and we stopped in the deserted parking lot of a grocery store, where Cleveland got out and went around to the trunk.

"What's in the trunk?" I asked Arthur, who yawned, stretched, and turned to face me, looking pink and unshaven.

"Oblivion," he said. "Oblivion is in the trunk."

Cleveland climbed back in with a six-pack from the cooler, and by the time we reached the house on the lake, he was well into his second green aluminum fist of Rolling Rock, and though his driving hadn't really fallen apart yet, I was glad we weren't going any farther. The road grew narrow and crooked, the trees grew denser, and to our left I began to make out, through rare gaps in the pine and sycamore, strips of silver lake, and the striped awnings of distant houses; soon we came to a gravel drive, to a cluster of rusted mailboxes like a row of tumbledown tenements, their red metal flags hoisted and falling at all angles. As we pulled, gravel popping, into the driveway, Cleveland stopped the car, threw it into park, and got out.

"I'm going to walk," he said. He slammed the door and set off, carrying a can of beer. Arthur and I sat a moment, watching him shamble toward the empty house, something determined yet wary in his tread. The engine began laboriously to idle. Three or four minutes passed. Arthur put his feet up on the dashboard.

"Well?" I said.

"He always does this," said Arthur. "He'll be back."

"You mean we just sit here and wait?"

"Can you drive?"

"Can't you?" I scrambled over the seatback and settled

in behind the steering wheel, which was warm in just two places, as though from the heat of Cleveland's hands. "You really are a relic," I said.

"There have always been people willing to do my driving for me," he said, shrugging, as I put the car in gear. "People like you."

Although Cleveland had said that his father visited it every other weekend, the summer house looked long abandoned. It was white wood, trimmed in blue, with a veranda that ran all the way around and a white rowboat rotting on its wild front lawn; this lawn, weedy and filled with gnats, began at the edge of the lakefront beach, surrounded the house, and then ended abruptly in a sagging, vine-covered slat fence at the treeline, as though it could barely withstand the encroachments of the forest around it—indeed, here and there amid the weeds, packs of saplings and even young trees were closing in. One of the front steps had come unnailed, the paint peeled from the white columns of the veranda, the bench of a broken porch glider dangled by a single chain under the wide front window, and standing on the threshold, I felt keenly aware of all the vacations that had been passed here over the last half century, all the ghostly cries of "A hummingbird!" "A meteor!" all the bitter sighs and campfires of a dozen vanished families.

When I came into the dark, cedar-smelling house, Cleveland was standing in the living room with his back to me, looking at a photograph framed over the fireplace. I came up behind him and looked. It was a picture of himself at the age of fifteen or sixteen, an angelic smirk on his face, eyes bright, hair long and of a lighter color; already he held a can of Rolling Rock in one hand, a cigarette in the other, but there was something different in this characteristic pose, something enthusiastic, gloating; and the smirk was that of a novice who had only just learned the Secret and couldn't quite believe that it was so simple. In the picture he looked handsome and nearly famous, and looking at him now, big and scarred and immobile, I saw, for the first time, what Arthur and Jane must have seen when they looked at Cleveland: diminution in growth, loss through increase, a star that has passed from yellow to red. Perhaps I read too much into this photograph, but Cleveland's reaction to it soon confirmed my own feeling. I couldn't help but say, "Gee, Cleveland, you look really terrific in this photo."

"Yes," he said. "I was happy."

"Was it summertime?"

"Uh huh. Here at the lake."

"Doesn't summertime always make you feel kind of the way you look in this picture, though?"

"Sure," he said, but I could tell he said it only to humor me, and his tone more honestly said: Not anymore; no. He tapped the glass of the frame once with his finger, and then turned toward me.

"Let me show you your bedroom," he said, avoiding my gaze. He started off, then turned back toward the photograph and tapped it once again.

My bedroom was the back porch, which, when the tide was in, overhung Lake Erie. I changed slowly into my swimming trunks and then, stiff from the long ride in the car, ran down to the beach, where I found Arthur and Cleveland already stretched out on towels and laughing, their cans of beer little bunkers half-buried in the sand. There was a light breeze off the water, and they had kept their shirts on; Arthur's said LAST CALL. We drank, we swam, we lay on the dingy sand and looked out at the boats on the lake. Cleveland disappeared into the house for a while, and returned with an air rifle and a trash bag full of tin cans. I stayed on my towel and watched as he erected a row of targets along the fence, took aim, and blew them off without a miss.

"How can he do that when he's drunk?" I asked Arthur.

"He isn't drunk," said Arthur. "He's never drunk. He just drinks and drinks and drinks until he passes out, but he never gets drunk."

This reminded me of the photograph on the mantel, the can of beer.

"What kinds of things did he used to write?"

"Oh, essays, I guess you'd call them, odd essays. I told you about the one on cockroaches. We had this teacher in high school, a terrific woman. He started writing because of her."

"And," I said.

"And later she met with, of course, some kind of disaster."

"Which kind?"

"Death." He rolled over and faced away from me, so that I could see only the back of his head and hear his voice only in an unsatisfactory and into-the-wind way. "So, theoretically, that's why he stopped. But that's just his same old Cleveland bullshit. Every one of his failings has a perfectly good excuse. Usually some kind of disaster."

"Like?"

"Like his mom kills herself, his dad becomes about the scariest queer I've ever seen—and I've seen scary ones, believe me—so Cleveland is pardoned from ever having to do anything good, or productive, ever again." He pulled off his T-shirt and draped it over his head, baring his slender, rosy back.

"Did he want to be a writer?" I said, and tried to pull the shirt from his head, but he grabbed hold of it and remained hidden.

"Sure he would have liked to be a writer, but see, now he has these great excuses. It's so much easier to get fucked up almost every night."

"You drink a lot."

"It's different."

"Look at me."

"No. Look, he's gotten a lot of mileage out of this Lost Weekend thing. I'm as guilty as anyone of laughing at him and respecting him for being a fuck-up. He knows lots of people, and most of them want to be his friend. At least initially. They do change their minds."

This was true. He had already deteriorated in charm and in drunken brightness to the point where one occasionally met someone who, at the mention of Cleveland's name, would say, "That creep?"

"I told you that when his mom died she left him about twenty thousand dollars. It's gone. He spent it. Mostly on dope and beer and records and trips to see the Grateful

Dead play Charleston, or Boston, or Oakland, California, once. On bullshit. Do you know what he does now?"

"Yes," I said.

He threw off his shirt and whirled to face me, though of course his face didn't betray any surprise.

"Did he tell you?"

I stood up.

"I'm bombed," I said. "How many cans do you think I can hit?"

I took a nap on the screened porch, over the lapping tide, and suddenly I smelled chili. I lay on the cot, waking slowly, in stages, the warm red odor working its way into my brain until my eyes opened. I went into the kitchen and stood next to Cleveland as he opened one can after another, until he had two dozen targets for tomorrow and a gallon of chili in the pot. He was shirtless and had a drunk's bruise on his left shoulder, as he did on his shin and forearm.

"Gee, you have a big stomach," I said.

He stopped stirring the aromatic brown slop in the tureen and patted his belly proudly.

"Of course I do," he said. "I'm in the process of eating the entire world. Country by country. Last week I polished off Bahrain and Botswana. And Belize."

We sat down at the scratched, old, fine oak dinner table with our bowls of chili, and I started drinking beer again, which was cold and cleared my head. After dinner we went out. It was still, though barely, light. Arthur found a Wiffle ball and a fungo bat, so we went out into the water, and he skillfully hit long flies that we swam yards and yards to field. After we'd waded in to shore, we stood shivering in the breeze and put on our sweatshirts. Cleveland taught me to cup a windblown match, "like the Marlboro Man," and then how to flick the cigarette butt twenty-five feet when I was done. The sun went down, but we stayed on the beach, watching the fireflies and the momentary bats. The woods were full of crickets, and the music from the radio on the porch mingled with the sound of the insects. I sat on the sand and thought, for a moment, of Phlox. Cleveland and Arthur wandered down to the water's edge, too far for me to hear their talk, and smoked two long Antonio y Cleopatra cigars, then put them out in the sand. They pulled off their sweatshirts and ran into the water where years before Cleveland had brutalized his little sister.

I felt happy—or some weak, pretty feeling centered in my stomach, brought on by beer—at the sight of the fading blue sky tormented at its edges with heat lightning, and at the crickets and the shouting over the water, and by Jackie Wilson on the radio, but it was a happiness so like sadness that the next moment I hung my head.

"How can you spend so much time with her?" Arthur was saying, as he threw pine needles into the heart of the fire that Cleveland had built on the beach, where they caught, flared, and disappeared, as my little moods had all day. "She thinks she's such a glamour girl."

"So do you," said Cleveland. Two small campfires burned in the lenses of his black glasses. "And what's *wrong* with thinking that? She exaggerates herself. It's healthy."

"It's unbearable," said Arthur.

"It's genius," said Cleveland. "A genius you don't possess. Do I myself not claim to be in the process of eating the entire world? A patent exaggeration. Do I not claim to be Evil Incarnate?"

"Yes," I said. "Yes," and I told them about my skyscraper, and my zeppelin, and the hurtling elevator, and Arthur snorted and drained another beer, and said that was a little unbearable too.

"No, it's big—he's got it, it's big," said Cleveland. "Bigness is the goal of life, of evolution, of men and women. Look at the dinosaurs. They started out as newts, little newts. Everything's been getting bigger. Cultures, buildings, science—"

"Livers, drinking problems," said Arthur, and he stood up and went back into the house for some more beer.

"He doesn't get it," I said.

"Yes, he does," said Cleveland. "He's heard this a million times before. We used to have this thing, this image of ourselves—not ourselves, but, well, it was exactly like your thing with the hotel. What would you call that kind of thing, Bechstein?"

"An image. An image of the big stuff you wanted?"

"Come on, you can do better than that."

"How about 'a manifestation of the will-to-bigness,'" I said.

"Exactly!" He threw a pebble at my head. "Asshole. Okay, this was about women. Back when Artie was still ambisexually inclined. Bambisexual. Iambisexual."

"Come on."

"Shut up. We had this vision—imagine your skyscraper

hotel, only think of the whole city around it, think of a whole skyline like that, big and art deco, with searchlights, the beams of searchlights, cutting across the sky, all crazily, frantically. And then you see them. In the sweeping beams of the searchlights."

"See what?"

"Giant women! Gorgeous women, like Sophia Loren, Anita Ekberg, but the size of mountains, kicking over buildings, crushing cars under their manicured tremendous toes, with airplanes caught in their hair."

"I see it," I said.

"That was the manifestation of our will-to-bigness." There was a long silence. I heard the toilet flush inside the house. "You know, ah, Bechstein . . ."

"Hmm?"

"When do I get to meet your father?"

"You're crazy."

"No, I can tell I'd like him. He's big too. I've heard about him. I hear he's one of the real wise guys. I'd like you to introduce me. If you don't mind. Even if you do mind."

"What, exactly, are you into with Dave Stern? Numbers?"

"P and D."

He meant pickup and delivery for a loan shark: dropping off the principal to the unfortuante borrower and then stopping by once a week to collect the ridiculous interest.

At first I hadn't taken Cleveland's supposed involvement with the underworld seriously, but now, suddenly, I did. Cleveland would do it. He would breach the barrier that stood between my family and my life, and scale the wall that I was.

"No, but, Cleveland, you *can't* meet my father." If a whisper and a whine can be combined, that was the tone of my voice. "Come on, tell me more about the searchlights and giant women."

"I remember them," said Arthur, who had just returned. "He wanted that, not me. I only wanted to know who built the Cloud Factory. Which, by the way, is rather small."

"God built the Cloud Factory," said Cleveland. "And God is the biggest of the big."

"Wrong," said Arthur. "There is no Cloud Factory. Or God, or giant women, or zeppelins."

"Fuck you," said Cleveland. "They'll come for me, one of these days. They'll come for you too. Prepare yourself. Prepare your father too, Bechstein." And he stood up and went into the house and did not come back.

"What was that about your father?" said Arthur.

"Who knows?" I said. "He probably has me confused with Jane."

As I stood looking in the mirror at my hangover the next morning, balancing my headache carefully between two hands, I heard shouts, then some thumping at the front of the house, and then a woman's voice, a familiar southern accent. I trudged out to see.

Cleveland and Jane were squared off just inside the front door, beside two bags of groceries, and Arthur, in his underpants, and wearing the T-shirt that said LAST CALL, watched warily, but with a thin smile, his eyes round. I thought of our first meeting outside the library. Jane, sunburned and fine, her hair bleached almost white, wore a

pink-and-yellow plaid cotton dress, which did not harmo-
nize with the fists at her sides, or with her muscled shoulders, or with her fierce eyes.

"Go 'head," Cleveland said. "I dare you."

"I will," said Jane. "I'll hit you."

"Hi, Jane," I said. "You look great."

She turned toward me, undid her fists, and smiled, then
turned back and gave Cleveland a right hook across the
jaw. He fell against the wall; he touched his finger to the
corner of his mouth and looked in bemusement at the blood
that came away on it. For a moment he smiled at Jane, at
me, at Arthur, before he threw himself at Jane and brought
her down with a hard sound to the wooden floor. They
began to wrestle, grunting and saying shit, you fucker, et
cetera. Cleveland had the advantage of weight, though I
doubted he was any stronger than she.

"Come on, Cleveland, Jane, cut it out," said Arthur
mildly. He looked at me, raised an eyebrow, did not move.
I went over to try to do something, and got smacked in the
groin by someone's fist. It hurt, and I fell breathless to the
floor. Jane, beneath Cleveland, brought her knee up to his
chest and pushed. He flew backward, and Jane leapt up and
threw herself upon him, screaming, "Cleveland!" Motion
ceased. They panted, I panted; I drew myself to my knees
and watched Cleveland begin to laugh and Jane to cry.

"Oh, Cleveland," she said.

"Did you drive a hundred and fifty miles just to beat the
shit out of me?"

"Yes," she said, and she sniffed, in a show of pride, and
snapped her head back and thrust out her chin.

"Really?"

"No," she said, dropping her forehead to his chest and kissing his big belly, and at that moment, Arthur, whom I had not noticed leaving the room, came in again, holding a saucepan full of water, which he emptied onto their desperate heads, grinning.

"They're fine," I said. "Pour some water onto my balls, for Christ's sake."

"I've been waiting so long for you to say that," said Arthur.

So Jane was among us now, and although I missed the intimacy of the previous day, I found her so thrilling, so prim and *sportive*, that I welcomed her arrival—we all did. She went back to her car to fetch her luggage, singing loudly and earnestly some sad hymn, like a young girl who had learned it only that morning at church. As she came back into the house, she stopped singing, looked around her, dropped her bags, and sighed. She unpacked two pressed, polka-dot dresses from her plaid dress bag and hung them from the living-room doorknob, then carried the groceries in their torn sack from the hallway to the kitchen, and dumped them out on the counter.

"Oh, no—a salad," said Arthur.

Jane had brought several pounds of vegetables with her, and she proceeded to make an enormous salad and, rather mechanically, to vent her spleen at Cleveland. "You raped our dog," she said, slicing thin, translucent wafers of cucumber into a wooden salad bowl as big as a bicycle wheel. "I mean . . ." Cleveland changed completely. He switched from drinking beer to drinking the orange juice that she had brought, and he kept going over to embrace her, to smell her, to assure himself that she was really there. Arthur and I sat down at the kitchen table, ate grapes, and watched them reunite; they forgot us completely, or pretended to do so.

"They said you were dead," Cleveland said happily. "Dead of dysentery."

Jane blushed and said, "You made them say that," changing carrots and scallions to orange nickels and green dimes. "You left them no option." She made as though to slice her rosy throat with the Sabatier knife, and stuck out her tongue. "I hear you took it very well."

"I was devastated," he said, and his face grew grim, and he looked, for a moment, like a devastated man. "How was New Mexico?"

"It was wonderful."

"Was it stark? Starkly sensual?" As she chopped, he orbited her, slow as Jupiter, regarding her from every angle, but on this last word his orbit decayed and he fell against her, softly.

"Starkly sensual doesn't even begin to describe it. You asshole," she said.

Jane and Cleveland had been an item for nearly six years, and although their manner with each other was utterly familiar, they nonetheless displayed all the intoxicated rancor of a brand-new couple. It was as though they still had not decided if they liked each other. When she looked at him lovingly, her eyes were filled with the strong regret and disapproval of a mother with a jailbird son. And though when speaking to her he came closer than with anyone else to ridding his voice of its smirk, nevertheless the smirk remained. I think that fundamentally he was jealous of her: not of any phantom lovers—for she never had any—but jealous of *her*, of her half-English crazy optimism and her manias for salad-making and endless walks. And I think that Jane was afraid for Cleveland, afraid of the inevitable day when he really would ruin everything.

"Do you all like chives?" she said. "I bought some fresh chives." She waved them hopefully. "I'll bet you haven't had a single vegetable since you got here."

"We had beans," I said.

There was silence while we all watched her make a vinaigrette, shaking flakes of this and that into the cruet without looking at the labels on the spice jars. I saw her shake nutmeg into the dressing, and curry. After she had held the bottle to the light and examined it closely for half a minute, watching the particles slowly sink through the line from oil to vinegar, she looked at Cleveland. "You know, I did like New Mexico an awful lot. So many interesting animals, and the Indians are so kind. I saw a rattlesnake, Cleveland. And tons and tons of motorcycles. I think you'd like it. I was thinking maybe the two of us could go out there sometime."

"Sure," said Cleveland. He fanned out his hands as though to say, Why not leave right now?

"You don't mean it," she said.

"Wait till I get some money. Then we can go anywhere. We can buy a trailer."

"You'll never get any money," said Jane. She shook the dressing, then dumped it onto the salad. "Or will you?"

I watched Cleveland's face, which revealed nothing, but when I turned back to Jane, she was staring directly at me, and I realized that I was blushing.

"That's a beautiful salad," I said.

"Well, let's eat it, Art," she said. "Come on, Cleveland, Arthur. Come eat some vegetables."

After lunch, to my surprise, Jane asked me to walk into town with her. Cleveland smiled, woodenly, and raised his can of beer to me; evidently she had warned him that she planned to do this.

"I can give you only glowing reports of his behavior, Jane," I said.

I put on my tennis shoes, trying to get up the nerve to decline her invitation. I had seen it coming at lunch—she knew something, she had heard something, she was worried about Cleveland. Arthur came into the living room, carrying a book by Manuel Puig, with a long Spanish title. He was always in love with some new Latin American writer or other.

"Where are you guys going?" he said, looking at Cleveland.

"Town," said Jane. "Need anything?"

"Can I come?"

"You have to keep Cleveland company."

"You can come," I said.

Arthur looked at Cleveland again.

"No, that's okay," he said. "I wanted to read."

Jane went to the door; I stood for a few seconds, embarrassed at having been singled out by Jane, and suddenly

afraid to talk to her. But when I got outside, the Sunday
was in full bloom, you could smell the lake, clouds blew
quickly across the sun. I jumped up and down a few times,
feeling the give of the dirt beneath my feet.

"Isn't this a nice place?" said Jane. "Next time you
should bring Phlox."

"If I'd known you were coming, I would have."

"I'm not scolding you. I know why you guys came
here."

"Good," I said. "I know why you came here too."

"Good. Look. Way up there, a vulture! I saw a lot of
vultures down in New Mexico. Aren't they beautiful!"

"I don't think they have vultures in New York," I said.

"They have vultures everywhere they have food
chains," she said. "This way." We walked down the gravel
drive, to the mailboxes, but, instead of taking the cracked
old blacktop road, she pointed to a dirt path that led up the
roadbank and away in the opposite direction from the
house. "It's shorter," she said. We walked through skunk
cabbage, Queen Anne's lace, cataracts of honeysuckle; she
picked up a tree branch and hacked lazily at the ivy and
brambles that overgrew the path. Stopping for a moment,
she uprooted a frail stalk of Queen Anne's lace and turned
it upside down, holding its thick brown root up to my face.

"Smell that," she said. "It's a wild carrot."

"Mmm," I said, inhaling an odor of dirt and soup broth.
I felt as though I were a vacationing child again, walking
with some older cousin. When we came alongside a tiny
rill, she pulled me to it and knelt down beside the sparkling

water. I found a twig and broke it in two, feeling a little self-conscious but willing to try to relax.

"Let's race," I said. We tossed our little boats and watched them bob until they disappeared from view. Then she recovered her alpenstock and we set off again, until we came to a place where the creek was wider, and a plain wooden bridge took you across. We leaned over the low rail for a minute.

"Let's spit," I said. We spat. It was amusing, and we spat again. I was still laughing when she took hold of my wrist, tears in her eyes, and we were no longer two kids on a nature walk. I was trapped.

"Art," she said. "I know you know. Tell me what Cleveland is doing."

"What do you mean?"

"I ran into this sleazy friend of Cleveland's, Dave Stern."

"He's my cousin," I said.

"I'm sorry; he isn't really all that sleazy."

"It's okay," I said. "He isn't my real cousin. What did he say?"

She kept herself from crying; she wiped a hand across her forehead, blew the hair from her eyes, and then started off again. Her pink plaid shift lifted as she ran a few steps, then she stopped and waited for me.

"He didn't say anything, really. Just hinted. I could tell he was trying to bug me. He said Cleveland was working for his father. So I asked him what his father did."

"And he said?"

"He said, 'My father makes deals.'"

"And then he laughed like a big donkey."

"Tell me," she said. Three syllables.

"I don't know," I said. It sounded so much like a lie that I bit my lip. "Did you ask Cleveland?"

"He said to ask you." She stopped and brought her chin up to mine, fixing me with her eyes, and I could feel her next words on my face. "So tell me."

"He said to ask me?" Was he testing me? Did he actually think that I might tell her the truth? "He's jerking you around. I have no idea what Lenny Stern does."

"Lenny Stern?" she said.

"He's kind of my uncle."

"Is he a drug dealer? Is Cleveland dealing drugs?"

I was glad for the opportunity to tell the truth.

"No," I said. "I know that, anyway."

She looked relieved despite herself, despite the fact that she knew she should still worry.

"Well, as long as you know that," she said, and she stepped away from me and looked at me very carefully. She knew that I had lied to her, and although she chose to believe me, she never entirely trusted me again.

When we got back, Jane and Cleveland started drinking, and Arthur and I watched them fight for the rest of the afternoon. For a while I tried, without saying anything, to let Cleveland know that I had not ratted. He ignored me and seemed to be feeling fine. He stood up, inhaled deeply, and cried, "Ah, the sweet piss odor of cedar!" Eventually we just tried to stay out of their way. Still we kept coming upon them kissing within the narrow triangle made by two open doors in the hall, or in the shadow of the chestnut that overhung the front yard. At sundown we laughed at their unlikely silhouettes moving side by side along the beach. We stood by the open door, leaning against opposite jambs and smoking. Then we stopped laughing. I envied them the hands in the back pockets of each other's jeans, and I envied them their history, the plain and the frantic days, the simple length of years behind them.

"No matter how long I know you guys, I'll never be able to catch up."

The cigarette hung slack from Arthur's peeling lower lip, and I saw that he'd had his own reasons for suddenly growing quiet.

"Catch up on what?" His Kool jiggled as he spoke.

"The time. All the days and evenings like this one."

"Ah." He smiled very faintly.

"What are you thinking?"

"Actually, I was just thinking that seeing Cleveland and Jane together again makes me feel tired. You know, all the days and evenings like this one. But it can't last much longer."

"What do you mean?"

"I mean—nothing. Here they come." He flicked the end of his cigarette in their direction with an exaggeratedly formal upswing of his arm, as though firing off a salute, or sending up a flare.

12

THE EVIL LOVE NURSE

♦   ♦   ♦

When I got back to the city, I was glad, alarmingly glad, to see Phlox again. At dinnertime that Monday, she met me on the hot pavement in front of Boardwalk Books, and without pausing to think, I lifted her and swung her and kissed her, through all three hundred and sixty degrees, like a soldier and his girl. We got some applause. I gathered in my fists the thin, rough cotton at the waist of her sundress, and squeezed, pressing her hips to mine. We talked a lot of nonsense and headed for the Wok Inn, heads together, feet apart, leaning into each other like the summit of a house of cards. I asked about the new auburn streaks in her hair.

"Sun and lemons," she said. "You wear a loose-weave straw hat and draw some strands of hair through the holes. Then you juice the strands. I spent a lonely weekend juicing myself."

"Same here. That's from *Cosmo*, that thing with the lemons," I said. "I read about it in your bathroom the other morning."

"You read my *Cosmo?*"

"I read all of your magazines. I took all the love quizzes and pretended I was you answering the questions."

"How did I do?"

"You cheated," I said.

We passed a thrift shop, its window full of battered no-head mannequins wearing sequined gowns, of old toasters, and of lamps whose bases were little Spanish galleons. In one corner of the window was a flat, multicolored box.

"Twister!" said Phlox. "Oh, Art, let's buy it. Just imagine."

She grabbed me by the arm and pulled me into the store. The saleswoman retrieved the game from the window for us, and showed us that it was intact; the spinner still spun and the game mat was fairly clean. At dinner it lay under the table, tilted against my foot and hers, and, first as we continued our happy, empty conversation, then as I summarized the weekend at the summer house, the Twister box stirred and tickled me with each kick of her restless ankle.

In the living room of her apartment, we shoved aside chairs and the coffee table and spread the plastic mat across her rug. Its primary-colored spots, and the off-kilter, go-go red letters that spelled out the word "Twister!" at its ends, brought back a flood of memories of 1960s birthday parties on rainy Saturdays in finished basements. Phlox hopped off to her bedroom, to "peel away the confining raiment of civilization," as she put it, and I sat down on the floor and unlaced my sneakers. An odd contentment came over me. Although the used Sears furniture, the fake Renoir, the cat statue, et cetera, still seemed kind of ugly and in bad taste, I discovered I had made one of those common aesthetic efforts that consists of just swallowing an entire system of bad taste—Las Vegas, or a bowling alley, or Jerry Lewis movies—and then finding it beautiful and fun.

In a way, I thought, I had done the same thing with Phlox herself. Everything about her that was like a B-girl or a gun moll, a courtesan in a bad novel, or an *actrice* in a French art movie about alienation and ennui; her overdone endearments and makeup; all that was in questionable taste and might have embarrassed me or made me snicker, I had come to accept entirely, to look for and even to encourage. She delighted me as did bouffant hairdos and Elvis Presley art. When she came out of her bedroom dressed in a nylon kimono and huge slippers of turqouise fur, I was almost dizzy with appreciation, and the gaudy plastic Twister mat at my feet seemed to be the very matrix, the printed plan, of everything I liked about her.

"Who's going to spin?" I said. "Is Annette home?" This was Phlox's roommate, a big, loud, attractive nurse, the vagaries of whose complicated work schedule I was never able to master.

"Nope. We'll have to keep the spinner here beside us and trade off."

I crawled around to the other side of the game and sat on my haunches, as did Phlox. We faced each other across the mat for one ceremonial moment. Then she flicked the black plastic arm of the spinner.

"Right hand blue," she said.

I leaned in and put my right hand in the center of a blue spot. She did the same, and as she fell slightly forward, the folds of her kimono parted, and her hair tumbled down over her bowed head. I peered into the shadows of her robe, through the spaces in her swaying two-tone hair. She spun again.

"Right foot green."

This put us both half on the mat and half off. The blue and green rows were closer to me than to her; I sat in a kind of elongated crouch, my right hand and foot on the mat, one behind the other, but Phlox had to come all the way across, her right foot in its furry slipper placed in front of her right hand. She lifted her shiny left leg a few inches into the air to help complete her reach, and wobbled for a few moments, before falling onto her side.

"You lose," I said, laughing, but she said it didn't count, and slid the spinner over to me before hoisting herself forward again, the soft skin of her lifted thigh shaking with effort. I spun.

"Left foot blue."

Since her right hand lay upon the blue spot where it would have been most convenient for me to place my left foot, and since she beat me to the second-best spot, beside my right hand, I was forced to run my left leg through the triangle formed by her right leg and arm, and I felt the muted contact of my left thigh in blue jeans against her bare ankle. We were on three points now, tilted forward, and our heads drew alongside each other, ears kissing. Her deep and Italian laugh, close to my ear, seemed to issue from that darkness within the parting of her warm kimono, and I felt the summit and base of my spine begin to trade anxious messages. I shifted my hips and spun again.

"Right hand yellow."

The balance moved to her side of the mat; she dropped

backward, right hand behind her, and I found myself almost atop her, laughing now too, her swinging hair so near my mouth that I opened up and chewed on the nearest stray ends, which crunched strangely, then fell from my lips and hung moistened and clinging to one another like the tips of little paintbrushes.

"Spin," she said.

"I'm spinning."

She watched me, her mouth pursed but her eyes ready to start laughing again, and then, with a sweet flex of the muscles of her face, she bit her lower lip and looked worried, as though she thought she might collapse. I spun again, with my left hand, which remained free for just one more second.

"Left hand green."

I went for the best spot, but she, going out of her way, wrenched her body into my path and forced me to go under both of her thighs with my left arm, and I had to bend my upper body around backward. I found myself looking up into the fragrant crook of her underarm, my head cradled between her hip and ribs. My fingers strained to touch the green spot, and my thighs trembled. I felt pain in my knees and shoulders. Somehow she had managed to remain upright. She laughed at my shaking, four-way struggle to keep from falling, but suddenly I was giving it everything I had.

"You spin," I said, teeth clenched.

"I can't."

"Spin, damn it, spin, spin it, come on." The contorted hold on my right foot on that green spot began to give.

"I can't."

"Phlox!" I let my head drop against the smooth nylon along her thigh. The Opium and sweat hurried out from her shaking breast. I had an erection—pardon me for once again mentioning the condition of my penis—and it labored against the cotton walls of its lonely cell. I felt my fingers begin to slide.

The telephone rang, once, twice, three times.

"Fall," she said. She leaned down, arching like a bird's her long neck, and kissed my lips.

"No." My slippery feet and hands jerked across the plastic, making quick and telltale squeaks. She bit the tip of my nose.

"Fall!"

I fell, at a rate of thirty-two feet per second per second.

During the first weeks of July my life settled into a pattern, which is how one knows that it is July. Nights I spent at Phlox's apartment, days at Boardwalk Books, and evenings alternately in the company of Cleveland and Arthur, or of the Evil Love Nurse, as Cleveland had lately taken to calling Phlox. Some compulsiveness inherited from my father, and also a kind of unnecessary delicacy, had always driven me to keep friends separate, to shun group excursions, but for this calm couple of weeks at the eye of the summer I felt free of the guilt that usually accompanied my juggling of friendships, and free of the sense of duplicity that went along with pushing the people I loved into separate corners of my life, and once in a while Phlox, Arthur, and I would eat our lunches on the same patch of grass.

Cleveland passed most of his nights with Jane. For years

she had maintained a fictitious friend named Katherine Tracy, an artistic, unbalanced girl who would occasionally attempt suicide, or fall seriously ill with colitis, anorexia, shingles, heartbreak, piles. During these times, Katherine Tracy required attention and constant company, and Dr. and Mrs. Bellwether, who had grown rather fond of the diffident, intensely self-conscious Katherine over the years, always gave their sympathetic approval to Jane's spending a few days out of the house to help care for Katherine, who had this neurotic fear of telephones and refused to own one. What Cleveland did with his days I was shortly to discover.

As for Arthur, the beginning of July brought two final exams in his summer-school classes, and a bad case of scabies, which, aside from herpes, was the worst venereal affliction anyone could imagine in those days. It kept him at home most of the time, studying and smelling of Kwell. I felt no pressure to commit myself more to one part of my life than to the other. Phlox (who sensed sooner than I did that she and Arthur were becoming irreconcilable, who perhaps had never really liked Arthur at all—in fact, she once said, "I never *like* boys; it's love or it's hate") and Arthur indeed ruined the one evening on which the five of us did go out together, after they had destroyed the afternoon that preceded it.

The evening began, once again, with a vision seen through the big front windows of Boardwalk Books. About fifteen minutes before I expected Phlox, Arthur, Cleveland, and Jane to come collect me, they went down the sidewalk past the shop, and there was one long moment in which I noted but did not recognize them. They were two and two.

The pair of women came first, one strangely dressed, in pied clothes of three or four eras, talking and examining the wrist and bracelet of the other, who wore a candy-striped skirt and bright yellow sweater. In the wind, their hair trailed from their heads like short scarves, and their faces looked cynical and gay. The two men followed behind, one with a great black lion head and black boots, and the other in white Stan Smiths, looking flushed and wealthy and bathed in sunlight, and each holding his cigarette in a different fashion, the heavy man with a negligent looseness, the thin man pointedly, wildly, as though the cigarette were a tool of speech. My God! I thought, in that spinning instant before they turned and waved to me. Who are those beautiful people?

They went past and I pressed my face against the glass to follow their disappearing forms. I felt like a South Sea Islander watching his white gods climb into their shining cargo plane and fly off, with the added and appropriate impression that I was somehow deluded in feeling this way. I turned wildly to see if anyone in the store had witnessed the theophany, but apparently nobody had, or at least nobody had been as commoved as I. I jumped up and down at the cash register, hopped from one foot to the other. I punched the clock. When they came back, at six sharp, I rushed out into the street and hung there, still confused after the lunchtime disaster, not knowing whom to embrace first; finally I shook hands with Arthur, before taking Phlox into my arms. I may have renewed with that error all the discord of lunch. As I held her she pinched my arm, lightly, and Arthur, of course, noticed.

"A handshake before a hug," he told her. "Look it up."

I hugged Jane too, was enveloped briefly in smooth arms and Chanel No. 5, and then stood facing Cleveland, who pushed up his big black glasses and frowned.

"Enough touching already," he said.

We headed back toward the library, where Cleveland had parked the Barracuda. I was in a state of perfect ambivalence, worse than ever before. My arm was around Phlox's waist, chafing against the funny white leather belt she'd used to hitch up her dress, but I kept walking backward, turning to face Cleveland, Arthur, and Jane. I could tell it annoyed Phlox, but I told myself I had recently spent plenty of attention on her, and when Jane dropped Cleveland's hand and came forward to talk to Phlox, I fell back among the boys. Jane liked Phlox, and said so all the time. Phlox thought that Jane was dull, that she was stupid still to be dragging herself through the mud for Cleveland, and, of course, that she was secretly in love with me.

"You're gonna get it," said Arthur, and smiled.

"Good to see you guys."

"Good to see you too," said Cleveland. He seemed to be in high spirits; he huffed along the sidewalk, boot heels pounding, gut pulled in. "Listen, Bechstein, when's your day off?"

"Wednesday," I said. I looked toward Phlox. She was laughing at some story Jane told with waving brown hands; I watched the pair of butts and the four high-heeled legs. I had promised Wednesday to Phlox.

"Meet me."

"Where?"

"Here. Oakland. Say by the Cloud Factory."

"To do what?"

He didn't say anything. Arthur, who was walking between us, turned to me, a look of mild annoyance on his face. I was surprised to note that apparently Cleveland hadn't told Arthur about my father. I felt a quick thrill when I saw that there was something between Cleveland and me that Arthur wasn't a party to, something outside their friendship, and then, just as quickly, I felt sadness and even shame at the nature of that something. It was not what I wanted us to have most in common. But the invitation, of course, was irresistible.

"Okay," I said, "but can we meet in the morning? I'm supposed to spend the afternoon with Phlox."

"Fine," said Cleveland. "Ten o'clock, say." He inhaled hugely, rattling all the snot in his nose. "Do we have to walk so fast?"

Phlox turned her head, squinting and opening and squinting her eyes in the light of sunset, her look changing from protective to vulnerable and back again.

We had planned on dinner and Ella Fitzgerald, who was playing Point Park that night. Cleveland claimed that they would be airlifting her into Pittsburgh with a sky hook, like Jesus in *La Dolce Vita*, and someday, he said, they would be doing the same thing with him. In the restaurant, I sat next to Phlox and across from Arthur; Jane was beside Arthur, and Cleveland took up all the space at the head of the table, making it awkward for the waitress, whom he apparently knew, in some connection that made Jane blush frequently. Arthur and Phlox had already started to go at each other in the car, in little ways, unfriendly jokes and a lot of smiling.

They were continuing that afternoon's show. The three of us, see, had been making an effort to meet for lunch now and then—behind the library, in the park, or on the lawn of Soldiers' and Sailors', but on this afternoon my luck had run out, and in the midst of a terribly important argument I had found myself siding with Arthur.

We were discussing *Born to Run*, by Bruce Springsteen. I said that it was the most Roman Catholic record album ever made.

"Look what you've got," I said. "You've got Mary dancing like a vision across the porch while the radio plays. You've got people trying in vain to breathe the fire they was born in, riding through mansions of glory, and hot-rod angels, virgins and whores—"

"And 'She's the One,'" said Arthur. "It's Mariolatry city."

"Right."

"'Killer graces and secret places.'"

"I hate that," said Phlox, splitting open a tangerine with two long thumbs. "I hate that thing about 'secret places that no boy can fill.' I don't believe in that. There are no such places."

"Now, Phlox," said Arthur. "Surely you must have one or two secret places."

"She does," I said. "I know she does."

"I do not. What good would boys *be* if they couldn't fill all the places?"

Arthur and I presented a united front in support of the

measureless caverns of a woman, Phlox sternly and with increasing anger defended her total knowability, and something about the situation upset Phlox. I guessed it was partly that the argument was so trivial, and partly that it was two against one, but mostly that the whole thing was so horribly in reverse.

Perhaps I did know all the reasons she could have for being upset with me, and perhaps there would be no mystery to women at all if I would just lift the corner of my own purdah. Anyway, it had been an ugly lunch, and now, over red plates of pasta, things were intensifying rapidly.

"That's because you're so insecure," Arthur was saying. "And besides, you love sitting in that window all day—admit it."

"I do not," said Phlox. "I hate it. And you just wish it was you."

"Okay, okay," said Cleveland, his mouth full.

"You're a crazy woman," Arthur said. "Those ladies have probably never even noticed you."

"You saw me crying! You should have heard the things they said about me!"

"What did they call you?" said Jane, very sweetly. As soon as she heard that anyone was or had been in any kind of distress, she became an engine of sympathy, hurtling to the rescue. She reached across the table and put her hand on Phlox's.

"I can't say it. I don't remember."

"I remember," said Arthur.

"*Okay*, Artie," said Cleveland.

"You said they called you a strange-looking white bitch

who thought she was hot shit waving her ass in a window to the boys all day."

Silence fell over our party. Phlox threw her head back proudly and her nostrils flared. I had heard this story already, a few times, but Phlox's life was so full of incidents in which other women vented their jealous rage at her that the impressive, rhythmic hatefulness of the Hillman Library cleaning ladies hadn't really affected me before. I felt terrible, unfamiliar, unwilling anger toward Arthur.

"Wow," said Cleveland, finally.

A few little tears pooled at the corners of Phlox's eyes and rolled down her face, one two three. Her lower lip quivered and then stopped. I squeezed her other hand. Both of Phlox's hands were now being squeezed.

"Arthur," I said, "um, you should probably apologize."

"I'm sorry," he said immediately, without much conviction. He looked down at his lap.

"Why do you hate me, Arthur?"

"You're terrible, Arthur," said Jane. "He doesn't hate you, Phlox, do you, Arthur?" She hit him on the shoulder.

I looked at my linguine in red clam sauce. All the heat seemed to have suddenly gone out of it, the dusting of Parmesan I'd given it had cooled and congealed into a thick lumpy blanket of cheese spread across the top, and the whole thing, with the gray bits of clam, looked smeary red, and biological.

"I'm leaving," said Phlox. She sniffed and snapped shut her pocketbook.

I got up with her and we struggled around Cleveland.

"Looks like we've all got a fun evening ahead," I said quietly. I dropped some money onto the table.

"Whom the gods would destroy," Cleveland said, "they first make pasta." He reached up and touched my elbow. "Wednesday."

"Wednesday," I said, and started to run.

Out on the street, Phlox was pulling herself together, snapping shut her purse. I came up behind her and pushed my face into her hair. She inhaled deeply, held her breath; exhaled; and her shoulders unbound. Just then—at the very instant she turned a fairly calm face to me—all the cicadas in the trees went ape, who knows why, and their music was as loud and ugly as a thousand televisions tuned to the news. In Pittsburgh, even the cicadas are industrial. We covered our ears and mouthed words at one another.

"Wow," she mouthed.

"Let's get out of here."

"What?"

"This is driving me nuts."

"What?"

I pulled open the door of a restaurant adjacent to the one we had just quit, a coffee shop; we stood in the lobby next to the Kiwanis gum-ball machine and kissed in the quiet of forks and Muzak.

13

PINK EYES

◆   ◆   ◆

By this time, Arthur resided at the Shadyside home of a rich young couple, his third residence of the summer. After leaving the Bellwethers', he'd spent ten exultant and sinful days, so he said, in a small, pretty Shadyside apartment with a genuine rose window, of which I got a brief glimpse one hectic Sunday when I dropped by. Now, with this third place, he'd continued his upward journey through the World of Homes. The rich young couple, friends of some friends, had gone to Scandinavia for July. I'd seen the wife many times on television (she read the weather), and it was strange now to look at the framed Maxfield Parrish postcard over her toilet, or to wear one of her husband's pale beautiful oxford-cloth shirts, or just to think that there I was, stretched out across the carpet of a lady I'd seen on television, her head wreathed in lightning and tiny paper storm clouds. Arthur had won his battle against the "little animals from hell," but now all the shaved hair was growing back, which itched, apparently, and made him unable to sit still for more than a few minutes.

The morning after Phlox and I did not see Ella Fitzgerald, I stopped by my house, to put on clean clothes for work. The telephone rang as I fumbled with the front door; in the mailbox was a fat wad of mail, most of it, at first glance, informing me of imminent bargains on beef, garden hose, and charcoal briquettes. The apartment felt stuffy, vacant, and the jangling telephone sounded somehow plaintive or lonely, as though it had not been answered in days. It was Arthur.

"Hello," I said. "No, I just walked in the door."

"I'm calling to say I'm sorry."

"Oh. Well." I couldn't think. It is always so simple, and so complicating, to accept an apology.

"I was very rude and I hate myself for it."

"Um—"

"Look, do you think we could meet today?"

"I don't think so. Oh, I don't know." There was an unusual warmth in his voice, a note of truth or of plainness. "Okay, maybe later today. I guess we have to talk about this?"

"I'm home today. Call me after work. Oh, and, Art—"

"Yes?"

"Have a nice day."

Not only did Boardwalk suffer under the curse of having to sell books; there seemed also to be a curse on the premises themselves, so that throughout the summer entire days of business were lost, here and there, to the need to remedy some minor disaster or other: Sometimes a pipe would burst in the basement, ruining overstock and making the place stink of wet books, and sometimes the air-conditioning froze and quit working, and once some vandals smashed the huge

display window; on this day, there was a fire. It was a small
fire, caused by a paramedic cigarette, but Valerie closed the
slightly blackened bookstore and sent us all home.

I decided to walk to the Weatherwoman House through
the clear, hot Monday morning. For some reason, many
crews of men with tar-burning wagons were scattered across
the rooftops of East Pittsburgh, and the smell of tar made
everything seem even hotter, more yellow, more intensely
summer. At the corner of St. James, a green Audi convertible passed, and then stopped short with a squeal ten yards
beyond me. Dark man, big smile; Mohammad. I came up
alongside and we shook. I said hello, *comment ça va*, where
are you going, and where are you coming from? Momo told
me one long semistory about both his having to appear in
traffic court and his sister's passion for Charles Bronson,
which were in some way connected. Periodically he stepped
on the gas pedal, making the engine race, to punctuate his
story at crucial junctures.

"What kind of mood is Arthur in today?" I said, just
after we shook hands again.

"He is in an ugly mind-state as hell," said Mohammad.
He smiled and put the car in gear.

Either Mohammad was inexpert at reading Arthur, or
Arthur's mood had changed on the Arab's departure, or perhaps the change came with my surprise arrival; in any case,
when Arthur opened the door, his smile was the one he occasionally gave Cleveland, loose and puckish. I was touched.

"Wonderful. Come in, come in," he said. "Nice shirt.
Nice pants. Nice shoes." We both had on the usual dun-

garees, white shirts, and brown loafers. I had shaved, he had not. Neither of us mentioned Mohammad.

He led me into the bright, uncomfortable living room. The decorator had made an effort, it seemed, to create the illusion that the whole house existed in some remote future, in the wan, empty years after the extinction from the planet of furniture and cushions. I sat down on three wide dowel rods and a piece of beige canvas and tried not to lean back.

"Is it as lovely outside as it looks? Yes? We should take a walk," he said. He spun on his heel and walked away. "Want coffee?"

"Please. Do you know why I'm off today?" I shouted after him, into the kitchen.

"Why? You quit?" I heard him pouring, then the little rhythm of cup and spoon.

"Sure, I quit. No, I didn't quit; there was a fire."

"My. What happened?"

"The one copy of anything by Swift in the store, *Gulliver's Travels*, finally couldn't stand the indignity of living at Boardwalk anymore, and burst into righteous flames."

"I see."

"It was a very small fire."

Arthur came back with two white cups. "How do you know Swift started it? Maybe it was *Fahrenheit 451.*" He let himself down onto another odd tripod and made a display of easily seating himself, with a look of mock hauteur.

"To the twenty-fifth-century manner born," I said. "Ha ha." I was a little nervous. We weren't talking about anything.

"Perfectly plain, isn't it? Do you have a smoke?"

I gave him a cigarette and a light, and my hand shook. Then we sat there, looking at the creamy walls. I decided I didn't really want to talk about Phlox, but it had been very good to hear him say that he was sorry, and I would have liked to hear him say it again.

"So," he said finally, and it came out in a wobbling ring of smoke. "Do you want to walk? We can walk through Chatham."

"Sure." I rose, or rather fell, from my chair thing. "What's this kind of furniture called, anyway?" I said. I drained the tepid sour tail of my coffee.

"That's called science furniture, son," he said. "For the spine of tomorrow."

He locked the door behind us; we stepped out into the stinking, lovely day and headed for Chatham College, a destination that made me think of the party the night we'd met, of our short face-off in the doorway at Riri's, of all the possibilities for brown women, in that already distant June, which I'd surrendered with the advent of Phlox. I thought for a quiet second or two; Arthur's antennae operated inexorably.

"We could drop by Riri's," he said. "Every time I see her she asks after you. She said she thought you were a very sweet boy."

His tone, this faint air of the panderer that he sometimes wore, brought to mind another picture from that evening, which until now I'd forgotten: the change that had come over his face in the Fiat, the aha! in his eyes, when first I asked him about Phlox.

"Arthur, did you . . . ? Why did you . . . ?"

"What?"

"Nothing. Never mind."

"Okay. God, what a stink in the air, huh?" We watched his feet take steps along the slow, hot pavement. "What about Phlox?"

"I just—I love Phlox, Arthur—"

"Ooh, stop."

"Stop. There you go, see; I can't understand it. We have to talk about this, right? I love her, and I love her because I *want* to love her, of course, but I always feel that somehow Phlox and I are together because of you. Except I can never figure out exactly why I feel that. It's like doing algebra. I can't keep the whole thing in my mind long enough to grasp it. But then every so often everything lines up just right, and I can see for, like, a second, that you made it happen. You're behind it. Somehow. And if that's the truth, then I can't understand why you say the kind of thing you just said. Or why you do the kind of thing you did last night."

There was another long silence, which took us across Fifth Avenue and up the steep drive of the college. Nearby I could hear lawn mowers, and the voices of women at play.

"I never thought you would like her," he said at last.

We came to the pond, and now we sat down in the grass, under some maples. The ducks chattered and splashed.

"Are you angry? Do you hate me? I hope you don't hate me, Art Bechstein. I'm glad you think Phlox is wonderful. Of course, I'm also shocked—no, that's a joke, honestly.

I'm very, very sorry. Really. I'm sure she's very good for you."

He put an apologetic hand on my knee, then pulled it away, and I felt filled with forgiveness, with the warm catch in his voice, and, having just exposed him at his manipulative worst—had he conceived of Phlox as some kind of punishment?—with a strange, airy manhood, as though we had just boxed. I tore off handfuls of grass and tossed them into the air.

"Arthur," I said, "why are you such a little Machiavelli?"

He crushed the end of his cigarette into the grass, flicked it away, and seemed carefully to weigh the label, and to be amused by it.

"Isn't it obvious?" he finally said. "My mother made me this way."

Horns honked, a cranked-up radio passed, the ducks beat water and quacked. We looked at each other.

"Let's go swimming," he said.

The rich young couple, I was mildly surprised to discover, belonged to the same country club as Uncle Lenny Stern, at which they had been kind enough to inscribe Arthur as their guest. Years before, in the club dining room, during the reception that followed Davy Stern's bar mitzvah, I had vomited vanilla mousse across my mother's lavender dress. The pool was Olympic-size and filled with boisterous children. Women with scarves and rigid hair sat under red umbrellas that threw shadows across the women and across the thermoses, kids' sunglasses, and stacks of fresh towels that lay on the white wire tops of the poolside tables; once an hour a whistle blew, children groaned, and the waters would grow calm, as the pool suffered a fifteen-minute invasion by pregnant women and small white infants. Families were all around us, without their men, and we lay beside each other on chaises longues, exchanging lazy sentences in the strong sunlight.

From time to time I would glance over at him, stretched out with his eyes shut, his lashes glinting, his body almost bare. I had never before given a man's body the regard I now gave his—but furtively, and through the flutter of a squint. I felt, I feel, almost as if I did not have the vocabulary to describe it, as if such words as thigh, breast, navel, nipple, were erotically feminine, and could not apply here. For one thing, each of the above-named parts was covered with thick blond hair, running to red-brown along the top of his bathing suit and on his chest. I realized that in looking at him I was trying to subtract the hair, the pads of muscle, the outline of the cock between his legs, the glittering stubble on his cheek. I stopped doing this. I looked at him. He was in a sweat; his stomach was flat; there was hair on the back of his long, damp hand. And I looked also at his crotch, at that strange—that shaven—fist wrapped in slick blue Lycra. But his skin was the most strange, and the most difficult to keep my eyes from; it was dappled all over with tiny shadows, which gave it a look both soft and rough, as of suede or fine sand; and it seemed, stretched so tightly across his bones and muscle, as though it would never give, like a woman's, to the pressure of my hand. He sat up suddenly, leaning on his elbows, face red, eyes like the water in the brilliant pool, and caught me looking at his skin. I was startled into thinking the sentence that I had all summer forbidden myself to think: I was in love with Arthur Lecomte. I longed for him.

"Yes?" he said, with half a smile.

"Ha. Nothing. Um, I've—I've been here before," I said. "A long time ago. I threw up on my mom at a bar mitzvah." My mom. I had not said this in years. It just slipped out, in my confusion, and I bit my lip. Arthur twisted onto his side and propped himself up with one arm, looking eager.

"And?"

I rolled over onto my stomach, as much to conceal the swelling in the bathing suit I'd borrowed from him—he'd already glanced that way—as to avoid the current discussion. I spoke through the slats in my lounge chair, staring at the damp concrete of the deck.

"And that's all. Just another cheesy story about a nauseated Jew."

"I've heard them all," he said, and after a long moment, he fell back into the path of the sunlight. I breathed out.

In the pool he swam laps, with a polished, rather old-fashioned Australian crawl; I watched the little waves he made catch sunlight and shatter his submerged body into blue and white smithereens. Then I jumped in and thrust all the air from my lungs, so that I settled onto the cold bottom of the pool. I lay on my back and looked up, through the shifting window of water.

.   .   .

We took the bus back to Shadyside and, at separate ends of the huge Weatherwoman House, changed into fresh clothes. We wore the fine shirts of the Weatherwoman's husband. Arthur said he would walk me home. When we got to the Terrace, my phone was ringing again. I threw the door open and ran into the house, but when I put the receiver to my ear there was only the sound of an empty tunnel. I hung up.

"Phlox," we said.

While Arthur went to the toilet, I took one of those giant canisters of Coke from the refrigerator and carried it out to the front steps. I swallowed a couple of blebby mouthfuls and watched a few little things happen: an ant, a faraway jet. When Arthur reappeared, he held in his fingers a marijuana cigarette.

"Look what I found in my pack of cigarettes," he said.

We smoked it with damp fingers and talked blandly, looking mostly at the sky, which was blue as baby clothes. I felt as if I were talking to a friend from the fourth grade, when talking with a friend and sitting in the sun had felt different, had felt like this, more full of possibility than of any real matter. This made me wish to the point of tears that I were wearing sneakers. I had on leather young-man shoes, which were impossible. I stood up and could see the arches and battlements atop the Cathedral of Learning, away off in Oakland. Oh, I thought, the Emerald City in the twelfth century. The sun was so bright. I distinctly heard the click of a woman's heels on the far sidewalk. Nowhere around me was there anything to remind me of the

year—no new cars, no rock-and-roll music; only sky, red
brick, cracked pavement, a breeze—and I underwent one of
those time slips during which one can say to himself, "This
is the summer of 1941," and nothing, within him or without, can prove him wrong. The sunlight was the sunlight of
forty years before. I looked at Arthur, shirtless, his hair still
damp at the ends, the corners of his eyes pink with chlorine
and grass, and the moment held. I touched his face. He
tilted his cheek toward me, almost warily, one skeptical
eyebrow raised. The telephone rang.

"You've got to do something about that girl."

"Quiet. No, I'll bet it's my dad." I ran, very clumsily,
into the house. "He's probably been calling every five minutes since nine o'clock this morning." When I reached the
phone I stood and watched it ring a couple of times more.
"I don't know if I can handle this."

"Let me do the talking."

"Hello? Pops. Hi. Oh, I'm swell. I'm dandy." I heard
Arthur say, "Uh oh." "How's Bethesda?"

"Bethesda? Bethesda is a sweltering hell. Very muggy,"
said my father, through the squeaks and clicks of the
ionosphere. "Very humid. We're all wearing Aqua-lungs
here. And through her breathing apparatus your grandmother says you should write to her."

I started to laugh—a bit too hard, I told myself. He
would know, he could tell.

"You really should write. Listen, I won't keep you, obviously you're in the middle of something—"

"Dad, no, not at all—"

"Ha!" said Arthur.

"I only wanted to tell you that I just found out I'll be in Pittsburgh tomorrow. Probably for a whole week. I should have several free meals. Maybe a movie."

I said I would look forward to it. After I'd hung up and come outside again, Arthur said. "What is this, high school? So what if he knows you're stoned?"

"I don't know." I sat heavily on the step.

"You're just afraid. You can't do anything to upset him, or you're cashless."

"No, it's not that."

"Look at it. You're an economics major when obviously you should be making movies, or traveling, or reviewing restaurants, or something frivolous."

"Okay."

"You live in Pittsburgh when you should be living in New York or L.A. or Tokyo, or someplace frivolous."

"Okay."

"You dumped your crazy girlfriend and got yourself another one, who's also frivolous but who at least wears lipstick and perfume and has a job. Your whole life is just one big 'Thanks for the check, Dad.'"

"Okay, *okay.*" For a few seconds I clenched my jaw and shook, wanted to punch his face, break his straight nose, but then I felt confused, and I laughed. "Okay."

All at once, I was insanely hungry.

14

MARJORIE

♦　　　　　♦　　　　　♦

Phlox, as it turned out, was the first one over the Wall.

I fretted all afternoon, after saying good-bye to Arthur, over how to describe my day to her, concocting and rehearsing various half-truths, but when she called that evening from her place, I didn't even get the opportunity to say I'd been at work, because she told me she'd dropped by Boardwalk at lunchtime and seen the crayoned closed-due-to-fire sign Scotch-taped to the glass door.

"So what did you do today?"

"Oh, just hung around."

"Did you see Arthur?" She ticked a pencil or pen or her fingernails against the receiver. It was a nervous habit of hers.

"Yes, I hung around with Arthur. For a little while."

"Ah." There was a long silence. "Well, come over, Art, please," she said at last. "Come quick."

"You sound so sultry when you say that."

"In the church of my heart the choir is on fire."

"Jesus, I'll be right over."

"Good."

"Who was that, anyway?" I tried to keep track of her

167

thousand quotes and citations, as though assembling a Bart-
lett's of Phlox. My love of her (I say this despite
Cleveland's caveat) was like scholarship (not falconry)—an
effort to master the loved one's corpus, which, in Phlox's
case, was patchwork and vast as Africa.

"Oh, some Russian said it. For me. Come." With that,
she hung up, just like in the movies.

I walked the quiet dinnertime streets, thinking of a
cold, simple meal and whispered sex, thinking, more guilt-
ily, that I would have to even out my day with Arthur by
speaking softly into Phlox's ear all evening, but when I got
to her apartment it was full of noise, and there was a heavy
smell of beef and herbs in the air. The phonograph played
Vivaldi full-blast, or some other twittering music, a kitchen
appliance ground gravel in the kitchen, and Annette and
two of her nurse friends had commandeered the living room
and were splashing enormous daiquiries across the carpet,
laughing. I yelled hello to them and then went into the
kitchen, where Phlox squatted before the open oven, poking at something with a long fork.

She wore a backless heliotrope minidress that threw an
auspicious triangle of shadow across the tops of her thighs.
She'd tied back her hair, and a few damp wisps that had
come free clung to her cheeks. Before she saw me she drew
a forearm across her slick brow, and blew an upward and
largely ornamental jet of air that stirred her bangs. She was
like a sweaty, smiling stoker in the hot engine room of an
apartment in uproar. When we embraced, my hands slipped
down her back and tumbled into her dress at the waist, and
she squealed.

"It's crazy here," I said. "You smell terrific."

"I smell like an athlete. I know, I'm sorry, I didn't realize that Annette was going to be entertaining this evening.
Let me at least cut the stereo."

She went out and I opened every simmering pot and
poked at the potatoes in the oven, tearing their crisp jackets with the tines of the fork. The meal was four or five
months too early, perhaps—some kind of pot roast, a thick
sheaf of asparagus, and baked potatoes the size of shoes—
but I knew better than to suggest that perhaps a chef's salad
or stir-fried vegetables would have been more appropriate.
Anyway, it was such a *beguiling* menu for the end of July,
and even though I'd eaten lox and bagels not three hours
before, I had this appetite. When Phlox cut the stereo, the
white noise that filled the apartment dropped abruptly to
the giggling blue-green of the waitresses' conversation.

I bounced around the kitchen, chattering, while she
pulled everything together. I steered clear of the subject of
Arthur, by embellishing, with a great deal of energy, the
story of all the smoke at Boardwalk, and Phlox, deep in
food thought, pretty well ignored me. My tale of fire carried
us through until just after we sat down to eat in the breeze
that came through the windows along the dinner table.

"Oh, yeah, I talked to my father today," I said without
a thought. "He's coming into town tomorrow. For a whole
week."

"Oh, Art, how exciting! I want to meet him!"

Why, that summer, was I so often the victim of astonishment?

"Sure, maybe. Sure," I said, unable to chew.

"Well, I can, of course, can't I?"

"Well, it's business, you know; he'll be busy almost all the time. I just don't know. It's hard to say." I began to recover myself.

"Well, he doesn't work at night, does he? We can have dinner." She laid down her fork and stared at me.

"We'll have to see."

"I think you're ashamed of me, Art Bechstein."

"Oh, Phlox, come on, I'm not ashamed of you."

"Then why don't you want your father to meet me?"

"It doesn't have anything to do with you. It's just that—"

"Why are you ashamed of me? What don't you like about me?"

"There's nothing. I love you, you're splendid."

"Then why can't I meet your father?"

Because nobody gets to meet my father!

"I don't want to fight about this."

"This isn't a fight, Art; this is you being impossibly weird again." One tear pooled and then spilled.

"Phlox." I reached across the table and ran my finger down the shining path. "Don't cry. Please."

"I've stopped. Okay." She picked up her fork, sniffed once. "Forget it."

"Can you just understand that it has nothing—"

"It's *all right*. Forget it."

We worked our jaws in silence.

Tuesday night, the downtown bus was full of kids headed to the Warner for the opening of a new science fiction movie, a mutational romance that later went on to become a sensation. (I saw it twice: once with Phlox and once not with Phlox.) The bus's air-conditioning had failed, and I was uncomfortable in my sport coat and tie; grit and exhaust blew in through the rattling open window.

"The bloom on my cheek has withered and faded," said Phlox.

I looked at her face, and saw, through her makeup, traces of unmistakable bloom. I said so, and she smiled, pensively.

"Art, is your father one of those silly fathers?"

"Pardon me?"

"Does he drink a lot, talk about money, get angry, tell dirty jokes, and laugh loud?"

She has just described my Uncle Lenny and his close friends Eddie "Bubba" Martino and Jules "Gloves" Goldman (a distant relative). "No, my father is a serious guy," I said. "He drinks only at weddings. He isn't vulgar. He hardly ever laughs. He jokes a lot, though. He's funnier than I am."

"Then how can he be a serious guy?"

"All Jewish comedians are serious guys."

"What about the Marx Brothers?"

"The Marx Brothers were very serious guys."

"You're not a serious guy."

"Well, I'm not funny," I said. I swallowed. "I'm nervous."

She laid her fingers against my sleeve. We were to meet at my father's favorite Italian restaurant. I'd listened for a hint of wariness in his voice when I asked if I might bring

Phlox along, but he said "Of course," very gamely. Phlox would be the first acquaintance of mine since Claire actually to meet my father—and Claire had met him just twice, the first time bravely and miserably, and the second time miserably. I could hardly recall what eating in a restaurant with my father and a third person was like, but I had vague, sweet memories, from years before, of my father being hugely entertaining at birthday parties in pizza parlors and on miniature golf courses. I might have been even more nervous than I was (I certainly had the capacity), but we ate in this restaurant together so often, my father and I, that I knew it would be a comfort at least to be there, in the old red darkness. An unfamiliar restaurant can be a very disorienting thing.

Phlox and I arrived only two minutes late, and came with a sigh into the cool and the garlic. I spotted my father at the table—halfway back, toward the toilets and the cigarette machine—that we had come, over the years, to think of as our table. The first thing I noticed was that his heavy face was even more pink than usual, almost red, and I remembered his saying that he'd lately begun to reclaim the garden gone wild in my grandmother's backyard. He had on a beautiful beige summer suit, with a salmon tie. I knew that Phlox would find him good-looking. "Tsk," I said; he looked so handsome and large.

My father stood for her and took her hand, the gleam in his eye growing more distinct as he pronounced her floral name, which amused him, I could see, as much as it once had me; he admired her dress (the blue-and-white flowered one she'd worn on our first night together) and smiled a

delighted, paternal smile; he said something that made her
laugh, right off. All this civility meant nothing, of course.
He was an extremely civil man. I wouldn't know what he
thought of her until tomorrow. We lifted our menus and
complained over their gilt tops about the hot weather. My
eyes flitted blindly across the cirrate names of pastas; I have
never been able to read a menu and talk at the same time. I
managed to maneuver my father and Phlox into a conversation about the library, and took advantage of these thirty
seconds to select ravioli filled with sausage. My father ordered the same.

He turned to Phlox and made a grave face. "Is Art polite with you?"

"Hmm. Oh, yes, unfailingly."

My father lifted his eyebrows, smiled, and turned bright
red. "Ah," he said.

We ordered, and the waiter expertly spilled a little red
wine into each of our glasses, and my father talked, and the
food came, and my father talked some more. Over the
minestrone and salads, he put me through one long moment of heartbreak, by telling Phlox about a memorable
Sunday at Forbes Field with my mother and my infant
self—a very old, very pretty story that raised goose bumps
along my arms. Phlox didn't take her eyes off him. She
asked short, tactful, and very basic questions about my
mother. What was her hair color? Did I look like her?
What were her virtues and rewards? Didn't she just love her
boy? After each question my father would look at me, puz-
zled, and I would watch my food. You idiot, I thought, you
should have known this would happen.

"She was a very beautiful woman," said my father. "She looked like Jennifer Jones. I don't suppose you know who she is?"

"Jennifer Jones!" said Phlox. "Of course I know who she is! *Portrait of Jenny* is my favorite movie in the whole world!" She tossed her head, pretending to have been insulted.

"Indeed? My apologies," said my father, and he pursed his lips and lifted one eyebrow, pretending to have gained new respect for her, or perhaps her admiration for Jennifer Jones really did impress him.

"I can see it in Art," she said, turning to run a slender finger along the ridge over my left eye, and I thought: Oh, no. "He has Jennifer Jones eyebrows."

"And you," said my father, mocking and flirtatious, "have the eyebrows and the nose of the young Joan Crawford. In, say, *Grand Hotel.*"

"That's my ninth-favorite movie in the whole world," said Phlox.

"She ranks everything," I said. "She has it all figured out."

"I can see that," said my father, and from his tone one knew that he thought her either delightful or the most frivolous young woman he had ever met. Then he glared at me again, for one instant.

Over the main course he explained the Diaspora and carbon 14 dating (which Phlox just as easily could have explained to him) and gave a short history of Swiss banking. Cannoli were accompanied by coffee and an embarrassing account of my first visit, as a small child, to the ocean,

which I had mistaken for a vast expanse of fruit juice. My
father was wonderful. We laughed and laughed. Everything
was exactly as it had not been when I first presented Claire.
Phlox kept administering gentle squeezes of delight to my
thigh, under the table.

At last she rose and excused herself, with a downward
look of modesty which seemed to suggest that we shouldn't
hesitate to discuss her while she was away. And although I
was in terrible doubt about my father's feelings just then,
and although I knew better than to expect him, even under
the best circumstances, to comment on her before he'd
passed a night of careful and jovian consideration, her
blush, her murmured farewell-for-now, her lowered eyelids,
all seemed so confident that nothing ill would be said about
her in her absence that I risked it.

"Isn't she nice?" I said.

"Mm." My father stared at me, his big eyebrows knotted
over the pink top of his nose, and I saw the muscles gathering along his jaw. I began to recoil even before he spoke.

"What's wrong with you? I don't understand you." He
pitched his voice high and spoke quickly, but not very
loud. I knew that it wasn't Phlox who had upset him. My
father was hurt, and extremely hurt, or this, too, would
have waited until the next day.

"I'm sorry, Dad."

"Don't you remember your mother? You were almost
thirteen years old when she passed away." He wiped his
fingers angrily on his napkin and threw it down.

"Of course I remember her, Dad, Of course I do. Dad,
can we please not talk about this now? I don't care if you

make me cry again, but I'd rather not do it in front of Phlox."

"Don't you tell her anything about your mother? Obviously she must have asked you; she practically interviewed me." I hoped this wasn't some kind of insult. "What did you say when she asked you all those things she just asked me?"

"I—" My chin shook. I watched the red light of the restaurant wink across my water glass. "I don't know. I told her . . . I didn't feel like . . . going into it. She understood. And . . . you and I never . . . talk about it, do we? So why . . . Tomorrow, Dad, please."

I felt as though I were attempting to hold down all the blind pale things that lived in the black waters of my gut, and that if he asked me one more plaintive question in that wounded tone of voice it would all be over. I studied as deeply as I could the drops of condensation on the glittering sides of my glass. Then I heard feet along the thick carpet behind me, and my father made an odd sound, a short cluck. I let go my breath and turned to face Phlox and comfort. Instead there was a fat stomach.

"Art!" said Uncle Lenny Stern. "Joe! Art and Joe, father and son, man to man, hey? Hee hee. Man to man!"

"Uncle Lenny," I said, managing to remember to take his hand, which was sweaty as ever. It didn't occur to me that perhaps I was still expected to kiss his scratchy cheek. He wasn't really my uncle, after all. "I must be dreaming."

He laughed again; however, I was, for a moment, half-serious. I thought I must be dreaming a horrible transformation dream in which my blue-and-white-flowered Phlox had become a short, giggling, egg-shaped Jewish gangster. What my father had said to me, indeed, was what he often said in my dreams. But then, behind Lenny, I saw a section of Elaine Stern—her shoulder, I thought—and, behind her, part of Phlox, who stood, eyebrows raised, mouth open, watching as this tremendous woman and her attendant miasma of White Shoulders engulfed me. Aunt Elaine's kisses always hurt one's face; I used to call her the Pincher.

"Actually," said my father, "it isn't quite man to man. Introduce your friend, Art."

He pointed to Phlox, and there was a general whirling around.

"Uncle Lenny Stern, Aunt Elaine, this is Miss Phlox Lombardi. Phlox."

"Oh, isn't she gorgeous!" said Aunt Elaine. She crushed the back of my neck in her fingers. "And how do you like this handsome young man, eh? A prince!" She shook my head like a pompon.

"They aren't really my uncle and aunt," I said.

"I like him very well," said Phlox, and she held out a limp, pretty hand to one of the most notorious lieutenants in Pittsburgh organized crime. We made space for them at our table, which was wrecked, strewn with napkins and spots of red sauce, and two menus were brought, and more coffee. I leaned over to Phlox and whispered that we weren't going to be free for a while yet.

"That's all right," she said. "They're fun."

"Please," I said. I sat back and watched my Uncle Lenny; I hadn't seen him for a long time. He drew my father into a discussion of mutual funds and waved his arms around. His skin was Florida brown; as he got older he spent less and less time in the city of his birth, and the FBI listened in on more and more long-distance calls from West Palm Beach. I knew I was not the only one in the restaurant who watched him. I turned around and saw a couple of dark-haired men at a far table, probably brothers; they nodded to me, and without even thinking I sought out the bulges under their jackets, an ancient reflex of mine, and in the next moment I underwent the equally ancient fantasy of running around to the other side of the table to strangle Lenny Stern. I didn't want to kill him, really. It was a just a ten-year-old's desire to see a little shooting.

Elaine asked Phlox a bunch of questions about her "people," then recited an impressive list of Pittsburgh Italians with whom she was "like that," laying one finger over the other. It developed that Phlox's maternal grandmother was the aunt of a woman whose home and card table Elaine had graced with her giant presence many times in the 1950s. At this revelation, my feelings, interrupted at a crisis moment by the new arrivals and held in dazed suspense for the past ten minutes, began to wriggle and stretch and prickle, like frozen toes under a stream of warm water. They were very mixed. I found it strangely pleasing that, beyond all the new and crucial connections between me and Phlox, there could also be this old and silly connection of families; I felt the lover's shocked but unsurprised love of anything that appears to suggest the whimsical engines of destiny.

And yet this link also confirmed that Phlox was now hopelessly mixed up with my family. She'd met not only my father, which I hadn't wanted, but Lenny Stern, and if she

just turned around she would also see Them, the two ugly
men with guns, who were the lion and the unicorn of my
family's coat of arms. I gripped the edge of the table. All of
the people I spent time with and loved, rather than helping
to take me out of the world into which I'd been born, were
being pulled into it: Phlox, the cousin of some dead Mafia
wife, was eating a dinner paid for by the Washington Family; the fat, powerful man slapping my father's sleeve and
eyeing her across the table was, though distantly,
Cleveland's boss; and now—I remembered with alarm—
Cleveland, too, was threatening to come into contact with
my father. I might have doubted that he would do it, had
he not been Cleveland. The more I thought on these
things, the more I felt the heavy food sliding slowly and
murderously, like pack ice, through my stomach. There are
head people, who suffer from sudden migraines, and there
are stomach people, like me.

"Ah, yeah, Marjorie, my God." Lenny's voice rose up
out of his quite conversation with my father, and occupied
the table. I sat bolt upright. "Floss, it's a real shame you
couldn't of met Art's mother. She was a wonderful girl.
Played the piano like an angel. She—was—beautiful.
Laine?"

"I could forget? An angel. Art? An angel."

I looked at Phlox, who looked at me as though I looked
upset, and then at my father, who sighed. He seemed suddenly very tired.

"I remember," I said. "Excuse me." I stood up and went
into the men's room, where I knelt with my head over the
toilet, and was sick, on and off, for two hundred and forty

thundering clicks of the quartz watch my father had given to me at graduation.

"Art," said Phlox, later. We were in her bed. There was the green glow of her radio dial and the faint, lost voice of Patti Page singing "Old Cape Cod." "What happened? Tell me. It was rude to leave like that. I'm embarrassed."

I spoke into her pillow, which smelled of Opium and soap. "My father understood. Don't worry about Lenny and Elaine."

"But what happened? Is it your mother? Why can't anyone mention her without you getting upset?"

I pressed up against her, spoonwise, and spoke over the soft and slightly damp lip of her ear. "I'm sorry," I whispered. "Everyone has some things he doesn't like to discuss, no?"

"You have too many," said Phlox.

"This song always kills me," I said.

She sighed, and then gave up. "Why?"

"Oh, I don't know. Nostalgia. It makes me feel nostalgia for a time I never even knew. I wasn't even alive."

"That's what I do to you too," she said. "I'll just bet."

It was what everything I loved did to me.

15

THE MUSEUM OF REAL LIFE

◆ ◆ ◆

Hanging out at the Cloud Factory on the hottest day of the
year, shoulders to the wire fence, the sky still that yellow
Pittsburgh gray, but the sweat already pasting the hair to
my forehead and the cotton to the small of my back.
Cleveland was ten minutes late. I looked at the black win-
dowless flank of the Carnegie Institute, watched people slip
down the back stairs to the rear door of the museum cafeteria; they had nice old Slovak ladies in there who wore
clear plastic gloves and served spaetzle and ham and other
heavy things. I thought about how I used to prefer that
cafeteria to the dinosaurs, the diamonds, and even the
mummies. Then I watched the impenetrable Cloud Factory, which was running full tilt, one ideal cloud after another flourishing from its valve and drifting off; they looked
dry somehow, crisp and white against the dull, humid sky. I
tilted back my head and blew big tangles of cigarette smoke
into the air in time with the clicks of the Factory. That
morning after breakfast, Phlox and I had screamed at each
other for the first time. Now my hands were shaking.

She hadn't wanted me to leave her bed, or her breakfast
table, or her lap as I sat in it, lacing my shoes. But I was

getting anxious; it had been three days since I'd last spoken to Arthur or Cleveland, and three days, I calculated, was three percent of my summer, which seemed a terrible amount of time to lose. My clear June Technicolor dream of a summer spent fluttering ever upward, like a paper airplane over the heat and hubbub of Times Square, had not faded; all my stupid hopes were still pinned to the stupid two of them. I had to see Cleveland, that was what I felt, even if it was to enter with him the world I had said I never would enter. What I had screamed at Phlox was something else, however; I have no memory of what I said, but I'm sure it was irrational, nasty, and petty.

One cigarette later, I heard the loud, slobbering cough of Cleveland's motorcycle. He popped the curb at the end of the Schenley Park bridge, and I started over to him, but then I saw that he'd killed the engine and was swinging off the saddle and hanging his helmet on the bar; so I stopped, and stood, and waited some more.

We shook hands, then he walked right past me, up to the padlocked gate of the Cloud Factory, where he put his fingers through the diamond-shaped gaps in the fence and looked up at the magic valve. I went to stand beside him, but watched his face and not the hissing white production, except for what I could see of it in the lenses of his eyeglasses. He was unshowered, his long hair limp and sticky, a black smudge on his cheek. From something about the expression on his face, the tense fold of his eyelids, the dry lips, I guessed that he was hung over, but he smiled up at the infant clouds and rattled the gate—happily, I thought.

"Careful," I said. "You might tear it off."

"I did once."

"Sure."

"You know, this damn Cloud Factory . . ." He tightened his grip on the wire and pulled.

"What?"

He looked at me. I watched his knuckles turn pale.

"Do you know where I'm taking you today?"

"I guess. Cleveland, what?"

"I'm broke, Bechstein, I don't have a dime." His voice sounded sandy.

"So? Look, I know why people start working for Uncle Lenny."

"No, you don't." He pulled harder on the thick wires of the fence. "No, you don't. To hell with money. And *from* hell with money. To and from hell with money. I'm broke. . . ." His voice trailed off. "Something has to change. I love Jane, Bechstein."

I saw now that he was not just hung over; he was still drunk. He probably hadn't been to bed yet.

"You always tell me you love Jane when you're drunk." He didn't answer. "Okay, so let's go, Virgil. Shock me."

We went over to the big black BMW, leaving behind us two hand-sized bulges in the fence. You could still make them out from fifty yards away, two little blurs in the pattern of wire.

We rode through strange sections to a part of the city that I hardly knew. I knew, in fact, only that there was another good Italian restaurant somewhere around there; my father often mentioned it. We were at the foot of one of the hillside neighborhoods, its houses sparse up along the

distant ridge, but coming thicker and thicker toward the
bottom, like a cataract, one atop another, sideways and
backward and connected by crazy catwalks and staircases,
and all tumbling downhill to the river—the Allegheny or
the Monongahela, I was not sure which. I made out some
children playing on one of the few high streets that cut
across the hillside, and a car, and two women talking on a
far back porch.

Before he stopped the engine, Cleveland said something I didn't catch. In the sudden silence I asked him to
repeat it.

"This, this is my country," he said, with a broad
Charlton Heston sweep of his arm, "and these, these are
my people."

We started up one of the concrete stairways, which
shifted back and forth among the knots of houses, all the
way to the top; it looked like a long way.

"There's a road, but I like to make a stealthy approach.
Don't worry, we only have to go as far as the Second Cir-
cle." His heels tocked concrete, steadily, slowly, and our
breath came more quickly with each landing.

"Is this a poor neighborhood?"

"About to get poorer."

"How much poorer?"

"Depends on the vig."

"The vig."

"Depends."

"Oh."

That was it for a while. Cleveland stopped once and
mopped his forehead with a rose bandanna. He said the

agents in his bloodstream were being oxidized too quickly. We were up in the midst of things now, and I looked back down to the motorcycle, and beyond it to the river, its water the color of the water in a jar of used paintbrushes.

"The lovely Monongahela," I said.

"That's the Allegheny, Doctor Fact," said Cleveland. "Okay, I'm better now. Come."

Another few minutes of silent climbing brought us to a long road that ran perpendicular to the staircase. On the left the road curved all the way down the hill, and on the right it rose to the ridge, which, I now saw, was not as sparse as it had seemed from the bottom. There was a church up there, with a big red sign that said Jesus did something: saved, lived, gave—I couldn't make out the verb. Cleveland and I gasped for a few moments, then I followed him up the road. Two motorcycles flew past with a huge racket, and we hugged the shoulder to get out of their deafening way. They came extremely close, the near bike with its helmeted enormous rider almost nicking my hip. Cleveland tried to pound its back fender as it pulled away.

"Assholes. Jesus, I just relived every cigarette I ever smoked," he said, panting.

"Cleveland, why are you taking me here? Do I need to see this?"

"What do you think you're going to see?"

"Sad people."

"Never hurts to see sad people. Anyway, it'll give you something to tell your dad."

"Right." Dad. "Do you know what my dad would say if I told him I made the rounds with one of Lenny Stern's pickup boys? He'd say, 'I want you out of Pittsburgh. You've developed too many unsavory associates.' No, he'd say, 'Are you doing this to punish me, Art?'"

He spun and faced me. "I told you I'm not Lenny Stern's anything."

"Okay, okay."

"And what—is your father ashamed of what he is?"

"I'm ashamed."

"Well, maybe I'll tell him what we've been up to, then. You know I want to meet Joe the Egg."

I must have flinched at this nickname. "So you've said."

"Sorry," he said, not very apologetically. "Look, here we are."

We reached the first house in a row of houses all built across the tiny stretch of earth that lay between the road and nothing, empty air. The houses were supported at the rear by an intricate and feeble-looking system of peeling gray two-by-fours that worked their capricious way down to concrete anchors set into the hill. The greenish paint was also peeling from the side of the first wooden house, which had one newspapered window cut into it, toward the top. We picked our way to the front door along a cracked walk littered with old toys, an enormous Sony television carton, and a soggy pink sneaker.

"I really would like to talk to your father," he whispered, knocking.

"Cleveland."

He patted me once on the shoulder, and then tapped again on the door, with the same hand.

The woman who answered Cleveland's three lazy

knocks had a nice smile that lasted for the fifth of a second before she realized who was at the door.

"He ain't here," she said, looking back and forth between us several times, not nervously but with annoyance, and as though memorizing our faces.

"Well, I am." There was an instant and very convincing meanness to his voice. "And there is that invisible man who has been so generous to your brother. He's here too. In spirit."

She glanced at me before realizing whom Cleveland meant: probably not Uncle Lenny, or whoever was over him, but one of the Stern soldiers. The woman, or girl— she looked about sixteen—had narrowed the space between the door and the jamb, and drawn her body back into the house, so that now only her face showed.

"Who is it?" a man shouted from somewhere within.

The girl blushed. Cleveland smiled.

"Wait," she said, and shut the door in our faces.

"Come in? No, thank you; I'll just wait right here on the porch." He turned toward me and smiled again, lit a cigarette, and leaned against the crumbling side of the house.

"Get a load of this ménage," he said. "I always come here first; it's my favorite."

"Ha."

"They're your father's kind of people."

"Come on, Cleveland, stop."

This time a tall, unshaven young man in an undershirt, with long black hair like Cleveland's, opened the door, wide. His smile did not fade as his sister's had, but lingered too long, big and yellow and pitiful.

"Come on in."

We stepped into the house, which was full of odors. There was an immediate tart and sweaty smell of marijuana, and then, beneath or woven into that smell, fainter ones of tomato sauce, sex, and old furniture. The place looked grandmotherly and clean: easy chairs, frilly lamps, a beat-up china closet. The girl, her hair black like her brother's, sat on a sofa beside another young woman, who held a toddler on her lap. The little kid didn't look at us—he played with a toy helicopter. On the television, a game-show audience screamed out counsel.

"Who's this guy?" said the tall man, jerking his head at me.

"My dad," said Cleveland. "He doesn't believe I have a steady job."

We all laughed: we men, that is; the two women glared at Cleveland. Then we listened awhile to the television.

"Well," said Cleveland.

"Just give it to him and get them out of here." It was the woman with the baby; she spoke into the top of the bald little head.

"Why don't you shut up." He reached into the pocket of his jeans, pulled out a black plastic wallet, which looked new, and took from it two crumpled twenties, which he handed to Cleveland. "Not this week," he said.

"No problem," said Cleveland, producing a small manila envelope from his own pocket and poking the bills into it. "No problem at all."

"They say they're going to be hiring back some guys before September, you know, so, like, well." He smiled that awful smile again.

Now the little boy climbed down from the woman's lap and lurched across the living room, stopping when he reached the three of us. He looked up at me, with a crease in his brow, and uttered a few syllables, very seriously.

"Yes, I know," I said.

After the door had closed behind us and we came down the shattered walk, I asked Cleveland what he found so remarkable about the household.

"They're both his sisters," he said.

There was a short silence while I digested this.

"Whose. . . ?"

"I don't know. Maybe it's not even his. You should see them on a good day, though. Today they were all stoned. On a good day, that place is like a circus."

This made me angry.

"Cleveland. You— This is horrible. You're taking advantage of this unemployed guy, you walk into their house once a week and you ruin their day, I'll bet they have huge fights after you leave, and you think the whole thing is funny. You get a kick out of it. Those people hate your guts. They hate you. How can you stand to look at that guy's shit-eating grin every week?"

"The world of business is built on shit-eating grins."

"You can cut the fake cynicism, Cleveland."

"You're the economist. You know what economics is."

"I don't remember."

"You remember. It's the precise measurement of shit

eating, it's the science of misery. Look, I have to think it's funny, don't I? Okay."

He stopped. We were halfway along the row of houses, and the sun had just come out, making it hotter than before. He bent down to pull the fabric of his jeans away from the backs of his knees, and I realized how stuck together I felt, too, and bent down alongside him.

"Okay. Look. I brought you along, Bechstein. I've never brought anyone before. No one else except Artie even knows that I do this. Jane doesn't know. And I would never have brought Lecomte. Why? I don't know. I'm not supposed to bring anybody at all. But for some reason I wanted you to see this. You should understand this. Can't you see why I do this?" He was almost shouting, seemingly angrier than I had been a moment before. Drops of sweat had pooled over his eyebrows and poured down the sides of his face. But I didn't believe him. I felt all at once like Arthur with his X-ray heart, and I was sure that Cleveland was misleading me somehow, that he did know why I was standing on that hill with him, soaking wet, ashamed, and in a sudden rage.

"Because it's easy," I shouted. "Because it's easy, and it pays well, and it makes you feel like you're better than the people you exploit."

I thought he was going to punch me. He made fists and kept them, barely, at his sides. Then the anger went out of his shoulders; he unballed his hands and smiled, faintly.

"Wrong. No. Wrong. I do it because it is fun and fascinating work."

"Ah."

"See, I'm a people person." He gave an airy toss of his great head.

"I see."

"And also—I'm surprised that you haven't guessed this, Bechstein—I do it because—"

"I know," I said. "Because it is Bad."

He grinned and said, "I wear a rattlesnake for a necktie."

I laughed.

"I have a mojo hand," he said.

It was very difficult for me to admit it to myself, almost as difficult as it would have been to express admiration for my father's job and associates (and still I took his money), but collecting illegal interest on loans, although perhaps not fun, was terribly fascinating work. I had always felt pleasure on looking into the houses of strangers. As a child, coming home at sunset through the infinite chain of backyards that led from the schoolyard to our house, I would catch glimpses in windows of dining rooms, tables set for supper; of crayon drawings tacked to refrigerators, cartons of milk standing on counters; of feet on low hassocks, framed photographs, and empty sofas, all lit by the bland light of the television; and these quickly shifting tableaux, of strange furniture and the lives and families they divulged, would send me into a trance of curiosity. For a long time I thought that one became a spy in order to watch the houses of other people, to be confronted by the simple, wondrous fact of other kitchens, other clocks, and ottomans.

Cleveland took me to ten or twelve houses on that hill,

and I stood in kitchens, on patios, wanting so little to watch the smarminess and resentment passed along with each ten-dollar bill that I noted every thing in each room, feverishly—the silk flowers on the televisions, the statues of Our Lady, the babies' stockings on the floors. At first I pretended that Cleveland was conducting me along the galleries of a Museum of Real Life, a series of careful, clever re-creations of houses, in which one could almost but not quite imagine plain and awful things happening, as though the houses were uninhabited, fake, and for my amusement; but by the seventh or eighth house, with its blue-veined pair of legs, filthy child, pretty sister, spoiled lunch hour, I was out of the museum. His "people" had me in their spell. They did not like him, nor did he care very much for them; but there was a basic, hard, genuine acquaintance, an odd kind of comfort between them and him, and I felt as though I were being shown, in this world that seemed somehow better than mine, yet another way in which I would never come to know Cleveland.

"Cleveland," said one older woman, whose husband had borrowed one hundred and fifty dollars at an endlessly compounding rate of interest long enough ago that she now thought of Cleveland in the same way she thought of the mailman, "you look more like Russell every day. It makes me want to cry." She'd been treating her hair when we arrived and now wore a see-through plastic babushka that crinkled when she shook her head. The whole place smelled of bad eggs.

"Why is that?"

"Do you know where Russell is right this minute?"

"At the mill?"

"Nope, he's in the bedroom sleeping off a hangover. And you've got that same swoll-up face that he does. You got a girl?"

"Yeah." I was surprised to see that he put his fingers to his cheeks and pressed them tentatively.

"Well, I feel sorry for her. You get uglier every week."

16

THE CASA DEL FEAR

♦ ♦ ♦

As we crossed the cracked flagstones on the lawn of the last house, he stopped short, stood rigid. I bumped into him from behind, hard enough to knock his glasses off.

"What's the matter?" I said.

He hissed, "Shit," then took an unlucky and false step. I heard the flat crack of boot heel against lens.

"Shit!" he said again, but he kept on running downhill, a bit tentatively, holding out his hands before him; I bent down quickly to pick up the rubble of his Clark Kents and then went after him. In the road, farther down along the row of houses, sat the two motorcycles, one of which had almost torn off my pelvis earlier that morning. A very fat man was leaning against a kickstanded bike, smoking a cigarette, and it was toward him that Cleveland so faultily ran. I caught up just as my friend stumbled over a pothole, fell, and slid hugely across five feet of blacktop on his stomach, like a parade float.

"Jesus."

"Are you all right?"

He was instantly on his feet and running again, although now it was with more of a lumbering sideways hop, his long hair whipping out to one side with every step. I'd seen a flash of blood and black gravel on his palms, and I ran behind him, frightened by that flash, by the thud of his impact, and by his silence. The fat man had noticed us immediately and had stood up straight, and as we drew near to him he flicked away his cigarette and did the twist on it with one foot. Cleveland flew right up against him until their faces were an inch apart; I didn't know whether this meant battle or myopia.

"Feldman."

"Hey, Peter Fonda," said Feldman.

"What the hell are you doing here?"

Feldman was maybe in his late twenties, drenched in cotton undershirt, sweat beading on his little black mustache. He had a big, bushy chest and on his thick left arm a tattoo that said GONIF. His eyes and his entire face looked smart, mean, and amused; he reminded me a little of Cleveland, whom he pushed lightly away with the tips of his fat fingers, as he tugged another cigarette from behind his ear.

"I'm leaning against my motorcycle," he said. He lit a match with one hand and smiled. "Took a hell of a fall back there, Fonda." Feldman snickered: Ss-ss-ss, like a pool float being deflated by a bouncing child. "And who's this? Dennis Hopper?" He blew a cloud of smoke at me.

I looked away, and I recognized the battered blue watering can on the front porch of the house where an ugly husband named Russell was sleeping off a hangover in the bedroom.

"Damn," said Cleveland, and he ran past, up the

wooden steps and into the house, squinting back at me before he vanished, as though he expected me to follow, but Feldman put a heavy hand on my arm. I turned to him, beginning to make tentative sense of the situation.

"There's someone in the house," I said.

"At the moment, as far as I know, there are exactly four people in the house," said Feldman. He kept his hand on my arm. Silently I counted. Feldman had settled back against his motorcycle, an elephantine Harley-Davidson, and after a few minutes he launched himself from it with a lazy bounce of his beach-ball waist and started up the walk, dragging his toes. He was a big, sweaty bundle of tough mannerisms in an undershirt. As he walked away, he tilted his head over backward and looked at me from that odd vantage.

"Coming, Bechstein?" said the upside-down face.

Inside the house it was like this: The egg-bad smell was still everywhere, but it had its locus on the sofa in the living room, where the old lady was stretched out flat in her cellophane kerchief, breathing quickly, one trembling blue-and-white hand on her breast. Her eyes were open, and she looked at us wildly as we entered the house, but did not raise her head. I heard voices in the other room, Cleveland's among them, and then the groan of a table or dresser or something being shoved across the floor. Feldman, who knew my name, walked the hall as though it were the hall in his childhood home, dragging his fingers along the walls, looking at his feet, like a boy who has been sent to his room but is unafraid of punishment or of his father. Another piece of furniture creaked and then crashed

to the floor, and the sound of broken glass went everywhere. I jumped. As we reached the half-open door at the
end of the hallway, I heard men grunting, feet shuffling, a
curse. Feldman nudged the door open with the lizard toe of
his fancy loafer.

Cleveland and a black giant were locked in each other's
arms, tearing at each other's hair and clothing; the giant,
who looked to be about seven feet tall, apparently had as
his goal the messy old man who was scrunched against the
wall at the head of the bed, his eyes wide with terror. The
ruins of a vanity lay at their feet, its mirror scattered across
the floor around it, and an old electric fan, grille caked
with webs of dirt, whirled uselessly on the windowsill.
Cleveland had set himself between the giant and the goal.

"Lurch," said Feldman. "Lay off." He had a revolver in
his hand, and suddenly I could not swallow the spit in my
mouth, or move, or think; the abrupt black fact of a gun
always acts on me as a kind of evil jacklight, transfixes me.
At once, the giant freed Cleveland, or freed himself of
Cleveland. He unbent his body, and his slick, processed
ringlets nearly grazed the low ceiling of the room. He came
to stand beside Feldman and draped his vast arm across his
partner's distant shoulders. They smiled at each other across
a foot and a half of bad air. Feldman lowered the gun
slightly. The old man had not moved; his chin was wet.

"Cleveland," Lurch said, his voice deep and beautiful as
a radio man's, "what is your *problem*, baby?" He wasn't even
winded. Cleveland, on the other hand, was a mess; he
could not see, his hands bled, his shirt was torn, he gasped

for breath; he didn't say anything, but he smiled at Lurch. It was a strange smile. It was knowing.

"Oh, Lurch, here's someone you've been wanting to meet," said Feldman. "This is a Bechstein."

"Wow," said Lurch. He held out a hand the size of a dictionary and showed me his expensive teeth. "I guess Cleveland's been showing you the other end of the family horse?"

I hate to say it, but I was incapable of the usual bubbly little comeback; I had my eyes on the bright black revolver.

"Feldman, Lurch, don't do this," said Cleveland, streaking his pant legs with the bloody palms of his hands. "He's an old guy. I got juice from the old lady an hour ago."

Amid all that, I admired Cleveland's slang. Juice. I made an immediate mental note of it.

"How much did you take?" said Feldman, and now he had put the gun somewhere; his hands were empty. "Seventy-five fifty? That's not enough."

"We aren't supposed to depart until Mr. Czarnic here has remunerated a certain person to the sum of three hundred and fifty dollars and thirty cents, cash. More or less. Cleveland. Or else we show his wrinkly old butt some impressive feats of strength."

"Unless," said Feldman. He turned to me.

"Unless what?" said Cleveland.

"Unless what do *you* think of all this, O Son of Joe the Egg?" said Lurch.

"What do you mean? What difference does it make what I think of it?" I looked from one to the other of their

faces, looked at the old man, who had stretched himself out
now and was trying to slide his legs over the edge of the
bed. He held one hand gingerly to his hangover. "This isn't
any of my business."

"Aren't you your daddy's little boy?"

"My daddy doesn't live in Pittsburgh. My daddy lives in
Washington, D.C.," I said. "We talk on the telephone
once a week."

"Oh, but, Dennis, that's just the next best thing," said
Feldman. "You can *be there*. Your daddy's right downtown
at the Duquesne, Dennis. Room six twenty-four, if I'm not
mistaken."

Jesus.

"So?" I said.

"Six *thirty*-four," said Lurch. He walked over to the old
man's dresser. Its top was covered with nickels and pennies,
a clip-on bow tie, a wallet, a bottle of Aqua Velva, a photo
of the old lady when she wasn't old. He swept his huge fist
across the dresser, and it all went onto the floor. The glass
on the picture frame broke with a gritty sound. I looked at
Cleveland, who seemed to be trying to stare into my eyes,
although without his eyeglasses he was unable to do more
than squint intently.

"Cleveland, what is this?" I said. "Is this a test?"

Lurch unhooked an old felt homburg from the doorknob
of the closet and walked over to the old man. He bent far
down and pulled the hat onto the man's head, and kept
pulling, until the hat came unblocked, the felt stretched
and took on the shape of the man's skull, and his eyes disappeared under the crumpling brim. Lurch pulled, the man

cried out and grabbed at his tremendous forearms, the felt stretched, a small tear opened.

"Stop!" I said.

Lurch stopped. He lifted the hat, delicately dented in its torn crown, and hung it from the doorknob. The old man lashed out at Lurch and hit him feebly on the thigh.

"Let's go," said Feldman.

"After you, Mr. Bechstein," said Lurch.

We went out. I turned my eyes from the sickening look of hatred and thanksgiving in the eyes of the old man—the look, that is to say, of respect.

They drove us down to the foot of the hill, Cleveland behind Lurch, me with a great view of the smelly expanse of Feldman's back; as usual, things were proceeding too quickly, and also as usual, I was hesitant to acknowledge the implications of these things; so instead I shouted through the sweaty wind to Feldman, whom, despite my-self, and despite my anger at Cleveland, and despite the lingering fear of guns and brutality, with which I was still trembling, I rather liked.

He said that he and Lurch had been members of rival motorcycle clubs—Feldman of the Pittsburgh chapter of the Outlaws, and Lurch of a black gang called the Down Rockers—who had met in the thick of a race riot, crow-bars in their hands, bitter curses on their lips, and had for some reason begun to laugh. After that they were in-separable. They'd quit their gangs to work as a team, and had been hired as muscle by Frankie Breezy, the same man who had hired Cleveland, and the man whose "fran-chise"—it certainly didn't belong to Cleveland—we were just now leaving.

We were almost to the bottom of the hill. I could see Cleveland's parked motorcycle and smell the cloying sugary stink of the algae roasting along the riverbank.

"Feldman. Tell me. This whole thing was a setup, wasn't it?"

"Sure."

"Why did he do it?"

"Hey, he's your friend, Dennis. And you know," he said, in a softer voice, easing up on the throttle, "you ought to take better care of him."

We pulled up behind the other Harley, I got off the bike, and we shook. Then he and Lurch roared away across the shimmering blacktop. It was quiet for a long time.

"Well," Cleveland said finally. "So your father's in town. That's interesting."

"You make me so angry, Cleveland, fuck. What was that? What was the point of all that?"

"The point? The point was those guys would have done your nails and made you a cheese omelet if you'd asked them to. Your father's a wise guy, Bechstein, he's big. I told you. And by extension, see, you're big too. You partake of the bigness of your father. What is there to be ashamed of? The point was—"

"If you think now I'm going to let you meet my father—"

"I don't need you to make the introductions. Dennis. I can just pick up the red courtesy phone in the lobby." He lit a cigarette and shook out the match. "Look, Art, I guess this is sort of insane."

I was overcome with a feeling of great, wary relief, the way one is when one grasps at a straw. "It is insane, Cleveland. Yes. It is. Let's not even discuss it."

"Of course you don't have to come along. I can drop you off at the bus if you want. Or you could just wait around, kill some time in Kaufmann's or something, and then I'll take you home."

"Oh."

"But I would like you to come with, you know, it would make everything so much simpler. I mean, what is the big deal? I'm your friend, am I not? You don't introduce your friends to your father? I take it he's met Phlox?"

"Yes, he has."

"Well? I just want to *meet* him, that's all. Just shake his fabled iron hand."

"No," I said. "I *won't*. I just won't. No, you are not my friend, Cleveland. You've played around with me too much. Forget it."

"Fine. I'll have to call for an appointment."

"You really would go without me."

I turned from him and walked down to the riverside and stood in weeds and rusty cans. I was hot, overcome by a feeling of brute sleepiness, and I was two hours late for my foredoomed rendezvous with Phlox. I saw that I'd been mistaken when I thought of myself as a Wall, because a wall stands between, and holds apart, two places, two worlds, whereas, if anything, I was nothing but a portal, ever widening, along a single obscure corridor that ran all the way from my mother and father to Cleveland, Arthur, and Phlox, from the beautiful Sunday morning on which my mother had abandoned me, to the unimaginable August that now, for the first time, began to loom. And a wall says no; a portal doesn't say anything.

"I'm not your friend?" He crunched into the grass beside me. An old, yellow flap of newspaper wrapped itself around his boot.

"Cleveland, do you realize what you're asking me to do? Do you appreciate the misery this means for me?"

"No. I can't," he said. "You never let me."

I looked at him. He almost smiled, but his eyes were fixed on me, unblinking, his forehead wrinkled. Then he started over to the motorcycle. I followed with his broken eyeglasses, and he fit the parts together as well as he could.

It is true, I know, that I failed to permit Cleveland any real sense of the world within me, which was, and is, a world of secrets (but that is putting it too grandly, for it was only a world of things that I could not—no, that I *needed* not to say), and I regret this failure all the more now, when I realize that he—oh, Cleveland—five times opened wide to me the doors of his strange world. Five times that summer I rode Cleveland's motorcycle, my head squeezed into the banana-yellow helmet that had once belonged to his little sister. Each time, as we set out, I would clutch the metal bar behind me, but he drove, of course, like a maniac, threading his way among speeding cars, running down yellow lights, even hopping briefly up and off the sidewalk to avoid tie-ups, and I always finished with my hands more securely upon his hips, and would shout and laugh into his helmet. It was at these times, these five quick, alarming times, my fists full of hot black jacket, my helmet clicking against his, that I felt most linked to him, most understanding. I knew why he did the things he did. There would be nothing but his wide back, his laughter, and Pittsburgh whirling past, each of its trees a short hiss. The speed and the roar and the nothing that isolated us were more exciting, more true and intimate, than anything I ever felt that summer with either Phlox or Arthur; there was no shadow of sex to mar or deepen it. There were only laughing fear and my hands, like so, on his hips. We were friends.

He took me to his house so that we could shower and he could change his torn clothes, dig up an old pair of glasses. If I have not already described Cleveland's own abode, it is because the first time I saw it was that day, when everything seemed new and newly foreboding, when I was filled with giddy fear and with curiosity. Arthur had already made me a little apprehensive of what he called the Casa del Fear, by alluding darkly to its ever changing roster of inmates, its collapses and minor fires, strange animals, dunes and towers of unwashed clothes and dishes. "It's not a house," he had said, "it's an implosion." It sat in the middle of a small wood in the middle of a Squirrel Hill city block, a forgotten place gained by a narrow, cracked drive that was barely visible from the street. It might have passed for haunted, had its exterior not been decorated with tricolor giant wooden cutouts of Felix the Cat, Alice the Goon, Beany and Cecil, Mr. Peabody and Sherman, Ignatz Mouse and his flying brick. But it had gables, a queer, peeling turret, an iron fence, its shutters dangled crazily, and there was something vaguely human about its visage.

"Who owns this place?" I said, unscrewing my head from the helmet as we climbed off the bike.

"No one knows."

"Ah."

"Every month, on the first night of the full moon, I leave the rent money in a little paper bag at the end of the driveway. In the morning it's gone."

We climbed the steps of the house and crossed the creaking porch, went through the living room. Paperback books were piled everywhere, on tables, on the floor, in corners, and I glanced at their titles, an eclectic assortment that ran from the true stories of famous murders to Knut Hamsun, from diet books and horoscopes to Vonnegut and comic books. I supposed that all this odd variety represented the many and multiform roommates and previous occupants of the Casa del Fear.

"Have you read all of these?"

"Of course. Why else would they be here?"

"You bought all these books?"

"I don't buy books," he said.

This was before I knew about Cleveland's magical coat of many pockets, which inexhaustibly brought forth cigarettes, canned goods, books and magazines, and the occasional rubber snake or chattering wind-up dentures plucked from a variety store. Perhaps the greatest single miracle that Cleveland ever performed was to have run through his mother's considerable legacy in six years without ever purchasing anything more expensive than his motorcycle.

We cleaned ourselves up, and while he changed I wandered the halls, looking into the bare rooms, each with a stereo and a mattress. None of the evil roommates appeared to be home, although traces of them, visual and olfactory, were everywhere. Some of the bedroom doors were padlocked, others were torn from their hinges and set tilted against a wall. I stepped into one room and stared absently for a few moments at a poster that promoted a rock-and-roll band, before noticing that it depicted a garish Aztec sacrifice atop a pyramid—the heart, bereft of its body, lovingly rendered. I was thinking that I had to call Phlox, and the thought of Phlox was so appealing that I almost decided just to go to her, to sneak out of the house and let Cleveland head downtown alone. Perhaps that would have been an even more foolish thing to do, although it is difficult to see how. In any case, he stuck his head in the door.

"Okay, Bechstein."

I turned. He had on round white-rimmed glasses that made him look rather fey.

"All right." I sighed. "Just let me call Phlox."

But there was no answer; so we went downtown, which was my fourth time on the back of Cleveland's motorcycle.

17

B and E

♦ ♦ ♦

On the way downtown, I considered the possibility that I might end up once again in the ill-starred Italian restaurant. It would have made, at least, for a kind of gruesome symmetry. But my father, as it happened, was in his hotel room, with several other men. Dimly we could hear them laughing as we came down the worn plush in the cool, faded hotel corridor. My cheeks tingled from exercise and anxiety. And then Cleveland astonished me: When I stopped at the numbered door and for a last look of encouragement turned to face him, he drew a necktie from the pocket of his leather jacket and began to loop it around his shirt collar. The tie was gray-brown, with an intricate pattern of unusual squares and ovals.

"Rattlesnake," said Cleveland.

Another round of guffaws from the other side of the door. I waited, so as not to cause an ominous, abrupt cessation of laughter; when I heard the final sound of my father clearing his throat, I knocked. After the several seconds that it took them silently to discuss and to delegate, a man opened the door, one of Them. I tried to look into the room, but there was a white vestibule—a bench, a mirror, and a gladiola in a vase—and nothing else. The man, in shirtsleeves and suit pants, had a pale face and an uncool haircut. He recognized me, and I wondered how many times I had seen him before. He smiled and stepped out into the hall, shutting the door behind him.

"Hey," he said. "How do you like that? It's Joe Bechstein's boy." He shook my hand. "Jimmy. Jim Breezy. Last time I saw you, you were a kid. Say, Art, listen." He put his hand on my shoulder and pulled me a little toward him, and a little away from the door, then he looked over my shoulder and seemed to notice Cleveland for the first time. "This a friend?"

"Yes; right. It *is* good to see you, Jimmy."

"Say, Art, listen—your dad's kind of busy right now, you know, he's talking to some people. So. He's busy."

"Oh, no."

"Yeah, you know? I think maybe you better come back in an hour, like an hour and a half, maybe."

"Oh. Okay, Jimmy, sure. Five o'clock, say?"

He said sure, without looking at his watch, and went back in; the door shut.

"Oh, well," I said, "five o'clock. My dad's busy."

Cleveland rolled his eyes.

"You're jelly, Bechstein, you're like fish jelly," he said, and knocked on the door.

"Yeah?" Jimmy Breezy said this time, still smiling.

"Couldn't we see Mr. Bechstein now, and not at five o'clock?" said Cleveland.

"Who are you?" said Jim, smileless now.

"I'm the friend. Cleveland Arning."

"Send them in," I heard my father say.

Jim Breezy swung out of our way, like a gate.

There were seven men in the room, not counting Them, sitting in a variety of armchairs around a long, low coffee table, on which lay a read and refolded newspaper, a key, and my father's airplane ticket: my father, dressed for golf and looking hard but relaxed; Uncle Lenny, also in white shoes and big pastel pants; and five other men, one of whom, also pale-faced, sat bolt upright when he saw Cleveland. He had to be Frankie Breezy, a bit surprised to find his motorcyclist employee in the same hotel room as he. Frankie was a frail-looking man who wanted you to know, I saw at once, that he had a lot of money invested in his clothes. He was the flashiest thing in the room, which was, like the whole hotel, old, stale, elegant, and large. The men were enjoying their long cigars and their drinks; my father and Lenny had the usual glasses of iced coffee, all the other men something ginger or clear with a twist; and everyone had his smile on, with the exception of Frankie Breezy.

"Hello, Dad; hello, Uncle Lenny," I said, deciding against going over to kiss my father's cheek. I nodded to the other men, who nodded to me. "I'm sorry to bother you. And this is my friend Cleveland."

My father rose toward me, and he gave me a kiss. He shook hands with Cleveland.

"Joe, I know Cleveland," Frankie said, in an intentionally very strange tone of voice. My father looked at me.

"I'm very glad to meet you, Mr. Bechstein," said

Cleveland. "And it's really all my fault that we're interrupting you this way. I wanted to meet you."

"Glad to meet you," said my father quietly.

"He's one of mine," Frankie said.

"Why don't you and Cleveland amuse yourselves downtown for a couple of hours, Art. Then I'll take you both to dinner." He did not blink.

"Yeah, some of us ain't got a summer vacation, Art," said giggling old Lenny. "Some of us have to work even on the hottest day of the summer."

"All right, fellows. I'm busy. Good-bye."

"Aw, Joe, let them stay a minute," said one man, an older, balding once-blond man with friendly water-blue eyes and a nose destroyed by boxing. He picked up the newspaper and laid it beside him. This was Carl "Poon" Punicki, although I didn't know it at the time. Three other things I did not know then about him were, first, that he was a big-time jewel fence; second, that he and Frankie Breezy had been feuding all year over a small piece of the Monongahela Valley; and third, that he had a son, whom he prized and ate dinner with every Sunday afternoon, who was a biker. "I never met your boy, Joe."

My father had been required to do business with this man; he turned and put his arm around me.

"Arthur, this is Mr. Punicki."

He went all around the room. I shook a bunch of hands; so did Cleveland. I saw Mr. Punicki eyeing with paternal amusement Cleveland's snakeskin tie.

"So?" said my father at last. "You just wanted to drop by?"

"Yes," said Cleveland. "That's it."

"No," I said. "There's a reason, actually."

Cleveland and I must have exchanged a pair of real Hayley Mills now-what-do-we-do looks, because everyone laughed.

"This guy doesn't belong in here. He's a squeeze," Frankie said. "He's an employee."

"Pops, Cleveland wants a job," I said.

Frankie Breezy stood up and made two partial but probably automatic fists. "Cleveland *needs* a job," he said.

"This is very foolish," my father said.

"I'll give Cleveland a job," Mr. Punicki said. He took a pen out of his pocket and wrote on the colored paper folder of my father's airplane ticket. He tore off a neat corner and handed it to Cleveland.

"I'll see you at five," my father said to me, in a near whisper. His forehead was so furrowed with anger that it was as though he had only one long eyebrow, running all the way across. He was very red. "Alone."

I felt, momentarily but acutely, that I had gone too far, this time, even to bother with another goddamn dinner.

"I can't, Dad," I said. "I have things to do. I'm sorry." I started to cry, then stopped; it was like a yawn. "Come on, Cleveland."

"And I'll bet it'll be a much more fun job too," said Cleveland softly as we went out through the pretty vestibule. "More suited to my zany tastes and idiosyncrasies."

We waited a long time for the elevator. It was very quiet in that chill hallway. At last the brass doors slid open. On the way down, Cleveland, directly under the NO SMOKING $500 FINE sign, lit a cigarette, which struck me, for once, as an unnecessarily theatrical thing to do.

·   ·   ·

I swallowed half a beer without noticing. Cleveland and I were both dazed, though his daze was a kind of nervous reverie, whereas mine was more akin to torpor. When I finally remarked the pale bread flavor of the beer in my mouth, I looked around the bar and did not remember having come in. I was on the last stool by a window and could see out into the bright day and sunny red bricks of Market Square, and I allowed myself to be relaxed momentarily by the warm air that blew down from the lazy fans, and by the tranquil, salt exhalations of dead shellfish that filled the air. Carl Punicki went past the bar, without looking in the window. As he vanished, he ran a hand through his thinning yellow hair and shook his shoulders once. An inch of ash fell from the tip of my trembling cigarette.

"Oh," said Cleveland. "Art. It just hit me. I'm sorry."

"Ha," I said. "Thanks."

"Really. This is going to damage things with your old man?"

"Yes. I don't know. No. Things were already damaged."

"Are you mad at me, Bechstein? Don't be." The white eyeglasses gave him an impish look, and he said, flatly, "I've got a glorious feeling." He finished his beer. "Everything's going my way. The corn is as high as an elephant's eye."

I laughed and, at last, looked at him. Sometime during that day at the boiling end of July, which broke the all-time record set in 1926 or something like that, my friendship with Cleveland began to take on some of the characteristics of a détente, that uneasy willingness to laugh things off.

"I have to call Phlox," I said, thinking: I have to call
Arthur. I slid from my barstool and went through the old
photographs and men to the back of the bar, fingering the
coins in my pocket.

"Hello?" said, my God, Phlox.

"Oh, hello!"

Operator, Operator, there's been some kind of mistake!

"Oh. It's you."

"Hello, Phlox. I feel really terrible and I don't want to
talk about this. How are you?"

"Angry." She tapped. "Where are you?"

"I'm downtown. With Cleveland."

"Fine. Stay there."

"How about if I come see you right now?"

"No," she said, more quietly. "I don't think so." Her
voice was cold. "Why don't you call Arthur?"

"Phlox! Fine. I will."

"No, Art, come over!"

"No, I'll call Arthur, like you said." There was a pause.
The computer inside the pinball machine to my left simu-
lated the sound of a woman in orgasm. I felt how stupid was
the thing I'd just said to her.

"Fine."

"Oh, Phlox, let me just come over, right now."

"No," she said. "I'm too angry to see you right now. I
might say things I don't mean. Come over later."

Things were happening too quickly for there to be a
later.

"I'll leave right now."

"Don't," she said, and hung up the phone. When I

called back, I got a busy signal. So I called Arthur, woke him up from a nap. He said to come right over. I went to tell Cleveland, but he had gone, leaving a note and a couple of crumpled dollar bills. I read the note, stuffed it in my pocket, and went to catch a bus to Shadyside.

Arthur chuckled in sympathy when he saw me, held out his hand generously. I threw my arms around him and clasped him to me. We parted. His face was sunburned and newly wide awake, a tiny flake of sleep in the corner of his blue left eye. He had bought himself a bottle of citron Christian Dior. I was so glad to see him.

"Poor guy," he said. "You look miserable."

"I am," I said. "Hug me again."

"You must have had an especially disturbing day."

"I'm disturbed. Arthur, can I . . . ?"

"Please do."

It wasn't all that different. He has just eaten a plum, I thought.

He pushed me lightly away, then held on.

"Are you in full possession of your faculties?"

"I can't be certain; no."

"Well, it's about time," he said. He pinched my earlobe. "Let's go exhaust all the possibilities."

"Could we please do it slowly?"

"No," he said, and he was right. We did it very rapidly, in the Weatherwoman's bed, passing from toothed kisses through each backward and alien, but familiar, station on the old road to intercourse, which loomed there always before me, black and brutal and smiling, more alien, more

backward, and more familiar than anything else. Then, perhaps ten or fifteen minutes after my arrival at the house,
with a hard, spongy fistful of him in my right hand, and my
left hand flat against his stomach, I was overcome with a
feeling that made our black destination cease to seem loom-
ing. My heart was simultaneously broken and filled with
lust, I was exhausted, and I loved every minute of it. It was
strange and elating to feel myself for once the weaker.

"Here," I said. "Right here."

"Are you sure?"

"Yes. Please. This is okay. Now or I'll never do it."

"We need some slippery stuff."

"Hurry."

He scrambled out of bed and ran around the bedroom,
tossing   newspapers   everywhere,   rummaging   through
drawers, then disappeared into the bathroom. I heard the
medicine chest squeak open, then slam. He flashed naked
out the bedroom door and I heard him thump down the
steps, stumbling with haste at the bottom. I lay on the uprooted sheets and blanket of the bed, looking without a
thought of time at the hands of the alarm clock. My sides
ached with rapid respiration and this feeling of a heedless
desire to be fucked. The clock moved, the loose old screen
on the window billowed; I heard Arthur's footsteps again on
the stair. He came back into the bedroom, gasping for
breath, but grinning and carrying a bottle of corn oil.

"Slippery stuff," I said, and my laugh was like an irides-
cent bubble rising to the surface of a pool of molten tar.
"Come on."

"Relax, I'm all out of breath, give me a minute, give me a kiss," he said.

It hurt a great deal, and the oil was cold and strange, but when he said that he had finished, I did not want him to stop; I asked him not to stop, and he did his best, but then I started to cry. He held me, I stopped crying, and we were laughing again about a sound he said I had uttered, our faces inches apart, when his eyes grew round and he sat up abruptly, then came back in for a closer look.

"Your nose is bleeding," he said.

He stood up and went to the tall, wide bedroom windows, parted the drapes, and threw open the panes. A breeze and the late sunlight came through the wrought-iron rail into the room, and a row of thin shadows fell across the floor. There was blood on my pillowcase. When I got up to find Kleenex for my nose, Arthur purposefully stripped the stained linen from the pillow and went to the window with it. When I came back, he stood by the sill, grinning with the wondrous news he had just published to the neighborhood.

18

PERSPICACITY

♦　　　　　♦　　　　　♦

"Every woman has the heart of a policeman." Later, much later, long after the summer had blown up and fallen to the earth in little black scraps of ash and Japanese paper, I sat in a café in a deserted Breton resort town, talking to a kid from Paris who gave me this aphorism. He drank Pernod, sweet and cloudy, bitter and calm, and to illustrate his maxim told me a story about the detective powers of an old fiancée of his. Throughout their engagement, he had lived on the third floor of an old building in the Fifth Arrondissement, and on the sixth floor of this building lived a young woman, who tempted him. She would stand waiting for him by his door, wearing only a thin robe, when he came home from work in the evening, would leave flowers and colored ribbon in his mailbox, would call him late at night and have nothing to say. But this woman was poor, and crazy, he said, and he was engaged to be married to the brilliant daughter of a prominent Jewish family, members of the Socialist elite.

He said that although his neighbor was pretty, for over a year he managed to avoid her embrace, and he never, of course, mentioned her to the rich fiancée. Then, one Sun-

day afternoon, and for no particular reason, he finally surrendered. Afterward, the neighbor woman rose from his bed
and pulled on her dress and sandals, to go down to the
corner for a bottle of wine. On the stair she passed the
fiancée, who was coming to surprise the young man with an
expensive gift. The two women exchanged a very brief
glance. The young rich girl came upstairs, knocked on the
door, and, when he opened it, slapped the man's face. She
threw the gift, a gold-plated man's toilet set, through his
television screen, then departed, and he never saw her
again.

The aphorism may be false (it sounds good, which is all
an aphorism need do), but I had not been in Phlox's apartment for forty-five seconds before she gathered up whatever
clues there were to gather in my face, voice, and caress—
perhaps even in my smell—and accused me of doing what I
had done once again at two o'clock that morning, after
which Arthur had fallen asleep, though I could not and so
had crossed empty Fifth Avenue and walked home through
the trafficless streets.

"Who was it?" she said, pushing me away, taking hold
of the back of a chair.

"Someone you don't know." I didn't have strength
enough to lie convincingly. I'd been taken by surprise. All I
could do was sink deep into her old sofa and dread hearing
whatever she might next divine. She had woken me with a
phone call that morning, and already, I realized, the knowledge had been in her voice, the urgency that had drawn me
over to her apartment all unready, on three hours' sleep and
a single cup of coffee. She stood in the center of the plain

little living room, in a torn gray sweatshirt and gym shorts,
arms angrily folded, but she didn't say anything. She began
to cry.

"I'm sorry," I said. I talked into my shirt. "It wasn't
anything. It was a mistake. I felt lonely and horrible and I
ran into . . . this girl I knew a long time ago."

"Claire?" cried Phlox.

I looked up. I couldn't help smiling at this thought, or
half-smiling, anyway. "No. God, no. What a notion. Look,
Phlox."

She came over. I pulled her down into my lap and
rubbed my cheek against the torn, nubby, soft cloth she
wore. Solace is in the fabric of sweatshirts. "Please, Phlox,
you have to forgive me, you have to. I don't have any feelings for this woman. It's nothing."

She whirled around, angry and curious, eyes red.

"What does she look like?"

"She's blond. Very blond and cold."

"As blond and cold as Arthur?"

"What's that supposed to mean?" I said.

She wrapped her arms around my neck and said she
didn't know. Phlox said that I could tell her anything; she
would believe anything I told her. She cried, on and off, for
the rest of the day. It was a wounded, slow, delicate Sunday; our feelings and the things we said to each other were
cautious and tender. It rained in the late afternoon. We
half-undressed, climbed out onto her roof, and stood barefoot in the puddles, and under the cool water the tar of the
roof was still warm against the feet. Across the neighborhood, drainpipes chuckled and rang, and we could hear

cars tossing up curtains of water in the street. I smoked a cigarette in the rain, which is the best way to smoke a cigarette. I looked at Phlox's beautiful sad lunar face and wet lashes. When we came inside, we dried each other's hair and ate with plastic forks out of cold Tupperware bowls. The day before, Phlox had bought a little bottle of bubble soap and a plastic pipe, and we filled the air of her bedroom with bubbles and damp little pops; in the evening I took her picture. I resolved that I would not see Arthur for a whole week.

When I walked into work the next day, Ed Lavella was manning the cash register, ringing up the fifty-seven-dollar purchase, an eight-inch tower of books and magazines, of my father, who held out a hundred-dollar bill. My father was dressed for business, in a blue suit and sober tie, and he had the closed, unreadable face he always adopted at ten o'clock in the morning of what he hoped would be a full day's work. I knew that he despised Boardwalk Books, so he was obviously here because he wanted to speak to me, but we both realized as soon as we saw one another that now was not the time. He had work to do and wouldn't want the wild words of his son ringing in his ears all day, and I would be frustrated, by his professionally blank look and by our being there for all to see, in any attempt to obtain his forgiveness or solicitude. So we stood in the aisle by the best-sellers, unable to speak. He smelled of aftershave. Finally he asked me to dinner and a movie on Wednesday night, slipped me a twenty-dollar bill, and went out. At lunchtime I noticed that the money, rolled into a little

green ball, was still in my hand. I had a dozen roses delivered to Phlox at the library. As I came out of the florist's, I
ran into Arthur. That morning he had had his hair cut
short, but a long, fashionable, forward-falling lock hid his
left eyebrow. He looked odd, boyish, and gay.

"You live," he said.

Women passed us on either side, carrying sandwiches
and ice cream cones, talking with their mouths full. The
weather, after yesterday's rain, was unusually dry and fine,
and dazzling Forbes avenue filled with nurses and secretaries
who had freed themselves from air-conditioning and fluorescent light. I laughed because the air was full of these
women's talk.

"Have you eaten yet?" he said. "Let's go sit over by the
law school."

Yes, I remembered my resolution. With a pang.

"Okay, sure," I said. I blew a puff of air at his face,
which lifted the lock of hair and bared for an instant the
familiar yellow arch of his eyebrow.

That afternoon I telephoned Phlox at work and lied
to her. I told her that I would be dining with my father,
that tonight was the night the reviews would come in. Of
course I had not said a thing to her about my most recent
audience with my father. As I lied, I saw that this lie
would tomorrow entail another whole set of lies, and that
this set might on Wednesday entail another set, after my
father told me what he really thought of her, as he was
sure to do if indeed I decided to meet with him. But the
first lie in the series is the one you make with the greatest

trepidation and the heaviest heart. She sounded neither disappointed nor jealous.

"The flowers arrived not five minutes ago," she said. "You're such a wonderful boy."

After work, we headed toward the steps where we had eaten lunch almost two months before, behind the Fine Arts Building, wanting to walk but undecided yet about where we would spend the evening and what we were going to do. I had suggested the Lost Neighborhood. We leaned against the rail and looked down. Arthur stood as though calm, but I caught from him a whiff of nervousness or ex-citement; his fingers on the rail tap-tapped. Down in the Lost Neighborhood they were grilling food; smoke rose in ragged fountains, and crickets talked in the dry brush that surrounded our perch. Arthur laughed. The sky was rosy red and orange with chemicals.

"Cleveland and I drove down there once," he said. "Right after he told me about this job of his. We took his motorcycle down along the junkyard, past the two Devil Dogs, and tried to pull into the neighborhood. But we couldn't get in; it was funny. That is, we really *could* have gotten in, but Cleveland didn't want to. There were all these little kids, and bicycles lying in the street, and Big Wheels, and toy trucks. He cut the engine. We sat there. Cleveland wanted to watch, I guess. I'm hungry. Where should we eat?"

"My choice this time."

"No, I believe it's *my* choice this time," he said. "In fact, you always choose."

"So choose."

"Chinese."

"Very good."

We went. The food was brown and wriggly and spicy as hell. We cursed the fiery soup and ate it up. The cashews in the chicken dish were quiet little bland islands in an ocean of pepper. My lips swelled and burned. We swallowed glass after glass of ice water and emptied three pots of tea. I plucked small naked tangles of rice from the bowl with chopsticks; Arthur used his fork and swirled the rice into the sauces that pooled on his plate. It was a meal that held one's attention. Arthur and I hardly spoke.

After we had finished cigarettes and read our fortunes twice—"It is the loosest string that sings the longest," mine said—we came outside. It was seven o'clock. I headed to the left, heard Arthur say the word "No," turned to the right, and there was Phlox, standing at the corner of At-wood and Louise with her hands at her sides. She whirled and walked off, and I ran after her, calling her name. I caught her at the avenue and took her elbow in my hand.

"Hey," I said, and then that was all I could think of. We looked at each other for a long time, and she did not cry.

"I'm a fool," she said. "I'm a complete fool. I'm an idiot. Don't say anything. Shut up. Go back. I'm a fool."

We turned toward Arthur, who walked our way. He looked serious, but it was false; I could tell by his smirking eyes.

"I hate both of you," she whispered.

"What are you doing here?" I said.

Rather than answer me, she looked up at Arthur as he came to stand beside us. They stared, Phlox angrily, Arthur furtively, shifting his gaze away from her to something that lay at his feet and then back.

"I was thinking of getting some lime sherbet," he said at last.

"That's a good idea," I said. "Let's all go get some lime sherbet."

"No!" said Phlox. "I'm not going anywhere with you, Arthur." She drew herself erect and threw back her shoulders, and her eyes glazed over with a kind of Vivien Leigh haughtiness; she enunciated. "Please come with me, Art. I'm only going to ask you this one time."

I looked at Arthur, who gave me a cool shrug.

"Okay, okay," I said. People on the sidewalk turned their heads our way. "That's enough. Stop. Okay? Can we cut it out? Can we just stop it? Okay? Okay, look, we have to get rid of this thing once and for all." I was surprised that I could speak. I turned to Arthur and said, "Arthur, I love Phlox." I turned to Phlox. "Phlox," I said, "I love Arthur. We have to learn to be together. We can do it."

"That's bullshit," said Phlox. Her teeth flashed.

"She's right," said Arthur.

"I hate you, Arthur Lecomte." She whirled. She was atavistic and gorgeous in her anger, with her splayed fingers, her cheeks. "I'll never forgive you for doing this."

"You'll thank me."

"What are you talking about?" I said.

"Come with me, Art."

"Go on," said Arthur.

"I'll call you."

"That's all right," said Arthur, "really. Don't bother."

Phlox and I started off, at first without discussion or destination. It was twilight, and the Cathedral of Learning, pile and battlements, threw great beams of light into the air, and looked like the 20th Century–Fox emblem. I took Phlox's hand, but she let her fingers slip and we walked with a breeze between us.

"Did he *tell* you we were having dinner tonight?"

"Why did you lie to me?"

She put her fingers around my hand, lifted it, and then threw it from her like an empty bottle.

"*Why?*"

"How did you know?"

"I *knew*," she said. "That's all. I knew."

"Arthur told you."

"How stupid do you think I am?" She ran ahead a few steps and then turned on me, her hair sweeping out around her head. We had come to the Schenley Park bridge, which hummed with the cars that crossed it. The two stacks of the Cloud Factory were ink against the inky sky. "I didn't need Arthur to tell me. I knew when I got those roses."

"I bought the roses—"

"Forget it," she said. "I don't want to hear it. You'll just lie. You poor dumb liar." She turned.

"—before I knew I was having dinner with Arthur tonight." Each time I mentioned Arthur's name I heard him saying, "Don't bother," and felt dizzy; it was like peering over a cliff, and now, as Phlox walked off, the ground on the other side of me split and began to give way. I thought, I fancied, that in a moment I would be standing on nothing at all, and for the first time in my life, I needed the wings none of us has. When Phlox, who had vanished into the darkness along the bridge, reached the other side, she reappeared briefly in the streetlight, skirt and scarf and two white legs, and then the park closed around her.

19

THE BIG P

◆　　　　　　　◆　　　　　　　◆

"Bechstein." Blackness. "Bechstein." Light. "Bechstein."
"Hey. What. Oh."

Filling my front doorway, in a welter of bloody twilight,
was the huge silhouette of a man, hands on his hips. He
raised one black arm and the red rays shifted around it like
the blades of a fan.

"Jesus." I blinked and sat up on one elbow. "Good
thing this isn't a Sergio Leone movie."

"Bang."

"I guess I fell asleep. Time is it?"

"Night is falling," said Cleveland. He came and sat on
the arm of the couch, down by my feet; the top of a paperback protruded from his jacket pocket, and he held a white
envelope. "Look at you—you're all sweaty," he said. With
a vast, rattling sigh, he leaned back, against the wall, and
patted his fat gut. "What do you have to eat?"

I twisted around, sat full up. Arthur's laugh pealed in
my ear for an instant, and I realized I'd been dreaming
of him.

"I can probably manage some form of cheese sandwich,"
I said. I tried to stand, tottered slightly, caught myself; I
was sore all over. "I may have a few olives."

"Great. Olives." He lit a cigarette. "You sick?"

"I don't think so. No." Hannah, the little girl next door, was practicing "Für Elise" again. There had been piano music in my lustful dream. "I'll get you a sandwich. Um, what have you been up to?"

I went into the kitchen and took out the necessary jars and packages. It felt nice inside the refrigerator.

"Oh, just a million and one things. Poon things, I'm afraid. This was on the doorstep, Bechstein," Cleveland said, clunking into the kitchen behind me. He handed me the envelope I'd noted, on which was printed only my name, in Phlox's schoolish handwriting, without stamp or address. It was a business envelope. My heart made a sudden violent motion—leapt, sank. It's the same feeling.

"Oh, it's from Phlox," I said. "Well. Hmm."

"Hmm."

"Well."

"Hmm." He grinned. "Jesus, Bechstein, are you going to read it?"

"Sure, yes—I mean, why not? Would you mind . . . ?" I said, gesturing toward the unassembled sandwich.

"Of course. Let's see. Ah, bread, fine, perfect. Just the heels? Fine, that's fine. Love the heels. Bread and cheese, cadmium-orange American cheese—perfect, exactly. You're a minimalist. Go, go read." He turned from me and gave his attention to the food.

I stepped out of the kitchen with the envelope, trying not to guess at its contents, then broke it open and unfolded the two-page letter, also handwritten, in dark-purple ink on pale-purple stationery with her monogram—"PLU."

"The past tense of *plaire*," she liked to say; her middle name was Ursula. My eyes skipped across the paper for a moment, before I could restrain them, and the words "sex," "mother," and "horrible" peered out at me like miserable inmates through the barbed tangle of her paragraphs. I forced myself to begin at the beginning.

ART,

I have never written to you before and it feels strange. I think it is going to be hard for me to write you a letter, and I am trying to decide why this is. Maybe it is because I know how intelligent you are, and I do not want you reading what I write, because you might look at my letter in a too critical fashion. Maybe it is also because I feel stilted when I express myself in a letter, confined. I am afraid to write long sentences or to use words wrongly. And then there's just the fact that before, everything I ever wanted to say to you I could just say, right into your ear. Isn't that how it should be? Writing is so unnatural. Nevertheless there are some things I must tell you, and since I cannot see you ever again, I must write.

You are probably afraid that I am mad at you, and I am. I'm furious. No one has ever done anything like this to me before. Not like this. Not so weirdly and horribly. Art, I have touched your throat and your sex, we have slept with each other as fierce and spoken to each other as close as a man and a woman possibly can. You must know that what you are now doing disgusts me utterly.

I keep hearing (and don't think this is stupid) a million Supremes songs in my head. Stop in the Name of Love, etc. Art, how can you have sex with a man? I know you and Arthur have slept together because I know Arthur. He has to have sex. He once said he always has to feel a man's hands on his body or he will die. I distinctly recall him saying this.

Oh, how can you? It is so unnatural, so obviously wrong, when you really think about it. I mean, think about it, really consider it. Isn't it ludicrous? There is only one place in the world where you are supposed to put your penis—inside of me. Anyway, all of this is beside the point now. It has been obvious to me for a long time that you have some kind of hang-up about your mother, but I did not think it was this grave. Believe me Art, because I do care about you— you need help, soon, and badly (from a qualified psychiatrist).

I still love you, but I will not be able to see you anymore. You say that you love me, but as long as you are seeing Arthur that just cannot be true. You don't understand how much this upsets me. You must know (I believe I told you) that this is not the first time I have fallen in love with a weak man who turned out to be homosexual. It's horrible. After you spend so much time looking out—not being jealous, just keeping an eye on the women who come around the boy you love—which is normal, after all, is it not?—they come and get you from behind. That's the worst.

Don't call me anymore, darling. I love you. I
hope you're happy. I'm sorry for the letter. I never
could have said any of this to you. It's easier this way.
Call me sometime, maybe a long time from now,
years, perhaps, when you have seen.

PHLOX

"Let's go sit on the steps," said Cleveland, pointing, a
hollow olive stuck on the tip of his index finger. The
cheese in his sandwich stood an inch thick. "You look like
you could use some fresh air, Bechstein. You really look
sick."

"Hmm? Oh, no, no, it's just, um, something."

"Oh, well, *something*. That's a relief."

"I had a bad night."

We sat down on the cracked steps and I wondered if I
really might be sick. It was nearly eight o'clock in the evening. I had a very dim memory of having woken up that
morning, come out to the living room, and lain down again
on the sofa; I'd slept for around seventeen hours. Cleveland
slipped the paperback from his pocket and chucked it into
my lap. It was a cheap old assortment of Poe, secondhand,
a skull and a bat on the cover.

"Ten Tales of Tension and Terror," I read.

"I'm rereading the Big P," he said, talking around the
cheese in his mouth. "I used to be crazy about him. I used
to think I might be Poe reincarnated." He lifted his lank
bangs to show me his pale Poe brow. "Whew. I'll tell you
something, Bechstein." He poked his thumb into another
olive and then flicked the olive, like a shooter, into his

mouth. "The evil Carl Punicki is an okay fellow. He laughs a little too hard, and he throws his money around a little too much, and he slaps me on the back a little too often, but I can work with him."

"Work with him how?"

"I'm afraid to tell you."

"Oh."

"So what did you *do* last night?" he said, eyeing the half-crumpled letter in my hand.

I looked at him. He'd been babbling, he was eating the cheese sandwich almost without stopping to swallow, and I wondered if he might be stoned. The usual tracery of broken blood vessels on the skin of his face, under his eyes and across his nose, looked darker than usual; his eyes were pink, his hair was filthy. Although part of me wanted just to tell him everything, I resented his being so out of it, his doing something for Carl Punicki that was evidently worse than what he'd done for Frankie Breezy, and, finally, I was afraid that he would make fun of me, or—who knew?— even get angry. And what *had* I done last night?

"Yes, I'm stoned and I've been drinking all day. I'm half in the bag," he said. "Okay?"

"So you came over because there was no food at your house?"

"Right."

"Oh."

"Asshole. That isn't why I came over. I came to converse."

"You did?"

"Sure." He reached over and patted my thigh, then

took the letter from between my lax fingers. "Disturbing news?"

"I'm not really sure. Confusing news."

"May I?"

"No. Come on, Cleveland." I reached for the letter, but he lifted it up over his head, out of my reach. "I can't believe you're going to work for that monster Punicki, I don't feel well, you're all fucked up—"

"I'm normalized. Look, Bechstein, you're upset; something's wrong. Here." He handed back the letter, tapping it against my knee. "Why don't you at least tell me something of what's contained therein."

My little neighbor started up again with her Beethoven. Cleveland wore a very sincere, if somewhat bleary, expression; there was only the faint trace of a sneer.

"It's a ransom note, right? She's taken herself hostage. 'Dear Art,'" he said, biting his lip in thought and rolling his eyes upward. "Um, 'Leave Arthur in an unmarked paper bag inside locker thirty-eight at the Greyhound station, or you'll never see me again.' Is that it?"

"Oh, here," I said. While he read Phlox's purple letter, which he did very slowly, as though he was having difficulty making sense of it, I listened to the music next door and stared down at a tiny white sliver of fluff that he had caught on a spider thread and was spinning in the breeze like a pinwheel, at the end of its miniature tether. Cleveland would ball up the letter and throw it to the ground; would stand and spit on my head; then he, too, would leave my life forever. I had ruined everything.

After a few minutes Cleveland raised his giant head and looked at me. He grinned.

"You little slut."

I half-laughed, through my nose, the way one does when one is also crying.

"Oh, stop it, you big baby. She doesn't mean any of this. The whole thing is nonsense. Here she says no one has ever done this to her before, and then here she says it happens all the time. She's jangling your wires."

"She never wants to see me again."

"Bullshit." Carelessly he folded the letter and slid it back into the ragged envelope. "It *sounds* like she's handing you your papers, but this is just a goddamn ultimatum. These things always are. It's like, 'I'll never see you again, ever. *Unless.*' Jane sends me these all the time. Quarterly. Relax. You can call her tonight if you want," he said. He picked at a cheese fragment that had lodged in a fold of his jacket. "Unless."

We sat for a few moments, not talking about Arthur.

"Cleveland?" I said at last.

"Well, I'm not surprised, anyway."

"You aren't?"

"It had to happen. It's pretty funny in the letter when she says they 'get you from behind.' Ha ha. Ah, Bechstein, you dope. What are you crying about? Cut it out. I hate crying. Tell me what happened."

I recounted to him, very briefly, the events of the previous evening.

"He said I shouldn't bother to call him anymore."

Cleveland snorted.

"There's a big 'unless' stuck onto that one too," he said. "They're both hedging their bets. Stop crying. Goddamn it." He reached into the pocket of his jacket and pulled out a ragged ball of old Kleenex. "Here. Shit. You haven't lost them both. It's either one or the other. Do you want to hear this?"

"I guess." I began to feel restored, unconfused, even less achy, simply from the weight of Cleveland's grouchy attentions. "Thank you," I said. "I'm sorry. I'm kind of upset to hear about your working for Punicki too."

"Working *with* the Evil Poon, Bechstein; we have an arrangement. It's nothing to cry about, Bechstein, Jesus. I'm being admitted to an ancient and honorable profession. I'm learning a valuable skill. Okay now, let that go for one second and listen."

"I know, I know. If I forget Arthur forever, call Phlox—"

"You could be back in her arms again, as Phlox, or Diana Ross, would have it, within the hour. Really. But I guess you would really have to forget Arthur. Or the other way around."

He picked up the envelope again and flapped it thoughtfully against the back of his hand. "So who do you love? Phlox or Arthur? Who do you love more, I mean?"

"I don't know. The same," I said.

"Invalid response," said Cleveland. "Try again."

I guessed that he was right, that my feeling for Phlox, which I was calling love, could not really be the *same* as my feeling for Arthur, which I was also calling love. I thought of her clear broad forehead, and of her closet full of spectacular skirts, and of the perfume of her bedroom, and when this didn't instantly move me to decision, I thought of her tenderness and care for me, of her so obvious and persistent affection. It seemed to me that I shouldn't have to think so hard. Something stood between me and Phlox—perhaps it was myself—which made loving her a perpetual effort; she was a massive collection of small, ardent details that I struggled always to keep in mind, in a certain order, repeating the Phlox List over and over to myself, because if I forgot one particular of her smile or speech, the whole thing came to pieces. Perhaps I did not love Phlox, after all—I just knew her by heart. I had memorized my girlfriend.

Or perhaps it was presumptuous and conceited of me, and of Cleveland, to think that Phlox would really have me back. Perhaps she was calling it quits because it was, in fact, quits.

"Um, Cleveland—do you really not find it a big deal . . ."

"Find what?"

"That I—that I'm—that I might be . . ."

"Queer?" He set the letter on top of the Poe and stood up, stretching his arms wide, as though to embrace the entire gathering evening, and emitted, simultaneously, a belch and a fart. "Wow! Do that often enough and you implode."

"Ha."

"Queer as my oldest friend? As my father?"

"Um."

"As a matter of fact, Bechstein, I don't think that you

are. In my corroded opinion, I think you're just clowning around with your sexual chemistry set. But go ahead—give yourself a rest from the Evil Love Nurse. You can call her— how does she put it?—years from now, 'when you have seen.'"

I protested that what I was doing was more serious than he thought. I wanted to express to him something of my feelings for Arthur, but I remembered all of his sodden protestations of love for Jane, and I kept silent. He stood in front of me, a few steps down, and I could barely make out his features in the near darkness.

"What did *you* do last night?" I said finally, anticipating another tale of excess and hilarity.

"Last night," he said, as the hem of the blue sky filled with purple, "I learned how to deactivate an alarm system."

"Jesus."

"Neat, huh?"

"No! What the hell for?"

"For a merit badge. What do you think? To get inside houses. Poon owns five jewelry stores in the Mon Valley."

"He's a fence."

"He's the biggest, Bechstein."

"And you're going to steal for him." I stood up.

"Like the big time. No kidding—Cary Grant in *To Catch a Thief.*"

I brushed past him, was halfway down the front steps, running away from my own house, when I turned to Cleveland, a vague shape in the light that filtered out from the distant kitchen.

"Cleveland, it's illegal! It's burglary. Burglary! You could go to jail."

"Quiet." He came down the steps toward me, and we faced each other tensely. "Sodomy," he said.

That produced a long silence, toward the end of which he turned and went the rest of the way down the stairs.

"I didn't get all upset and act like an asshole, either," he said in a loud whisper. "I certainly could have. You seemed to expect it. So why don't you just let me do what I want, and I'll let you boys do what you want, and maybe that way we can all stay friends." He started away, then turned toward me and whispered again. "And don't get the idea that you can stop me." He grabbed me by the shoulder and squeezed; it hurt. "Don't try to blow the whistle on me." He shook me once. "Don't you go talking to the heavenly father."

"Cleveland!"

"Quiet. Because I could just as easily blow the whistle on you." With a snap of his wrist he released my shoulder, and I fell back against the steps.

"For God's sake, Cleveland," I whispered.

He brushed the hair from his eyes, quickly, looking embarrassed.

"All right, then. Thank you for the cheese sandwich. Good night."

I watched him pass, dwindling, through three patches of streetlight, biggest, bigger, big, nothing. Then I went back into the house, switched on a lamp and the porch light, and stood in the middle of the living room with my hands jammed angrily into my pockets, in the left one of which I felt a scrap of paper that, when I unfolded it, turned out to be the cocktail napkin Cleveland had left at the bar, stuck to the damp side of my beer glass, after our first encounter with Carl Punicki. As I reread absently its three words— HAVE TO THINK—I remembered Phlox's letter, twang! but out on the front step there was now nothing but the huge whirling shadows of the moths that had come to smash their heads against the light bulb. Cleveland must have picked up the letter in the dark, when he'd reached for his book. I would call him the next morning; everything would be fine. I came back inside, walked around in circles for a long time, read part of an old newspaper, then circled the room again. Finally I reached into my pocket and flipped a quarter. Heads was Phlox, tails was Arthur. It came up heads. I called Arthur.

20

LIFE ON VENUS

◆　　　　　◆　　　　　◆

We slept together. He would get up in the morning and rush off to work, scrabbling through piles of our mingled trousers and briefs, running his head under the sink, slamming the front door in farewell, and after he was gone I would spend the luxury of my extra hour by bathing in the Weatherwoman's claw-foot tub and in the strangeness of it all. We lived well. Arthur cooked elaborate dinners; in the refrigerator there was always pasta in the colors of the Italian flag, a variety of weird wines, capers, kiwis, unheard-of fish with Hawaiian names, and stacks of asparagus, Arthur's favorite food, in the rubber-banded bundles that he never failed to refer to as fagots. We sent our dirty clothes out to be cleaned and they came back as gifts, tied up in blue paper. And, as often as possible, we went to bed. I did not consider myself to be gay; I did not consider myself, as a rule. But all day long, from the white instant when I opened my eyes in the morning until my last black second of awareness of Arthur's fading breath against my shoulder, I was always nervous, full of energy, afraid. The city was new again, and newly dangerous, and I would walk its streets quickly, eyes averted from those of passersby, like a spy in the employ of lust and happiness, carrying the secret deep within me but always on the tip of my tongue.

The rich young couple—who were due to return on the last day of July—employed a black woman to clean their house. Her name was Velva. At eight o'clock on my only Wednesday morning at the Weatherwoman House, she entered the bedroom and screamed. After a moment of keen observation, she ran from the room, shouting that she was sorry. Arthur and I separated, went soft, laughed. We lit cigarettes and discussed strategy.

"Maybe I should go downstairs," he said.

"Put some pants on."

"What will she do?" he said. "I don't know her well enough to predict. Black people confuse me."

"Pick up the extension."

"Why?"

"Maybe she's calling the police."

"Or an ambulance."

I thought of my fat friends from Boardwalk, arriving in their van to attach their electric paddles to the outraged, apopleptic cleaning lady collapsed on the living-room floor. Arthur picked up the extension, listened, set it down again.

"Dial tone," he said. "And I'm not going downstairs. You go. Slip her a five or something." He pushed me, and I fell out of the bed, trailing the bedclothes behind me. A tendril of cotton blanket wrapped itself around a lamp, pulled the lamp to the floor after it, and then muffled the bang! of the shattered light bulb. We stared at each other, eyes round, muscles tensed, listening, like two boys who have been warned not to wake the baby. But the pop of the

bulb was the incident's only repercussion. Velva contrived
to be in another part of the house throughout our respective
breakfasts and departures, and subsequent events indicated
that she never said anything to anyone. Perhaps she did not
care—I fantasized that she was Lurch's long-resigned
mother. In any case, we were lucky. Like any successful
spy, I felt frightened and lucky all the time.

Pittsburgh, too, was in the grip of a humid frenzy. The
day after my flip of the coin, the sun had disappeared behind a perpetual gray wall of vapor, which never managed
to form itself into rain, and yet the sun's heat remained as
strong as ever, so that the thick, wet, sulfury air seemed to
boil around you, and in the late morning veils of steam rose
from the blacktop. Arthur said that it was like living on
Venus. When I walked to work—arriving sapped and with
my damp shirt an alien thing clinging to me—the Cathedral of Learning, ordinarily brown, would look black with
wetness, dank, submerged, Atlantean. There were three irrational shootings that week, and two multiple-car pileups
on the freeway; a Pirate, in a much-discussed lapse of
sportsmanship, broke three teeth belonging to a hapless
Phillie; a live infant was found in a Bloomfield garbage can.

And in bed, as our last week in the Weatherwoman
House drew to a close, our dealings with each other became
distinctly more Venusian. The stranglehold, the bite, even
the light blow, found their way into our sexual repertoire: I
discovered purple marks along the tops of my shoulders. It's
the weather, I said to myself; or else, I added—once, and
only for an instant, since I was so firmly opposed to consideration—this is just the way it is with another man.

I'd given my father the phone number at the Weather-woman House, and I wondered what he imagined I was doing there, since I had a perfectly good house of my own. I'd been putting him off for days now, uncomfortable with him not only because of Cleveland and Punicki and Phlox and my mother and my new, willfully unconsidered activities, but because of the edge of pleading in his voice when we briefly spoke, because of the blatant genuineness of his desire to see me. Our seeing each other during his previous visits had always been neither a priority nor something to be missed. We just saw each other if we could, and then he would leave again for Washington. This time he'd gone so far as to extend the length of his visit by a few needless days, and the strangeness of his determination not to leave without taking me to the movies made me feel more acutely the distance between us, the sorry pass things had come to. I did not like to see my father bending over backward; it didn't suit him. And in the late afternoon of that Wednesday on which Velva was horrified, I got in from work and found a message from my father on the Weather-woman's answering machine, and I trembled at the sad charm in my father's voice, his amusement with the machine, his terrible confusion.

"Ahem. Art, this is your father," said his voice. "Can you hear me? Ahem. Well, I'm glad to know you're moving among the phone-machine set. It's the—ahem—last night of the Joe Bechstein Festival and our records show that you still haven't used your ticket. What about this science fiction film that everyone is so crazy for?"

"Is that your dad?" said Arthur, coming up from behind and surprising me, wrapping his arms around my throat.

"Does that sound like a good idea?" said the voice.

"Yes," I said. "Shh."

"He has a high-pitched voice!"

"Quiet, you made me miss it." I rewound the tape. "He wants to go to the movies."

"He sounds like the voice of Winnie-the-Pooh."

"—a good idea? Because I'm leaving town tomorrow morning. Art—"

"Sure, let's go. I'd love to meet him."

"Quiet! Don't make fun of his voice." I rewound the tape again.

"—town tomorrow morning, Art—"

"Does he know?"

"Please," I said.

"—is everything okay?"

I called him back and told him I'd be bringing a friend along. A different friend.

"Indeed," said my father, and suddenly, again, I didn't want to see him. "Is that necessary? Couldn't we be alone for once?"

"Well . . ."

I was sitting on the edge of the bed, and now Arthur knelt before me and began to undo my pants.

"Are you afraid to be alone with me, Art?"

"That must be it, Dad. Don't." I pushed at Arthur's burrowing head.

"Don't what?"

"Nothing. Oh. Yes. I don't know."

"Art, there's a good deal I have to say to you, and it isn't the sort of thing I want to discuss with one of your friends around."

"Ah," I whispered, pushing, grasping. "Please."

"Art?"

Jesus. "Yeah, then let's, ah, forget it, Dad, okay? I probably wouldn't want to hear what you have to say, anyway, would I? No, I wouldn't." Jesus! "Go back to Washington. Say hi to Grandma. Ah." Ah!

"Art." There was a terrible shrillness in the voice of Winnie-the-Pooh, the note of dispossession, of loss of control. "What's happening to you?"

"I'm sorry, Dad," I said, feeling myself slip, slip, through fingers and fingers, into the pitiless wave. I fell back onto the bed; Arthur very precisely hung up on my father. He stood, wiped the corner of his mouth, then put me back together and zipped me up, with neat, rather waiterly gestures.

"Which other friend did he meet?" he said.

I slid forward and knelt before the telephone, head hung.

"Cleveland."

"Oh? Why didn't I know that?"

"I suppose your intelligence service failed you." I stared at him. Didn't he know what he—what I—had just done? What had I just done?

"I guess I'm not paying those fellows enough," he said, and smiled unhappily.

"Well. I must have forgotten to mention it."

Cleveland. When I'd thought of him at all in the past

few days, it was only with a vague anxiety, easily dispelled
by Arthur's slightest syllable or caress, and at that moment
it seemed possible—no, forgive me, but it seemed desir-
able—that Cleveland, with his new career, was lost to us
forever, vanished into the vanishing world of my father,
two polar bears on an ice floe drifting off into a waste of
white fog. I might never see anyone but Arthur, my fancy
Arthur, ever again.

"Why are you smiling?"

"I'm free," I said.

Arthur was polishing off the last half-inch of wine, I
was rinsing the speckled film of herb butter from our dinner
plates, and we'd just decided to go for a walk, when the
doorbell rang.

"Who could that be?"

"'I must have forgotten to mention it,'" he said, rising
and heading for the hall. I turned the water off, so I could
listen, but Arthur had swung shut the door to the kitchen,
something he never did. Who could it be? I thought I heard
him say hello, in an uncharacteristically morose tone of
voice, then thought I heard a woman say, "'Lo." Something heavy was dropped in the hallway, and then there
was the sound of a loud kiss, a real smacker. I set the
sponge down, dried my hands on my pants, and went out
into the hall.

Arthur, blushing deeply, was tugging at a woman, trying to draw her into the living room. Her eyes were blue
and cold as his, though ringed with dark circles; she had his
straight nose, and his mouth, set between two deep lines,

and his blond hair, though long and full and veined with the colorless strands of age; her faded clothes fit her poorly; and a tiny silver Jesus writhed on a cross that hung from her neck. There were, in the ducking motion of her head, in the red devastation of her hands, the marks of submission to hard work and sorrow, and she looked at me now as though she expected me to deliver some very unhappy news.

"Art Bechstein, this is my mother, Mrs. Ondine Lecomte. Mother, this is my friend Art." He made the introductions quickly, with an odd chopping motion of his hands, then began almost literally to push her out of the hallway, into the living room.

"Wow, hello, Mrs. Lecomte, how great to meet you," I said, coming on strong. I didn't want Arthur to deny me this clue, this glimpse into the most secret of secret worlds. Mrs. Lecomte would not, however, look me in the face; her eyes went to her ruined hands, and she turned bright pink, a mannerism of Arthur's whose source I might have been charmed to discover, had it not made me feel painfully ashamed of myself. I felt as though it were I who'd corrupted Arthur; I felt the word "corruption."

"I just came over with some of Arthur's mending," she muttered. "Your shirts, honey. I sewed new buttons. Fixed that collar."

"Great, Mom, thanks. Okay, let's go into the living room, here. What a nice house." As they went out, he turned back toward me and said, "I'll be back to help you with the dishes in a few minutes. Then we can go for a walk."

"I get the message," I said, but I was determined. I put the kettle on, and in five minutes got pot, cups, spoons, and a sugar bowl on a little tray and out into the living room, where I caught them as they were about to stand up.

"Coffee?" I said.

Slowly they lowered themselves back onto their science-furniture chairs, at the same time and with an identical air of being trapped. I served the coffee and was disappointed, shocked, indicted, and disturbed by the plain fact of Arthur's mother. I had mythologized her, and this might have accounted for my feeling so disillusioned and at sea, but the really disturbing thing was that her sad, wrinkled face and worn smock forced me to recognize that, in some fundamental way, I knew absolutely nothing about Arthur. I had assumed, without his ever having said so, that his manners, dress, and taste were the product of a wealthy, summer-house, three-car, private-tutor, dancing-tea background. Now I began to see that he was largely his own invention.

"I don't know how you get yourself into these kind of houses," said Mrs. Lecomte with a thin smile, looking around her at the pretty-art on the walls. "Always so big and empty and fine. They're like—"

"Yes, Mom."

"Mrs. Lecomte," I said, "I really am glad to meet you. I've heard so much about you."

"Oh." She slurped her coffee, wincing, and stared deep into it. We gripped our cups and sat watching as four or five angels of silence passed through the room. "Did you go to Mass Sunday?" she said at last, already ducking her head in anticipation of her son's reply.

"Ah, no, Mom, I didn't. I haven't been since Ash Wednesday." This was a lie, and I was surprised at him. He'd been to Mass several times that I knew about, and he always claimed, without embarrassment, that it made him feel Good. "Do you know about Ash Wednesday, Art?" he said. "All the priests get together Tuesday night—"

"Please," his mother said, her cup rattling faintly on its dainty flat saucer.

"—and they have this really big party."

"Arthur." She set the coffee down.

"And then Wednesday morning," he said, smiling his hardest smile, "they empty all the ashtrays into this big bowl—"

"I'm leaving, Arthur," she said, and stood up, trembling, and I saw then that this, like all of Arthur's relations, was a game they played. He probably came as close to blasphemy as he needed to until she started to cry. Then maybe they had a forgiveness ritual.

"Oh, please don't go," I said. "Here, Mrs. Lecomte, have some more coffee."

"No, I should go," she said, finally looking at me—for a second or two—with her laughless eyes. "I've got to get up early tomorrow, but thank you, honey."

The last word was barely audible and probably automatic, but it touched me. She was, after all, Arthur's mother, and I didn't want her thinking I was some Emissary from Hell sent to despoil her son, or something. Mothers usually thought I was swell.

"Oh?" I said. "What do you do?"

Arthur came over and put his arm around her shoulders. He started to tow his mother again.

"Thanks for coming by, Mom. Thanks for doing the shirts."

"I clean houses," she said. "Like this one."

She cast a last wistful and derisive glance across the glittering brass and the rubber plants of the Weatherwoman's salon, and then Arthur kissed her cheek and got her out the door. After he'd shut it, he leaned back against it, outspreading his arms, panting slightly, as people do in the movies when they have at last got rid of the boring date or the terrible creature of slime.

We wound up, as usual, in the bedroom, only this time, for the first time, our rhythms were out of phase, the tongues and touching without effect, and it quickly became apparent that something was wrong.

"I don't attract you anymore," he said, throwing an arm across his eyes.

"Nonsense," I said. "You're more fascinating than ever."

"Because my mother's a maid?"

"Because your dream mother's a duchess," I said, and I described the childhood and upbringing that his ways and looks so clearly suggested.

"That's Cleveland," he said. "Private tutors, the summer house. He had all those things. Ha. And look at him."

"Maybe you were switched at birth."

"What you saw tonight is not who I am." He sat up on one arm and fixed me sternly with his eyes, as though administering an important lesson or a reprimand.

"No."

"You turn into whoever you're supposed to turn into."

"I hope you're right," I said, thinking of him and not of myself.

"Why, what is your father, anyway? A Jewish neo-Nazi? A proctologist?"

"Let's get dressed," I said. "Let's take that walk."

"No, just a minute. What is your father, Art? Tell me. Come on, it's only fair. You're one up on me now."

"I love you," I said, getting up to pull my trousers on.

We walked a long way, leaving behind the fragrant, dark streets of Shadyside, where you had to push aside low and wild-growing branches and to pass through curtains of spiderweb that overhung the sidewalks and left ticklish strands across your lips and eyelashes. We came far into East Liberty, where the neighborhood began to deteriorate, the vegetation dwindled then finally disappeared, and we found ourselves on a commercial street corner, amid a loose cloud of unhappy black men laughing outside the corner saloon and along the closed, barred, steel-shuttered row of storefronts. As we stood poised on the edge of the shut-down neighborhood, and Arthur said that we should turn around, I heard a snarling dog. A pickup truck had stopped at the traffic light, and in its bed was an enraged Doberman pinscher, doing near backflips of fluid hate. Each burst of nervous laughter from the street-corner men sent the dog over again.

"Jesus," said Arthur.

"I know," I said. "That dog's gone mad."

"It's Cleveland."

"Oh, come on," I said, "not quite," thinking maybe

he'd had an encounter with Cleveland, like my last one, that he hadn't told me about, but then I looked into the cab of the pickup and saw Cleveland, on the passenger's side, laughing, holding his cigarette out the window.

"What's he doing? Who's he with?" I said, trying to recognize the man sitting behind the wheel of the pickup. The dog continued to emit the same slavering snarl over and over again, without variation, like a machine specially designed to snarl at laughing black men.

"He doesn't see us," said Arthur. "Hey, Cleveland!"

Cleveland turned, his jaw dropped, and then he grinned, waving delightedly, and said something that I didn't catch. The light changed and the pickup truck squealed off, the Doberman clambering to put its forelegs on the lip of the truck bed and to thrust its head into the onrush of wind.

"What's he up to now?" said Arthur, laughing. "What a dog!"

"What a dog!" I said. "Who knows?"

We laughed, but on the way home, while Arthur continued to exclaim and narrate, I hardly spoke, and there was nothing he could do to cheer me—indeed, his chatter annoyed me, for forgetting everything I had felt only that afternoon, I was gripped by the fear that I would never see Cleveland again. Later we did make love, and it was hard and wordless as ever, but when we were through, and he reminded me that we had only three more days before the rich young couple came home, I tensed.

"Then what?" I said, the question occurring to me for the first time.

"Yes, then what?"

"Where will you go?"

"Well, I was thinking of that perfectly nice place you have on the Terrace, which has been so empty lately."

"I don't know," I said, beginning to feel, with an inward groan, the return of a familiar feeling of pressure, but he said only, "Fine," and rolled over.

So, on the following Sunday, very early and half-awake, we left the Weatherwoman House, and, because I did not know what I wanted, Arthur stayed with me for three strained, unerotic days before the house-sitting grapevine came through for him again, and he moved out.

21

THE END OF THE WORLD

♦   ♦   ♦

One morning about a week into the strange new August, I was awakened by a telephone call from a woman at the Hillman Library, who told me, in a stunningly icy tone of voice, that I'd been sent several notices informing me of Sigmund Freud's *Selected Letters to Wilhelm Fliess* having fallen due on June 10, and that if I did not return the book immediately, my grade transcripts would be frozen, or something like that, endangering all my future employment opportunities, and that if this did not persuade me, the matter would be referred to a collection agency.

"I returned that book in July," I said, rubbing my eyes, remembering the day very clearly. I'd received no notices, but since I'd moved at the beginning of the summer, I supposed they hadn't been forwarded.

"Um, well," she said, her voice melting for a moment. "If that's the case, you have to come down to the library, in person. Yes, to initiate a Search and Recovery."

Of course, I'd been carefully avoiding going anywhere near the Hillman Library. I walked into work along back streets, ate my lunch in the workroom of the bookstore, and I was constantly on the alert and ready to run at the

first glimpse of a certain aqua ribbon. Arthur and I, through
an unacknowledged and unspoken agreement, didn't discuss
his days at work, and if he had any nasty encounters by the
card catalogues or at the water fountain, or if vicious
rumors about him began to circulate through Reference,
Acquisitions, and Gifts and Exchanges, I never found out
about them. I begged the righteous librarian to allow me to
initiate a Search and Recovery over the telephone, but she
would hear nothing of it. I was in midsentence when she
hung up.

Arthur had the day off. I found the scrap of paper on
which I'd written down his new number, and called him to
find out what he knew about Searches and Recoveries, but I
got only his sleepy voice on his latest answering machine.
He was spending the day, I remembered, with the lovely
Riri, at her cousin's out in Latrobe, something he'd been
promising her for months.

"This is Art," I said, after the tone, "and I'm about to
enter the jaws of death."

Thus I resigned myself, thinking that at least it would
be simpler, somehow, if he was not at the library when I
finally reentered it, which, half an hour later, I did. Fans of
the unconscious will be interested to note that I'd taken
care to dress well, in summer colors—pleated khaki pants,
white shirt with salmon pinstripes, loosely knotted Hong
Kong cotton tie. I hurried up to the tall, actorish fellow
who worked behind the front desk, and I looked cautiously
around me as I approached him.

"I'm here to initiate a Search and Recovery," I said.

He blinked his entire face.

"P-pardon?"

"I got a call today from someone here who said that I had to initiate a Search and Recovery." I glanced over my shoulder, toward the elevators, expecting at any minute to be spotted and seized.

"Uh huh," he said. "I see."

Libraries, I knew, are frequently the haunts of twitching, mumbling paranoid schizophrenics, researching their grandiose conspiracies, and so I was embarrassed by the look he gave me, which suggested that my insistence on Search and Recovery was probably due to my fervent belief that Richard Nixon, Stephen King, and Anita Loos were intimately connected to the sinking of the *Titanic* and the disappearance of Errol Flynn's son in Cambodia.

"It's some form I'm supposed to fill out," I said.

"Oh? I've never heard of it. Do you know who you spoke to? No? Maybe you'd better go back to Administration and ask."

"Um. I was afraid—I was hoping—do you think you could go back and ask for me? Ha ha. See, there's someone who works in the back offices that I'd rather not run into."

His eyes lit up and he wiggled his eyebrows. With very dramatic deliberation, he reached behind him for a stool and sat down. He picked up a pencil and tapped it against his temple.

"Be brave," he said.

It was perfect. I stopped dead at the entrance to the elevator corridor, and there she was, behind her bars, dressed to kill, pearls, blue sundress. Her locks were lighter than ever, nearly strawberry blond, pulled up and wrapped into a palm tree of hair that rose from her head and spilled its bright ends outward in a silly, fetching spray. She raised her face, which was suntanned and barely painted, the stalk of hair swayed, and whatever expression I expected to see— rage, embarrassment, unrecognition—was absent. She grinned. It was all I could do then, in the flash of her old, unlooked-for smile, to keep myself from running to press my face against the grille, into the window that I loved so much. But I kept a grip on myself and slowly came, self-conscious, suddenly stiff-legged, and holding out my hands, as though to catch a spinning beach ball. As I passed the elevators, their Up arrows lit and chimed, one, two. The doors slid open with the sound of murmured approval, and the corridor behind me filled with a little audience.

"Phlox," I said, fifteen inches away from her lips. "Oh, Phlox."

"Do you love me?" she said, still seated, radiant with patience and anticipation, and obviously feeling that she held the strings. Her light, unconcerned tone of voice might as easily have said, May I help you?

I didn't stop to think, and said that I did.

"Wait," she said. She stood, turned from me, and walked out of the office, swinging her hips, and she came around to the other side of the window, where our hands went out, our fingers tangled, and I put my mouth to hers. After we'd kissed for a minute, with all her well-informed co-workers watching us through the magic grille, she drew back and looked at me, without a trace of hurt or anger on her face. There was only half-suppressed mirth, the rapid blinking of disbelief. She cocked her head to one side.

"I'm so sorry," I said.

"Hush," she said, and giggled. "Come on."

She took my hand and pulled me down the hall, into the stairwell, her white pumps tocking against the tiled floor. For a second I shut my eyes just to listen to the promising clatter, to think once again, Ah, there's a woman coming; here comes a woman. Under the staircase we kissed, pushing our hips together. We began to get the same wild notion then; she grabbed at my hand with both of her hands, walking backward, and pulled me up the stairs, to the third floor of the library, where there were, all around the outer walls, tiny dark rooms, with tiny desks, that the library rented to graduate students.

"They're locked, aren't they?"

"Not this one," she said, tugging me toward a door, which opened with a twist of her flushed hand.

"How do you know about this?" I slipped in behind her, whispering, and she closed the door.

"Hush," she said. "Everyone knows about this. Sit down, we'll have to be quick. Here."

She leaned forward to unzip my pants, like a child unwrapping a doll. They fell and puddled around my ankles. I sat.

"Oh," said Phlox, touched, when she saw my erection. "It's so lovely."

"It is?"

"It's so handsome and polite." She hitched up her dress; no panties.

"Were you prepared for this?" I said, this suspicion dawning on me, honestly, for the first time.

"I've been prepared for this for a week now," she said, taking my fingers. "Just feel how prepared I am."

Down upon me she settled herself, wiggling, making the necessary adjustments, and there, once again, were the aptness, the welcome give of giving skin, the warmth, the human and fragrant slipperiness, and I sighed as though I ached in every muscle and were sinking into a hot bath. In sixty seconds it was all over, and it had all begun again.

But it was different.

That evening, Phlox called to invite me to dinner, and without hesitation I said that I would be right over. Abandoning the necktie this time, I brushed my teeth, grabbed my keys, slapped three *flaques* of cologne around my open collar. Just as I was closing the door behind me, the telephone rang again, and knowing that it was probably Arthur, I clapped my hands over my ears and took the twenty-six steps two at a time. Walking the streets to Phlox's house, as so many times before—past that mailbox, past that airy, rampant bed of cosmos, past that old man, oh yes, with the neck brace and the Pomeranian—making the old approach to her apartment through that eternal oily puddle and the stink of that ginkgo tree, I was filled with a frail and sad exhilaration, which I really ought to have recognized for what it was and, perhaps, to have stopped right there—for it was nostalgia, and what inspires nostalgia has been dead a long time. There was nothing to eat when I arrived, nothing at all, and we threw our bodies together and fell onto the hard, scratching carpet. We didn't stand, this time, for two hours, until she could no longer hold her water.

"Mau Mau," I said, when she came back from the toilet. The forbidden name spilled out, although I'd forgotten it completely until this moment.

"Oh, Art, it's been so long."

I said yes, it had, but we were talking, I think, about two different things.

"What's happening?" I said. "What is this?"

"Lust," she said. "I believe it's frenzied lust." She giggled.

"Did you arrange that phone call this morning?"

"What phone call was that?" she said, meeting my eyes but turning a bit red.

"Mau Mau. It was never like this before, Mau Mau."

"We have to take each other back."

"I'm back," I said. And lying beside her on the floor of her living room, with my arm beneath her head, her breath against my shoulder, the orange plaid of last light falling on the carpet, I felt, for a little minute, that I really had returned. I felt weak, languid, as though I'd been for a swim. Phlox spoke into my ear, apologizing, scolding sweetly, and as she spoke, a breeze stirred the damp hairs of my groin, so that it was as though her words raised the goose flesh along my arms and legs, gently chilled me, and I curled myself around her and said, "I'm back." Yet as the aftereffects of the drug of sex began to wear off, as my worldly strength returned, as the circulation in my pinned arm was cut off and my hand fell asleep, I began to doubt,

to worry, to search my heart. I did not know if I was truly
still in love with Phlox or simply blowing off some final
heterosexual steam. I thought, with a guilty pang, of
Arthur, and remembered his having said once that there
was no such thing as bisexuality, that you were either one
thing or the other. I guess I still believed in absolutes. I
didn't know what I would tell him now when I saw him
again, or if indeed there was something I should be telling
Phlox, right this minute, before things went any further. I
grew more and more uncomfortable, bound up in Phlox's
arms on the rough carpet. I wanted a cigarette, wanted to
unstick my prickling skin from hers. When she began to
talk about the letter she'd left on my doorstep, laughing as
though it had been twenty years since then, I sat bolt upright.

"The letter!" I said.

"I know, and I'm so sorry, Artichoke. Come back
here," she said, pulling at my shoulders. "I can't even remember what I wrote. I know it must've been pretty silly."

"No!"

"You didn't think so?"

"No, I—well." I stood, ashamed, looking around and
around for the shirt that I'd thrown off. I took a deep
breath. "I lost it."

"Art!"

"No, I mean, Cleveland has it." The shirt was halfway
across the room, my cigarettes in its pocket, and I tore for a
while at the almost empty pack. Anything but meet her
gaze.

"Cleveland! Why does he have my letter?"

"I'll get it back, don't worry. He picked it up by mistake." The match flowered. "And lately I haven't seen him; he's been, ah, busy."

"I saw him the other day," she said, slowly. "He didn't say anything about it."

Now I turned to face her. "You did? Where?"

"But he was very strange. Art. He didn't read my letter?"

"Strange? What did he do?"

"Art, did Cleveland read my extremely private and personal letter?" She stood up now, hands on her naked hips, tossed her flyaway hair. Nearly all the light had drained from the room.

"No," I said. "Of course not."

"Well." She came over, took me in her arms, kissed me; I'd just inhaled a lungful of smoke; we parted and I exhaled gratefully, hating myself for having lied, and for having waited impatiently for the kiss to end. "I don't suppose it would really have mattered if he did," she said.

"And he might have, you know, by now," I said lamely. "Knowing Cleveland."

"It doesn't matter." She kissed me again, a happy, dismissive peck. "I'm starved. Let's get a pizza delivered, how about?"

We half-dressed and sat on separate sides of the windowsill, legs entwined, watching the street for the appearance of the pizza man.

"I've been walking a lot, Art," she said, running a finger down my shin. "Very long walks, since—since our problems. Sometimes it helps me figure things out. Sometimes I just go and go without a single thought in my head."

"Alone?" I said. It was difficult to imagine Phlox setting out for a long excursion, or for anything at all, all by herself.

"Yes, alone. I've gotten much better at being alone lately."

"It's only been ten days, Phlox. You keep making it sound like I've been off sailing around the Horn."

"Well, I'm not good at being alone. It was a long ten days."

She looked away, pretending to watch two hopping robins down on the little lawn, though at first I didn't see that she was just pretending. At first I saw only her profile, that outline I knew so well, and the dim light falling past it to her ear, the mass of familiar shadows and glints, the darkness along the side of her straight nose, the tiny lights in the hairs of her upper lip, and it pleased me, as it always did, her profile, so that I was impelled now to look more closely, to toss my gaze quickly across it as across a painting reproduced in an artbook, to try to see the whole and its parts at the same time, to bear in mind the regular profile but remark the Egyptian effect of her slightly pointed chin, the fine join of earlobe and jaw, the bone beneath her eye, and as I looked, it was no longer a profile, for profiles, really, don't exist; it was Phlox's face; and I had loved it. And then, suddenly, I saw motion, the tightening of her lower lip, the flaring of her nostril, the tears that dwindled down her cheek, and I saw that she pretended to look down at the birds in the grass.

•   •   •

When we went to bed that night it was loud and fast again, again she took control, and I found myself, inevitably perhaps, crouching on my elbows and knees—that way; I twisted and buried my face. She said, then, in an odd, clear voice which cut through everything, that she wished she could fuck me, that there must be a way, and something very primitive deep inside me awoke with a start. I rolled over, panting, but came to a definite halt. Phlox began to sob, and I wondered, unclenching my fists, if she was crying because the thing she'd wished for had frightened her, or because she could not have it, or if it was because she knew, now, that she could have it, because somehow I had been changed.

"I didn't mean it," she said, tumbling over onto the bed.

"All right," I said. I knelt beside her, ran my fingers through her faded hair. I said things that I forgot as soon as I said them. In ten minutes we were going at it again, and although I'd wanted it to be more gentle this time, had wanted to embrace, to linger, in no time at all it was exactly like wrestling; we bit and exclaimed, and I found myself twisting her into the pose I'd held just a little while before. I stared all the way down her glistening back to the tangle of her distant head.

"Can I?" I said.

"Do you want to?"

"Can I?"

"Yes," she said. "You'd better. Now."

I went to her cluttered vanity and scooped out a dollop

of cold petroleum jelly, prepared everything Arthur had trained me so well to prepare, but immediately on entering that pinched, plain orifice of so little character, I lost heart, because I simply could not understand what I was about to do; it was neither backward nor forward, or else it was both at the same time, but it was too confusing for me to desire it anymore, and I said, "It's all a mistake."

"It is not," she said. "Go, ah! go. Slow, baby."

When we were through, and we'd collapsed, she said that it had hurt and it had felt all right, that it was frightening as sex could be, and I said that I knew it. We stopped talking. I felt her grow heavy, heard the slow gathering of her breath. I slipped out of bed and went to find my clothes. Dressing furtively in the darkness, pulling on each sock, I felt very happy, for one instant, as though I were rising at three in the morning for a fishing trip, and there were sandwiches and apples to be packed away. I decided not to leave a note.

Halfway home under the clear, starry sky and the unhaloed streetlamps, I had yet to form a single coherent thought, a plan of action, when it came to me that I'd forgotten to ask Phlox about Cleveland and the thing he'd said or done that was strange, and I saw then that I didn't really care. Like that, like a spasm, I spat and wished that the summer were over. Immediately afterward I felt ashamed; I covered my mouth as though I'd blasphemed or something. But a strong desire overtook me to go away, to take a plane out that morning, to go to Mexico, as Arthur had done once, and live irresponsibly in a little pink hotel; or to Italy, to sleep through blinding afternoons in a half-fallen villa; or to vanish into the railroad wastes of North America. My only commerce would be with prostitutes and bartenders. I would send postcards without a return address.

"No," I said aloud, "don't give up." But I was still fantasizing halfheartedly about the places I might visit, and the simple life that I would lead in them, when I reached my front door and heard the telephone ringing inside.

"How was Latrobe?" I said.

"Been out?"

"Yes, I've been—" I was on the point of lying, but I saw, for once and with disheartening clarity, the outcome of whatever stupid lie I might manage. I would only involve myself over again in all the tedious nonsense of juggling Arthur and Phlox. I looked at my watch, exhaled, and told him he'd better come over.

"No," he said, "I'll meet you."

Arthur house-sat now for a poli-sci professor who lived up in the hills of north Oakland, and so we met roughly halfway, at the statue of Johann Sebastian Bach in front of the Carnegie Institute, not far from the Cloud Factory. It was cool for a summer night; I shivered, sorry I'd worn only a sweatshirt, sorry that we stood so far apart, on the sidewalk beneath the giant green Bach. I was sorry, too, that the air was cold between us, that even under the best of circumstances he could not just put his arm around me and hold me to him, because this was Pittsburgh and J.S. or somebody might see, and so we stood with our hands in our pockets, two young men struggling to be in love and about to have it out.

"I slept with Phlox," I said.

"Oh, Jesus, let's walk somewhere." He'd dressed quickly; his sneakers didn't match, his shirt was half-untucked—he'd already been to bed at least once before I answered my phone. And I have to admit that it was right then, as I blurted out what I'd just done, and his unshaven, stray-hair face creased with a kind of prissy annoyance, that I felt the first failure of the emotion I was about to profess.

"How did it happen?"

"How do you think?" I said, snapping because it looked as if things were going that way. "No, Arthur, I'm sorry; it happened very strangely, actually, and I don't really get it at all."

We passed the bronze Shakespeare with his great domed head, the bronze Stephen Foster eternally serenaded by the pickaninny with the bronze banjo, and I saw that we would end up in our usual place high above the Lost Neighborhood, which we did, silently, taking up our usual slouches against the iron rail. The sky glowed and flashed orange, off toward the mills in the south, as if volcano gods were fighting there or, it seemed to me, as if the end of the world had begun—it was an orange so tortured and final.

He took hold of my elbow, firmly, and turned me till I faced him. Again that day I expected to see anger, and again I was disappointed.

"Art, don't leave me," he said, an unfamiliar look on his face, cheeks hollow, eyes rolling. I'd never seen his face reveal anything before. "I've been so afraid that this would happen. I knew when you weren't home all night. I knew it."

"I had no idea," I said. "It was all a big accident. Or that is, she planned it. I fell into it. I can't say what it really means. It was so strange tonight, Arthur." My throat tightened. All the sexual battle and stress of the day, the confusion of my final bout with Phlox, the loveliness of her lacy bedroom, and the power of her face mounted within me and came spilling out. Arthur held out his fingers and lightly brushed my cheek.

"What is it? Art. Come on. Don't cry."

"I don't know what I'm like anymore," I said. "I do dumb things."

"Shh."

"Don't ask me to choose. Please."

"I won't," he said, shortly, as though it cost him some effort. "Just don't leave me."

I stopped crying. Everything seemed utterly upside down. The Arthur I thought I knew would be scorning me now, and ridiculing Phlox, and forcing me to admit that she'd suckered me. He would be forcing me to acknowledge that if I didn't love him, Arthur F. Lecomte, with all the hip places he had been, the perfect manner of the life he led, his sarcastic brilliance, his hard amusement, and, most of all, the male company he could offer me, then I was a fool, a loser, and entirely my father's obedient boy; cursed, doomed to lose the things my father had lost—art, love, integrity, and all that. A shift, another shift, had taken place. Somehow it was up to me now, and I wanted to know why.

"Did something else happen to you today?" I said. "Something with Riri?"

Arthur sat down on a step and looked down onto the miniature lights of the Lost Neighborhood.

"I took this test," he said. "I didn't tell you. I took the foreign service exam. I failed. I knew when I came out of the room, really, but I got the letter this afternoon."

I sat beside him and put my arm across his shoulders.

"So? You can take it again, can't you?" I tried to think of when he must have taken it.

"I'm twenty-five. I'm still in college. I'm queer. My lover is about to leave me for Deanna Durbin." He threw a stone. "I've been chasing after the same things for a long time now."

"I love you," I said.

"You're a sexual dilettante," he said. "You have no idea."

We made love on the steps. I threw up. He walked me home, told me a bad joke, and we climbed into my narrow bed. In two hours there was daylight at the window and a Wedgwood sky.

22

THE BEAST THAT ATE
CLEVELAND

♦   ♦   ♦

I imagine it was shortly before dinnertime on the twenty-
third of August that Cleveland reentered the world of his
earliest childhood, intent on doing it harm. Until just a few
days before this, I think, he hadn't set foot in Fox Chapel
in years and years, not since the distant winter morning on
which the Arnings had moved out to the country, and he'd
sat in his little rubber boots and silken, pillowy snowsuit in
the back seat of the family car, bewildered, watching the
bare window of his bedroom disappear. Now his boots were
of black leather, the air smelled like perfect lawns, and he,
Evil Incarnate, knew exactly where he was going. He went
slowly, keeping a light hand on the throttle so that the
giant growls of his German engine wouldn't draw too much
notice. As though his opaque helmet were not disguise
enough, he'd cut his hair short, had traded his glasses for a
pair of contacts, his black jacket for a twill sport coat, and
as he pulled off into the parking lot of a mock-Tudor shopping center whose rustic, pretty stores sold things of no
practical use, potpourris, artificial eggs, duck-related mer-

chandise, he did his best to look like the wayward, thrillhound son of a well-to-do Fox Chapel family—one of the local young black sheep who were always flipping over in their Italian cars on winding roads, vomiting on the golf courses at night, diving fully clothed and drunken into the runs and creeks—one of whom, really, he was. Only in my hands, he thought as he killed the engine, it goes further than simple bad behavior. It is an intellectual and moral program. It is the will to bigness.

He shed his helmet, left his bike in a space around the back of the shopping center, near the Dumpsters, where Tudor ended and blank cinder block began. Then he stood for a moment, patting at his jacket. Gloves, flask, penlight, pocketknife, Poe. From the straps that held it to the saddle he drew a little crowbar and slid it under his watchband, up into his sleeve, until it jabbed at the soft crook of his arm.

A wood began behind the shopping center, fairly dense with pin oak and brambles, shot through with tiny rills, but he knew that it held sudden clearings, it was passable, and that it continued for almost two miles until it stopped abruptly at a certain concrete wall whose dimensions, by now, he knew quite well. He grinned at the sight of the colonnade of trees before him, he dallied a minute more to enjoy the quick leap of his heart and the warmth that mounted in his stomach. Although he supposed it was a stupid thing to have done, he was what he was—so on the way over he'd stopped at a bar for two lucky shots of Jameson's Irish whiskey, and now, drawing a hot half-inch from his own flask and contemplating the lovely, dark world he was about to enter, he was filled with alcoholic courage; with

a habitual head toss, he started into the trees, twigs crunch-
ing underfoot; but he no longer owned his tossing long hair,
and he rubbed at the bristly back of his head.

The trip through the woods took him a little over an
hour, so he had far more than enough time to think about
what he was about to do, and anyway I think he loved the
act of considering himself a jewel thief, like this: "I am a
jewel thief"; for he was learning a profession, and, as with
doctors, and priests, and the other few true professionals
(people, that is, who are trained to recognize peril), merely
pronouncing the words "jewel thief" served him as a kind
of instantaneous reminder of his many skills and respon-
sibilities, as a restorative slap. It jerked him into bleak,
hungry readiness, like the snap of the wrist that frees the
humming switchblade.

Twice or three times the odd cry of a bird, the yell of a
jay, would stop him dead, and he'd duck behind a tree for
several seconds, watching, breathing. He wasn't frightened
by the many things that could go wrong in the natural
course of a job, because these things were more or less the
whole point, along with the proverbial fat wads of dough.
But he'd been troubled, even mildly spooked, by his teacher
Pete Arcola's uncharacteristic anxiety during the previous
couple of days. Somebody had been telling Poon to watch
his step, to keep a leash on his protégés, and although
Punicki laughed and told Pete to tell Cleveland not to
worry, he'd also set up elaborate precautions for the fencing
later on that night. Arcola, ex-Special Forces, trained to
steal by the army and then set loose, said it was Frankie
Breezy making vague, "probably bullshit" threats, but

Cleveland had a dim suspicion that my father might be lurking somewhere behind them, as he clutched a tree and listened hard.

When he drew near the house, however, his mind cleared again, his heart hardened, and he began to apply himself to his task. There was a young oak five or six feet from the base of the concrete wall; he grabbed its lowest limb and yanked himself up, then inched forward along the limb until he was almost level with the wall's lip. He studied the house that stood not sixty feet from his already damp forehead. The bough rocked under his weight. It was a great brick house, red and hung with ivy, two dozen windows in the back alone, three chimneys. Arcola had chosen it, after their sightseeing tour a few days before, because there appeared to be no guard dogs. Perhaps their last adventure with the snarling bitch in the back of the truck had been a near disaster, or perhaps she was no longer in heat; in any case, they were for the moment unprepared to deal with Dobermans. Cleveland loved dogs, of course, and would never have employed the poisoned wiener.

All of the downstairs lights were on, all of the upper windows dark, as he'd hoped and expected—it was dinnertime, and Cleveland could see them, Dad, Mom, Junior, Sis, and Baby, sitting around the vast dining room table with their beautiful food, could see the uniformed maid disappear through swinging doors into the kitchen (glimpse of copper pots, flowery wallpaper), and he felt briefly wistful at the familiar sight of the father and the son, and the butter being passed in silence along the unbridgeable distance between them. He spat thick whiskey spit, then climbed out onto the top of the wall, squatting. He looked down along the wall's inner face, to the grass by its foot, for signs that the perimeter was alarmed, though he knew that if there were an alarm system, it would not be activated, surely, at this hour of happiness and safety; but there were no such signs, and he let himself slowly down into the hostile territory of the well-groomed yard.

Shrub to shrub he went, avoiding the swaths of light from the windows, which gathered now in the twilight and fell across the grass; avoiding the dining room; trying to decide which of the still-dark upstairs windows was the master bedroom. Master bedroom, he thought. The phrase reminded him for some reason of Jane's parents, and as he scanned the dozen upstairs windows he permitted himself to engage in deep fantasy for a second or two. With a fat enough wad of dough, he would buy thirty feet of chrome Airstream camper and set out across the Fatherland with Jane, culminating their voyage at Mount Rushmore, where they would surpass Cary Grant and Eva Marie Saint by doing the holy deed in the chapel of Teddy Roosevelt's right ear. There it was! down at the opposite end of the house from the dining room—two thin, tall windows, nearly doors, behind a rail of spiraling wrought iron, about ten feet off the ground. They would be opened every morning, no doubt, for the master's deeply satisfying survey of his domain.

It was at this point that he began to wish he had a partner. Pete Arcola had lost half a leg in a car accident six months before, and Cleveland, Arcola said, was the first guy Poon had found who was even worth training. Punicki fenced only for the true artists and craftsmen of Pittsburgh jewel theft, of which there were perhaps four, or three. Now Cleveland needed someone to crouch and make a platform of his back, to lace hands together and give a boost. He ape-walked over to the dark window and stood beneath it, looking up.

As he took another pull from his flask, he noticed that the window directly in front of him was open. Hey. He stuck his head into a dim, empty room, library or study, big desk in the middle, on which burned a tiny lamp in the shape of a heron. The lamp threw its cold light just far enough for him to make out the thousand lawbooks that lined the walls. He put on the gloves. As quietly as possible, he climbed into the library, which smelled of pipe, and then carried back out the thickest, largest books, the tomes. He intensely disliked cold, plutonian libraries like this one, and was actually glad to get outside again, to find himself at last rocking at the peak of the cairn of books, like Buster Keaton, with a firm grip on the wrought-iron rail. He pulled himself up.

Drawing the slender crowbar from his sleeve now, he forced the window in the patient, incremental, silent way that Pete had taught him; then he was inside the cool, perfumed, silent, black bedroom; panting, with a taste of fire in his mouth from the whiskey that jostled in his gut, he waited for his eyes to adjust to the darkness, then went to Mom's vanity and took the chair. He wedged it, softly, against the door, pushing in the lock button. The important part was also the easiest and swiftest. Some of the watches and bracelets were just lying around like pennies;

feeling like the Grinch Who Stole Christmas, he swept them up, then went through the socks and panties in the antique dresser, the funereal jewel box, until he had himself two big handfuls of heirlooms and anniversary presents from the master.

Something to put them in—he thought of using a sock, but decided on a pillowcase or sheet, and tiptoed over to the bed. On the left-hand night table was another gold bracelet—snik!—and an old blond doll, the kind with eyes that close for doll-like sleep when the rubber baby is laid on her back. He grinned, pulled the head off with a rather disturbing soft pop, and poured all the jewelry into the hollow body. It took him a grisly minute to get the head screwed in again; then he shook the weird maraca once, and, unable to resist, rewarded himself with another pull from the flask—he was, after all, under a good deal of stress—and it was thus that mighty Cleveland made, at last, one too many fine, brilliant demonstrations of his mighty nonchalance. He should have deferred the moment of exultant glee, left just a little sooner. As he dropped down onto the lawn with a thud that was as quiet as he could manage, he heard the first call of the sirens.

At this point I should probably say that my father, since our last bizarre, miserable attempt at conversation, had entered into a state of rage that was reportedly terrible, biblical, in its fatherliness and bare restraint, in the fear and trembling it inspired. My father was wroth. Through Lenny Stern he let it be known that Frankie Breezy should call him at once, and when twenty minutes later Frankie did, he encouraged Frankie to see that Cleveland was Frankie's responsibility. Frankie could see that. What did Frankie Breezy, feeling perhaps a bit numb as he hung up the phone, imagine could be the reason for Joe the Egg's sudden malignant interest in Frankie's old pickup and delivery boy, a stupid motorhead? He would have known what everybody else knew, that ever since his wife got dead, Joe Bechstein had been funny about his boy. Now the boy had ended up down in the dirt playing with the rest of the boys, and Joe the Egg was crying about it. He'd told Frankie to teach Cleveland a lesson, but Frankie probably smirked when he heard this, guessing for whom the lesson was really intended.

He had no reason not to want to do it, either, since Punicki was currently his least favorite person in the whole world. He sent a few ears out into the street. It took very little time to get wind of the Fox Chapel job; and an anonymous phone call at sunset, with a guess at the general address, did the trick neatly. The cops came screaming into the neighborhood, and Cleveland, making a lot of noise, which alerted the Master, tossed the doll over the wall, then scrambled up after it. He heard the rip of the seam at the shoulder of his jacket. Through the woods he crashed, with Baby under his arm, losing his way twice. He imagined the scene back at the house, the crying children, Dad rushing out into the yard, Junior into the street. Police, Police! A branch jammed into his cheek, near the eye, and he saw a flash of red. At last he pounded out onto the blacktop of the deserted parking lot, started his bike, and took off.

It was as he pulled out onto the road, turned unthinkingly to the right, that he realized two things: He didn't know where he was going, and he'd had too much to drink. The alcohol had deserted him during his run through the woods, but now it returned, with all the rancor of an I-told-you-so, and he swung around in the road and started off in the other direction, back toward Highland Park, unable to decide what to do next, since it was too early to go around to Carl's store; anyway, he was supposed to pick up Pete beforehand, in Oakland. As he considered running a stop sign and slowed to a near halt, it occurred to him that more than just the police might be looking for him; and he thought of me, because he had a vague, wild idea that I might be able to say something to someone and take some of the heat off, if heat there was; then he thought of Jane, of that safe, other, tender world, and wondered if he could risk returning to her house, where he had not been now for two months.

He roared past two police cars headed in the opposite direction, heard their distant squeals as they whirled around and gave chase. The doll still under his arm, he crossed the Allegheny, determined to lose his pursuers. Ten minutes later he stood astride his motorcycle in an empty East Liberty parking lot, behind a cluster of old buildings that hid him from the street, loading docks on three sides of him, empty crates, a forkless forklift. On the fourth side there were a small office trailer and an illuminated pay phone rising up from a patch of weeds. He drained the last draft from his flask, then dug a quarter out of his pocket.

"Cleveland!"

"What are you doing, Bechstein?" he said. "Drop everything."

I'd been lying on the sofa, trying to read an essay ana-lyzing the notorious transience of the Clash's drummers, and of drummers in general, but I was continually distracted by the thought that I had no plans at all for the evening, and that I'd had no plans at all since the previous Friday, an evening with Phlox, which I'd destroyed by failing to conceal from her my new, terrifying inability to attend to her speech or body; there'd already been a more subdued but similar evening with Arthur, and I was beginning to doubt that I now had sexual feelings at all, of any prefix. I didn't know whether my lack of plans was blessing or pain. The ambiguous note on which I'd last parted with Cleveland—scrapping on the steps of my house—seemed insignificant now, small-time ambiguity, and his call prom-ised salvation.

"Where are you?" I said. "What's up?"

"How soon can you be at the Cloud Factory, Bech-stein?"

"Twenty minutes? Five if I make a bus. What? What?"

"Just come on."

"To do what?"

"I need to crawl beneath your aegis," he said, dryly. "Just come on."

"You're liquored," I said.

"Fuck, Bechstein, just come on. This is your big chance." Faint thrill of pleading in his voice. "Just come."

"It isn't Crime?"

"I'm coming to get you," he said. "Stay put." There was a lot of noise and rattle as he hung up the phone.

I shaved and, on an odd impulse, changed into the

clothes I considered my battle dress—as close as I came to battle dress, that is—jeans, black pocket T-shirt, high-top black sneakers, then stood in front of the mirror lamenting my feebleness, trying to narrow my mouth, harden my gaze, while laughing. I felt giddy, anxious, and what once was called gay, assuming that I was in for the same taste of fear, illumination, and strange liberty I'd found in our two previous rounds of Crime. I ran out to Forbes Avenue to wait for him, and my first disappointment came when I saw that I'd dressed all wrong. Cleveland, in his blazer, looked ready to eat an obligatory luncheon with a lonely old aunt. I looked ready to vandalize her house and steal her bird feeders. We'd exchanged our usual uniforms. He lifted his visor; I saw the fiery red mark on his cheek, below the eye.

"Look at you. Ha." He smiled for half a second. "Get on."

I got on, afraid to ask about the doll, put my arms around him, held on tightly; something was very definitely the matter here; I sensed the fatalistic bluntness of Cleveland's speech. His ever present alcoholic aura of having gone to far was now a rank smell around him.

"Your father is an asshole," he began, and then told me, quickly, shouting into the wind, what he'd been doing for the past two hours, and from whom he imagined he was running.

"Why would my father care?" I shouted. "You're paranoid. Why would he care what you do for Carl Punicki?"

He slowed as we turned into Schenley Park, and the wind died for an instant. "Because he's an asshole! Because, hell, because I corrupted your youth. I don't know. I took you out to the stockyard behind the family hot dog stand. God knows there's a lot more you could stand to find out. It would probably kill him."

I didn't answer. We came upon the Cloud Factory, dim in the streetlight, and had just begun to pass it, when there was the hint of a police car in the distance, by the library. We both saw it. He swerved into the museum parking lot, by the cafeteria door, and cut the engine.

"We'll wait here for a second," he said, craning his head around toward me, so that I caught a full whiskey blast. "I want you to stick with me for a while, okay, Bechstein, please?" He was opposed on principle, I knew, to the word "please." "Just be my rabbit foot."

The police car passed, a bit slowly, but passed, and the shadows of the cops within it seemed serene and unpursuing. I exhaled.

"Okay," I said, free from doubt for the first time in four days. I clutched his shoulder as kindly as a shoulder may be clutched. "I will. What's with the doll?"

He shook it.

"I see," I said. Actually, I would have loved to see. Stolen jewels. Who is not stirred by these two words?

"Just a minute," he said, sliding off the bike. He started toward the Cloud Factory with the doll.

I watched him disappear down the hill. It had never occurred to me that my success at remaining aloof from the business of my family all that time might be the fruit of my father's will as much as my own. I'd always thought I disappointed him by my shame, my lack of interest, my adolescent scorn. And then I thought: Wait a minute, am I going to get arrested? Hold everything.

"What'd you do with it?" I said, when Cleveland strolled easily back, patting the pockets of his too-small jacket. "Did anyone see you?"

"No evidence on me n-now," he said, sounding frazzled, a bit winded. "No one saw. May the Cloud Factory bless and k-keep my little baby. Now listen. Here's what we're going to do. I've got to run over to Ward Street to gather up my mentor. I'll get his truck—he has a beautiful truck—and we'll be back for you."

"Why do I have to wait here?"

He grabbed my elbow with one hand, my upper arm with the other, and lifted me into the air, about four inches off the saddle. It hurt.

"Off," he said, dragging me brusquely onto my feet. To an observer it would have looked as though he were about to beat me up. "You're staying here because you're going to be very busy while I'm gone." He reached into his trousers pocket and drew out a half-dozen quarters. "Here," he said. "Start calling all the magic names you know. All the wise guys. Your Uncle Lenny, whoever. Ask them—with all the filial humility you're so good at—to lay off. As a favor to you."

"I don't know any wise guys, Cleveland. I can't call Uncle Lenny."

He climbed onto the BMW, pulled on his helmet. His voice came distant and nasal through the lowered visor, as though he were talking to me from inside a bottle.

"Sure you can," he said. "Call your dad, if you have

to." He jumped down hard on the starter, and his drunken foot slipped, pounded on the ground. "Jesus. Call collect."

"This is not a good scheme, Cleveland. This is a bad scheme. You can't even start your motorcycle." I saw that I was trying to welsh on my promise to help him, so I grinned. "You're impaired."

He jumped again, and the bike began its controlled explosions.

"I'm huge," he said, poking his finger into my chest. "I'll be back in ten minutes."

Kneading the damp pieces of metal in my hand, I watched him pass again through the shadows between streetlights, shrinking as he went. I wished, with sharp, strange regret, that I had kissed his cheek.

I stood with a quarter half-slid into the coin slot, my thoughts a jumble of preambles and strategies, having decided firmly but in some bewilderment that I could not call Uncle Lenny. It would have to be my father. I say bewilderment because I still did not really believe that the premature arrival of the police had anything to do with my father, and so I couldn't quite see why I should call him, except that I'd told Cleveland I would. It was intolerable enough to have to alarm my father for a good reason, but for more of Cleveland's nonsense! I pinched the quarter, full of dread, wondering whether I shouldn't just call to say hello. I read fifteen times an obscene graffito on the aluminum corner of the phone booth.

"Collect call to Joseph Bechstein from Art," I said, and in a minute I heard my father saying that he would not accept the charges. In the second before my heart sank, I felt how odd it was to hear his high, clipped familiar voice and not be able to speak to him, as though the operator had raised an unhearing ghost or oracle; this woman held the switches and wire that connected us. My father would hang up, and then I would, and she would be left wherever it is that operators are.

"Dad!" I said. "Please talk to me!"

I heard the sudden silence as the woman broke the connection; then, as she blandly suggested that I dial direct, I heard the sirens growing in the distance. I dropped the receiver with a loud clunk and ran back toward the parking lot. For a few seconds I saw his motorcycle, very far away, before it disappeared from view. He must have flown past the wrong street corner, past two cops in a car with a description and an APB. One, then two, three squad cars went red and glittering after him. For the next few minutes I jogged helplessly back and forth, hopped into the air, climbed the steps of the museum, trying to catch a glimpse, aware of nothing around me but ceaseless demonstrations of the Doppler effect. I knew so little what to do that it actually occurred to me to call the police.

"Help, oh, help," I whispered.

Then I saw Cleveland emerge from a street over behind the library, the street I had walked in my efforts to avoid Phlox, and simultaneously heard the drone and terrible flutter of hundreds of beating dove wings. The helicopter swung low and hung, it swept its single straight beam across Cleveland, and its metal voice issued an incomprehensible command. Cleveland hesitated a moment, probably from

the shock of suddenly finding an uproar of wind and brilliance above his spinning head, then shot toward me,
toward the Cloud Factory, as the police cars appeared behind him. The helicopter jerked upward, then dropped
down again onto Cleveland. He reached the curb not
twenty yards from me, let his bike fall, with its rear wheel
still whirling, and ran toward the Cloud Factory, pursued by
the light from above. I ran after him.

"Get back!" said the helicopter. "Keep away!"

Cleveland scrambled up over the chain-link fence, tot-
tering at the top, and then I lost sight of him. The police
pulled up, left their cars, and came jingling and rattling
toward me. One of them detached himself from the group
and, with a shove and a hammerlock, took me into
custody. I could not say that I had nothing to do with this.

We watched, I and my cop. The searchlight caught
Cleveland on an iron ladder, drunk and terrified and climbing very badly, a flash of white-pink under his arm. I cried
out. Down, I thought, down, go down. But he continued
his upward climb, running wildly along each catwalk to the
next ladder, encased every step of the way in the solid tube
of light, until he reached a ladder fastened to the side of the
building itself, a series of bars like staples punched into the
brick.

"Go down!" I said.

"He can't hear you," said the cop. "Shut up."

Cleveland's pursuers were already scaling the building
around him, from all sides, when he attained the summit of
the Cloud Factory. I saw him, legs apart, in the shadow of
the magic valve, one waving hand extended toward the on-

coming helicopter to shield his face from its light, the other clutching the naked doll. In that one long second before he lost his footing and fell head over heels over head, the spotlight hit him strangely, and he threw a brief, enormous shadow against the perfect clouds, and the hair seemed to billow out from the shadow's head like a black banner. For one second Cleveland stood higher than the helicopter that tormented him; he loomed over the building, over me, and over the city of secret citizens and homes beneath his feet, and the five-foot shadow of the doll kicked and screamed.

23

XANADU

◆   ◆   ◆

It seems I resisted arrest when Cleveland fell, and had to be violently restrained. I have no memory of this, or of the other things that happened before the sunny instant I awoke, among bed sheets stiff as white shopping bags, my name around my wrist, suffering from what I thought at first was an atrocious hangover but turned out to be the effects of two sharp blows to the head with a rubber truncheon; I could actually see the ache, a web of phosphenes behind my eyes. As I tried to sit up, I heard a deep sigh of pleasure. I dragged my head around to find Uncle Lenny beside the bed, deep in a white chair that was too large for him. I started.

"That's the boy," he said, giving a little kick of his legs, which didn't quite reach the floor. "Hee hee. Good morning! So? How's the head? It's all better, huh?"

I looked away, too quickly, so that a black, starry wave broke over my eyes, and I said, "Ah."

"You like the room, huh? Not bad? Private. Very costly. I got you switched soon as I heard."

He waited a moment for me to thank him.

"Now don't worry, Art. Your dad, he's coming, proba-

bly's already at the airport. Don't worry about anything.
You ain't in any kind of trouble with the police. You got
friends, Art." He leaned forward, grunting, to touch my
shoulder with two tan fingers. "You got your Uncle Lenny.
And your Aunt Elaine; she's downstairs. She came too. To
comfort you."

I was conscious, then, of a different ache, deeper and
more sharp than the feeling of bereavement that a hangover
will sometimes uncover in the heart.

"What happened?" I whispered. My voice cracked,
thick and new. Through the window I could see the cascad-
ing houses on the distant high banks of the Monongahela,
the spread red-and-green dirty tartan of Oakland. So I was
in Presbyterian Hospital.

"You got hit by a cop, a lousy Polack of a cop. We'll
take care of him too."

"Great," I said. "Take care of everything." I had
Friends. I had Friends who owned police chiefs, who killed,
who did all the things I'd always regarded as though they
were the alarming, unfortunate, faintly interesting plot elements of a television program that I did not myself watch.
And now my father and my other Friends were coming to
receive thanks for the fix they'd put in, for all the terrible
trouble they'd saved me. I looked around my pillow for the
call button, and then remembered, or seemed to remember,
that Annette, Phlox's roommate, worked at Presbyterian. I
felt trapped, though I wasn't exactly certain of how; I no
longer had a clear impression of where the alliances and
fissures lay among the people I knew, of who stood on
which side of me and in what relation; which was tanta-

mount, when you consider it, to my forgetting who I was.
For a moment, staring at the button I couldn't bring myself
to press, I was terrified, disconnected, falling, and to pro-
tect myself I invoked, automatically, the only magic name I
knew. What would Cleveland do, I thought, in this situation?

He would have pushed things too far.

"Uncle Lenny," I said, "why did my father have
Cleveland killed?"

"Hey! Art! What are you saying? You been conked on
the head, honey. Your father didn't have nothing to do
with it. Your friend, poor guy, I don't know, he was a be-
ginner, he got careless. He brought the heat down on himself." He pulled intently on his ear.

"Lenny, I'm here in the hospital with a broken head.
I'm in pain, Uncle Lenny; please don't lie to me." I knew
him well enough to know that an appeal from suffering
might have some effect. Aunt Elaine, who complained mer-
cilessly of migraines, gallstones, rheumatism, cramps, had
transformed her husband over the years into a kind of human palliative; all of his other appetites, for cash, domination, a famous name, had long ago found satisfaction, borne
their admirable fruit, and the lone desire left him—doomed
to disappointment in his Florida of the ancient—was that
everyone should get better.

"Who called the police on him?" I said, and groaned.

"Oh, my. Who knows? The guy he robbed, probably."
His long lobe continued to occupy him, but I could see I
had him worried. I attempted another groan, and found
myself, for a few seconds, unable to stop.

"My God, Art, I should call the nurse?"

"I'm okay. Just tell me. Cleveland said my father set him up. Did he?"

"Art, look, your father'll be here any minute; you can ask him all the questions you want, and everything. I'll call the nurse, she'll get you a pill." He struggled out of his chair, then looked at me, face twisted as though he were imagining the pain in my head, his hands palm up and helpless before him. "Art, he was only looking out for you. He didn't like it you were mixed up with the wrong people. He was mad, I guess. Yeah, he was really furious. Jesus, you should of heard him on the telephone; I had to keep the thing this far from my ear. Look, you know how he is about you ever since, I mean, ever since . . ."

I sat forward, all the pain flown away, and reached out to grab him by the nubby sleeve of his sweater, as Cleveland would have done.

"*Ever since what*, Lenny? They killed my mother instead of him?" For an instant this seemed to explain everything, and then, abruptly, ceased.

Lenny backed toward the door, sad and alert, suntanned and old.

"I'm going to get your Aunt Elaine," he said, word by slow word, as though I were waving a crazy gun around. "All right? You wait here. I'm going out now."

"What happened to my mother, Lenny?" What happened to my father? What happened to me?

He went out. The pain in my head receded before the mounting uproar in my stomach. I pressed the call button, remembering despite everything to wonder if Annette was

my nurse, but it was an older woman who swept in, looking
crisp and happy, cap perched upon her head like a stuffed
dove.

"I'm going to be sick," I said, and was, though there
was very little inside me. I lay back on the crackling sheets.

"I won't be able to see anyone today," I said, accepting
a glass of sweet water. "I don't feel very well at all."

My valiant nurse (whom I now, belatedly, thank—a
kiss upon each of your lined cheeks, Eleanor Colletti,
R.N.) fought off intense outbursts of paternal concern and
gladioli until the first set of visiting hours was over, although each time I heard his high, soft, contrite voice in
the hallway I was terribly tempted to relent, since my in-
clination, as I have said before, was always to accept apologies, which feed on nostalgia. Throughout the afternoon a
thunderstorm came tumbling and spilling against my window, as I heard my father plead and hector and sigh; I
watched the door to my room remain firmly shut and ached
for that return of everything to its previous condition which
is the apology's false promise. But I knew that if he stayed
long enough, it would be I who ended up apologizing,
which was something—and this is exactly how I put it to
myself—that Cleveland would never do. At seven o'clock
Nurse Colletti, her jaw grimly set, came in to say my father
had gone, and with him the bouquet. She blew upward at a
stray gray lock.

It was, in fact, this continual demand of myself to think
as my dead friend had thought that finally led me out of bed
and to the tiny closet of my room, where I found my

clothes, my battle dress. I dressed slowly, among the faint rattle and ring of hangers, feeling weak and sad in my sad uniform, found my wristwatch, my wallet, my keys, crept out of my room and into the elevator. I informally checked myself out of the hospital, which was not too difficult to do at seven-thirty, and caught a bus back to Squirrel Hill.

Riding on a city bus along the route that you have taken from your job, from the movies, from a hundred Chinese meals, with the same late sun going down over the same peeling buildings and the same hot smell of water in the aftershower air, can be, in the wake of a catastrophe, either a surrealistic nightmare of the ordinary or a plunge into the warm waters of beautiful routine. I watched, among the forty hot, plain people, a mother brush her daughter's hair into ponytails wrapped kindly and tight with pink elastic bolos, and by the time I pulled the bell cord for the Terrace stop, I knew that everything would be all right, and that soon, very soon, I was going to be able to cry.

There was no mail in my mailbox; I came in the door and found Arthur sitting on my sofa, looking at a magazine, his large plaid suitcase on the floor in front of him. He looked ashen and sleepless. A cigarette trembled in his thin fingers. I went to him, we embraced, we wept, wet each other's shoulders and throats, wiped our streaming noses a hundred times.

"I have a problem," he said at last, sniffling. I felt his shoulders tense suddenly. "And it's your fault, in a way."

"What?" I said.

"Some of your father's associates came to see me today. At my mother's." Through the paleness and shadow of his face there was a hint of his usual wry expression. He could still see the joke. "You never told me you were such a, well, such a scion," he said.

"What do you mean? What did they want?"

He gestured toward the great valise.

"They wanted me to know I was lucky they didn't tear off my pretty fag face, for one thing. They requested that I leave town."

"How did they—what are you doing?"

"I'm leaving town. I'm going to New York. I'm just staying long enough to say good-bye to you and clean out my bank account. Can I spend the night here?" He attempted a smile. "Is it safe?"

"You don't have to leave town."

"Oh, no? Is there something you can do about it?"

I thought a moment.

"No," I said, "there isn't."

I gave myself a moment to feel alarm at my father's discovery, but none came. "How did they— Oh. The letter."

"I believe that's it," he said.

"It was on him when he—when they found him? Why?"

"What was it?"

"A letter from Phlox. A very distraught one."

"Maybe he kept it around for laughs."

I had an idea and stood up, looking about my summer apartment at all the boxes I had never opened, all the piles I had formed.

"I guess," I said, "I guess there's going to be. Well. A funeral. So. Aren't you going to stay for it?"

Arthur stared into his lap. I saw the color mount along his neck, up to the pink tips of his ears, but he was not blushing.

"No," he said. "I don't think that I am. All funerals are stupid, but Cleveland's will be the most stupid funeral in the world."

"I want to go."

"Fine," he said, without looking up. "Let me know how it is."

"I mean, I want to go with you."

There was a pause. He raised his face to me.

"I'm surprised," he said, but of course he didn't look it at all. There were only his even, bright gaze and the slight arch of his left eyebrow. "I thought you were gathering around you the tattered shreds of your heterosexuality."

I went to sit beside him again, thigh to thigh on the little couch.

"Well, I don't know. I might be. Can I go with you, anyway?"

"I was thinking maybe Spain," he said.

Perhaps it was foolish to be afraid, but I packed a bag too, and we spent the night at a hotel; and perhaps it was foolish not to be more afraid, for we took a room at the Duquesne, under the name of Saunders. The dim, faintly humming corridors, the motionless drapes on the window, reminded me of my last visit to the hotel, with Cleveland; everything, in fact, recalled him to me, as though he'd left the whole world to me in his will. By the time I slid between the fragrant sheets of the day's second foreign bed, I was far too aching, aggrieved, too set adrift, to do anything but fall immediately into uneasy sleep, and dream of my father, shouting.

Among the few things I took with me—clothes, passport, Swiss Army knife, three thousand ancient, inviolate bar mitzvah dollars converted into slick, ethereal blue traveler's checks—were a photograph of Phlox, and a gold lamé sock that she left in my bathroom, sometime in July. I have often thought, since, that I know I loved Cleveland and Arthur, because they changed me; I know that Arthur lies behind the kindly, absent distance I maintain from other people, that behind each sudden, shocking breach of it lies Cleveland; I have from them my vocabulary, my dress, my love of idle talk. I find in myself no ready trace of Phlox, however; no habit, hobby, fashion, or phrase, and for a long time I wondered if I had loved her or not. But as I have found that I may fall quite completely in love with a man—kiss, weep, give gifts—I have also discovered the trace a woman leaves, that Phlox left, and it is better than a man's.

My father I will never see again, Cleveland is dead, Arthur is now, I believe, on Majorca. But because I can find them so easily in myself, I no longer—say it, Bechstein— ·I no longer need them. One can learn, for instance, to father oneself. But I can never learn to be a world, as Phlox was a world, with her own flora and physics, atmosphere and birds. I am left, as Coleridge was his useless dream poem, with a glittering sock and a memory, a garbled account of my visit to her planet, uncertain of what transpired there and of why precisely I couldn't stay. To say that

I loved Phlox implies no lesson, no need or lack of need for her. She is a world I gained and lost. I have this picture, this stocking, and that is all. I wish that I had seen her one last time.

In any case, it is not love, but friendship, that truly eludes you. Arthur and I made it from New York to Paris, and as far as Barcelona, meeting and making brief excursions into a handful of young men and women, before we found ourselves barely speaking to each other; at last, when we spoke, it was of Cleveland, as though he was the only thing left between us, and we would look sadly into our glasses of sea-dark Spanish wine. We closed ranks only imperfectly, because each was subject to a deep mistrust of the other, as well as a true and radiant affection.

I'm told, by the way, that Cleveland's funeral was a strange affair, attended by drunks, mysterious riffraff, and all his shadowy family. Feldman and Lurch, with a dozen other bikers, formed the usual MC funeral formation around the hearse. The service itself was conducted by Cleveland's great-uncle, the Reverend Arning, who was a dwarf; Cleveland's sister Anna, flown in from New York City, wore his leather jacket at graveside; his father's lover, Gerald, wept hysterically and had to return to the car. Mohammad stood the whole time, so he has said, with his arm across Jane's shoulders, dreading the moment that she should begin to cry, but, like the lover of a cancer victim who has been dying for a long time, she seemed strong and resigned and without bowing her head, watched impassively the Reverend's sorrowful, tiny hands, the subdued antics of the crowd. She wore a weird, pointy black dress that had been her mother's forty years before in rural Virginia, so that she lent her own touch of comic sadness to the funeral Cleveland could not have designed any better himself. I now regret very keenly that I missed it. I wanted to say good-bye.

When I remember that dizzy summer, that dull, stupid, lovely, dire summer, it seems that in those days I ate my lunches, smelled another's skin, noticed a shade of yellow, even simply sat, with greater lust and hopefulness—and that I lusted with greater faith, hoped with greater abandon. The people I loved were celebrities, surrounded by rumor and fanfare; the places I sat with them, movie lots and monuments. No doubt all of this is not true remembrance but the ruinous work of nostalgia, which obliterates the past, and no doubt, as usual, I have exaggerated everything.

Insights,
Interviews
& More ...

Meet **Michael Chabon**

MICHAEL CHABON'S first novel, *The Mysteries of Pittsburgh,* was originally written for his master's thesis at the University of California at Irvine and became a national bestseller. His second novel, *Wonder Boys,* was also a bestseller, and was made into a critically acclaimed film featuring actors Michael Douglas and Tobey Maguire. Chabon's philosophy behind his success as a novelist is based on three requirements: talent, luck, and discipline. As he says, "Discipline is the one element of those three things that you can control, and so that is the one that you have to focus on controlling, and you just have to hope and trust in the other two."

Chabon's third novel, *The Amazing Adventures of Kavalier & Clay,* catapulted him to literary prominence. A sweeping, epic tale of the adventures of two boys through New York City's cultural and commercial life in the 1930s and 1940s, the novel weaves together themes of the relationship between art and political resistance, the Holocaust, McCarthyism, homophobia, and friendship. An immediate bestseller, earning praise from reviewers and readers alike, *The Amazing Adventures of Kavalier & Clay* went on to win the Pulitzer Prize for Fiction in 2001. His fourth novel, *Summerland,* for young adults, casts back to an adolescent boy's Technicolor world of baseball and fantasy. Chabon is also the author of two collections of short stories, *A Model World and Other Stories* and *Werewolves in Their Youth.*

Michael Chabon has also written articles and essays, and a number of screenplays and teleplays (including the screenplay for the second *Spider-man* film). His story, "Son of the

Michael Chabon

Patricia Williams

Wolfman," was chosen for the 1999 O. Henry Prize collection and for a National Magazine Award. *The Amazing Adventures of Kavalier & Clay* was selected by the American Library Association as one of the Notable Books of 2000. In November 2004, his detective novella *The Final Solution* was published to great critical acclaim by Fourth Estate, a division of HarperCollins Publishers. ∿

66 Chabon's philosophy behind his success as a novelist is based on three requirements: talent, luck, and discipline. As he says, 'Discipline is the one element of those three things that you can control, and so that is the one that you have to focus on controlling, and you just have to hope and trust in the other two.' 99

Michael Chabon on Writing *The Mysteries of Pittsburgh*

I STARTED TO WRITE *The Mysteries of Pittsburgh* in April 1985, in Ralph's room. Ralph was the Christian name of a man I never met, the previous owner of my mother's house on Colton Boulevard, in the Montclair District of Oakland, California. His so-called room was in fact a crawl space, twice as long as it was wide, and it was not very wide. It had a cement floor and a naked lightbulb. It smelled like dirt, though not in a bad way—like soil and coal dust and bicycle grease. Most people would have used it for suitcases and tire chains and the lawn darts set, but at some point this Ralph had built himself a big, high, bulky workbench in there. He built it out of plywood and four-by-fours, with a surface that came level to the waist of a tall man standing. It might have been a fine workbench, but it made a lousy desk, which is how I used it.

I was living with my mother and my stepfather that spring, working as an assistant in my stepfather's optometry office and trying to get the hang of California. I had moved from Pittsburgh in December with the intention of applying to an MFA program out here. At the University of Pittsburgh I'd had three great writing teachers—Dennis Bartel, Eve Shelnutt, and Chuck Kinder—and of them Bartel had an MFA from the University of California at Irvine, and Kinder had studied writing at Stanford. Both gentlemen had said they would put in a good word for me at their respective alma maters. I'm sure Kinder did his best, but his effort could not avail, and in the end I found myself headed to UCI.

That winter I had been down to check out Irvine, whose writing program was staffed by a couple of novelists, Oakley Hall and MacDonald Harris. Of the seven first-year MFA candidates I met during my brief visit—they would of course be second-years when I showed up the next fall—all were at work on novels (three of which, by my count, were subsequently published—a pretty high rate). I rode the ferry and ate a frozen banana at Balboa Island, and looked at the ocean, and wondered if southern California would ever feel less strange to me than northern California did, less of a place where people I would never know led lives I couldn't imagine. There were lots of young women walking around in swimsuits and negligibly short pants, and I suppose I probably wondered how many of them I would never get to sleep with. I was kind of on a losing streak with women at the time. I was in a bad way, actually. I was lonely and homesick. I missed Pittsburgh. I missed the friends I had made there, friends of whom I felt, with what strikes me now as a fair amount of drama-queenliness, that 1) I would never see them again on this side of the River Styx and 2) they were indissolubly bound to me by chains of fire. My loneliness and homesickness were of intense interest to me at the time, as were young women in short pants, and novels, and my eternal-yet-forever-lost friendships, and when I read a page of *Remembrance of Things Past* (as it was then known), the book that was my project for the year, I felt all those interests mesh like teeth with the teeth of Grammar and Style, and I would imagine myself, spasmodically, a writer. I hope you can infer from the above description that I was not yet twenty-two years old.

I returned to chill, gray Oakland from sunny Orange County, to the little basement room ▶

66 My loneliness and homesickness were of intense interest to me at the time, as were young women in short pants, and novels, and my eternal-yet-forever-lost friendships. 99

Michael Chabon on Writing *The Mysteries of Pittsburgh* *(continued)*

in my mother's house where I did some of my finest feeling lonely and homesick. There I ventured through a few more pages of *Swann's Way* and fretted about all those people I was soon going to be surrounded and taught by, people who were and knew themselves to be proud practitioners of novelism. Was everyone obliged to write a novel? Could I write a novel? Did I want to write a novel? What the hell was a novel, anyway, when you came right down to it? A really, really, really long short story? I hoped so, because that was the only thing I knew for certain that I could manage, sort of, to write.

Now here I was, basically required by law, apparently, to start writing a goddamned novel, just because all of these windy people down at Irvine were unable to contain themselves. What kind of novel would I write? Had the time come to leave my current writing self behind?

The truth was that I had come to a rough patch in my understanding of what I wanted my writing to be. I was in a state of confusion. Over the past four years I had been struggling to find a way to accommodate my taste for the fiction I had been reading with the greatest pleasure for the better part of my life—fantasy, horror, crime, and science fiction—to the way that I had come to feel about the English language, which was that it and I seemed to have something going. Something (on my side at least) much closer to deep, passionate, physical, and intellectual love than anything else I had ever experienced with a human up to that point. But when it came to the use of language, somehow, my verbal ambition and my ability felt hard to frame or fulfill within the context of traditional genre fiction. I had found some writers, such as J. G. Ballard, Italo Calvino, J. L. Borges, and Donald Barthelme, who wrote at the critical point of language, where vapor turns to starry plasma, and yet who worked, at least sometimes, in the terms and tropes of genre fiction. They all paid a price, however. The finer and more masterly their play with language, the less connected to the conventions of traditional, bourgeois narrative form—unified point of view, coherent causal sequence of events, linear structure, naturalistic presentation—their fiction seemed to become. Duly I had written my share of pseudo-Ballard, quasi-Calvino, and neo-Borges. I had fun doing it. But no matter how hard I tried, I couldn't stop preferring traditional, bourgeois narrative form.

I wanted to tell stories, the kind with set pieces, and long descriptive passages, and "round" characters, and beginnings and middles and ends. And I wanted to instill—or rather I didn't want to *lose*—that quality, inherent in the best science fiction, which was sometimes called "the sense of wonder." If my subject matter couldn't do it—if I wasn't writing about people who sailed through neutron stars or harnessed suns together—then it was going to fall to my sentences themselves to open up the heads of my readers and decant into them enough crackling plasma to light up their eye sockets for a week. But I didn't want to *write* science fiction, or a version of science fiction, some kind of pierced-and-tattooed, doctorate-holding, ironical stepchild of science fiction. I wanted to write something with reach. Welty and Faulkner started and ended in small towns in Mississippi but somehow managed to plant flags at the end of time and in the minds of readers around the world. A good ▶

66 If my subject matter couldn't do it—if I wasn't writing about people who sailed through neutron stars or harnessed suns together—then it was going to fall to my sentences themselves to open up the heads of my readers and decant into them enough crackling plasma to light up their eye sockets for a week. 99

> **“** Most science fiction seemed to be written for people who already liked science fiction; I wanted to write stories for anyone, anywhere, living at any time in the history of the world. **”**

science fiction novel appeared to have an infinite reach—it could take you to the place where the universe bent back on itself—but somehow, in the end, it ended up being the shared passion of just you and that guy at the Record Graveyard on Forbes Avenue who was really into Hawkwind. I wasn't considering any actual, numerical readership here—I wasn't so bold. Rather I was thinking about the set of axioms that speculative fiction assumed, and how it was a set that seemed to narrow and refine and program its audience, like a protein that coded for a certain suite of traits. Most science fiction seemed to be written for people who already liked science fiction; I wanted to write stories for anyone, anywhere, living at any time in the history of the world. (Twenty-two, I was twenty-two!)

I paced around my room in the basement, back and forth past the bookcase where my stepfather kept the books he had bought and read in his own college days. All right, I told myself, take the practical side of things for a moment. Let's say that I did write a novel. Your basic, old-fashioned, here-and-now novel. Where would I write it? Novels took time, I assumed. They must require long hours of uninterrupted work. I needed a place where I could set up my computer and spread out, and get my daily work done without distraction: Ralph's room. It had served Ralph as a room of his own; perhaps it would also serve me.

I lugged my computer in there and up onto the workbench. It was an Osborne 1a. I had bought it in 1983 with all that was left of my bar mitzvah money plus everything I had managed to save since. It was the size of a portable sewing machine in its molded plastic case, with two 5 1/4-inch floppy disk drives, no hard drive, and 64KB of memory. At twenty-five pounds you could schlep it onto an airplane and it would just barely fit under the seat in front of you. Its screen was glowing green and slightly smaller than a three-by-five index card. It ran the CP/M operating system and had come bundled with a fine word processing program called WordStar. It never crashed and it never failed, and I loved it immoderately. But when I hoisted it onto the surface of Ralph's workbench, and opened up one of the folding chairs that my mother stored in the crawl space, and sat down, I found that I could not reach its keys. Even standing up I could not reach the computer's fold-down keyboard without bending my forearms into contorted penguin flippers. So I dragged over the black steamer trunk my aunt Gail had bequeathed to me at some point in her wanderings and set the folding chair on top of it. The four rubber caps of the chair's steel legs fit on the trunk's lid with absurd precision, without half an inch to spare at any corner. Then I mounted the chair. I fell off. I repositioned it, and mounted it again more gingerly. I found that if I held very still, typed very chastely, and never, ever, rocked back and forth, I would be fine. Now I just needed to figure out what novel I was going to write.

I went back out to my room and shambled irritably back and forth from the door that led to the hot tub to the door that went upstairs, mapping out the confines of my skull like the bear at the Pittsburgh Zoo. And my eye lighted on a relic of my stepfather's time at Boston University: *The Great Gatsby.*

The Great Gatsby had been the favorite novel of one of those aforementioned friends whom I had decided that, for reasons of ▶

Michael Chabon on Writing *The Mysteries of Pittsburgh* *(continued)*

emotional grandeur and self-poignance, I was doomed never to meet up with again in this vale of tears. At his urging I had read it a couple of years earlier, without incident or effect. Now I had the sudden intuition that if I read it again, right now, this minute, something important might result: it might change my life. Or maybe there would be something in it that I could steal.

I lay on the bed, opened the book's cracked paper cover—it was an old Scribner trade paperback, the edition whose cover looked like it might have been one of old Ralph's wood shop projects—and this time *The Great Gatsby* read *me.* The mythographic cast of my mind in that era, the ideas of friendship and self-invention and problematic women, the sense, invoked so thrillingly in the book's closing paragraphs, that the small, at times tawdry love-sex-and-violence story of a few people could rehearse the entire history of the United States of America from its founding vision to the Black Sox scandal—*The Great Gatsby* did what every necessary piece of fiction does as you pass through that fruitful phase of your writing life: it made me want to do something just like it.

I began to detect the germ of *The Mysteries of Pittsburgh* as I finished Fitzgerald's masterpiece: I would write a novel about friendship and its impossibility, about self-inventors and dreamers of giant dreams, about problematic women and the men who make them that way. I put it back in its place on the shelf and as I did so I noticed its immediate neighbor: an old Meridian paperback edition of *Goodbye, Columbus* by Philip Roth, the one with the lipstick-print-and-curly-script cover art by

Paul Bacon, a master of American jacket illustration who would, in a few years, design a memorable cover for the book I was urging out of myself that day. I had never read *Goodbye, Columbus,* and as I got back into bed with it I remarked—in its lyric and conversational style, its evocation of an Eastern summer, its consciously hyperbolic presentation of the mythic Brenda Patimkin and her family of healthy, dumb, fruit-eating Jews, and its drawing of large American conclusions from small socio-erotic situations—how influenced Roth had clearly been by his own youthful reading of the Fitzgerald novel. That gave me encouragement; it made me feel as if I were preparing to sail to Cathay along a route that had already proven passable and profitable for others.

There were two more crucial observations that came out of my reading of *Goodbye, Columbus* on the heels of *The Great Gatsby.* One was that Roth's book was a hell of a lot funnier than Fitzgerald's, which almost isn't funny at all, especially when, as in the famous party-guest catalog, it tries its hardest to amuse. The second observation, one of the most striking parallels between the two books, got me so excited once I noticed it that I rushed through the whole Mrs. Patimkin-finds-the-diaphragm sequence to get up again and resume my caged-bear perambulations: both books, I noticed, coincided precisely with a summer.

This was a parallel both deeply resonant and lastingly useful. I had just been through, in the years preceding my decampment for the West, a pair of summers that had rattled my nerves and rocked my soul and shook my sense of self—but in a good way. I had drunk a lot, and smoked a lot, and listened to a ton of ▶

> 66 I lay on the bed, opened the book's cracked paper cover, and this time *The Great Gatsby* read *me.* 99

great music, and talked way too much about all of those activities, and about talking about those activities. I had slept with one man whom I loved, and learned to love another man so much that it would never have occurred to me to want to sleep with him. I had seen things and gone places, in and around Pittsburgh, during those summers that had shocked the innocent, pale, freckled Fitzgerald who lived in the great blank Minnesota of my heart.

So there was that. At the same time, the act of shaping a novel, as Fitzgerald and Roth had done, around a summer, provided an inherent dramatic structure in three acts:

> I. June
> II. July
> III. August

Each of those months had a different purpose and a distinctive nature in my mind, and in their irrevocable order they enacted a story that always began with a comedy of expectation and ended with a tragedy of remorse. All I would need to do was start at the beginning of June with high hopes and high-flying diction, and then work my way through the sex, drugs, and rock and roll to get to the oboes and bassoons of Labor Day weekend. And then maybe I would find some way, magically, to really say something about summer, about the idea of summer in America, something that great American poets of summertime like Ray Bradbury and Bruce Springsteen would have understood. Maybe, or maybe not. But at least I would be practicing the cardinal virtue that my teachers had so assiduously instilled: I would be writing about what I knew. No—I would be doing something finer than that. I would be writing

> 66 I had seen things and gone places, in and around Pittsburgh, during those summers that had shocked the innocent, pale, freckled Fitzgerald who lived in the great blank Minnesota of my heart. 99

about what I had known, once, but had since, in my sad and delectable state of fallenness, come to view as illusory.

I put Roth's book back on the shelf and went into Ralph's room and shut the door. I switched on the computer with its crackling little 4-MHz Zilog Z80A processor. I was cranked on summertime and the memory of summertime, on the friends who had worked so hard to become legends, on the records we listened to and the mistakes we made and the kind and mean things we did to one another. I slid a floppy disk into drive B. I paused. Was this really the kind of writer I was going to become? A writer under the influence of Fitzgerald and Roth, of books that took place in cities like Pittsburgh where people took moral instruction from the songs of Adam and the Ants? What about that sequence of stories I'd been planning about the astronomer Percival Lowell exploring the canals of Mars? What about the plan to do for romantic relationships what Calvino had done for the *urbis* in *Invisible Cities?* What about that famous sense of wonder, my animating principle, my motto and manual and standard MO? Was there room for that, the chance of that, along the banks of the Monongahela River? I took a deep breath, saw that I was properly balanced on my perch, and started to write—on a screen so small that you had to toggle two keys to see the end of every line—the passage that after a certain amount of wrestling became this:

It's the beginning of the summer and I'm standing in the lobby of a thousand-story grand hotel, where a bank of elevators a mile long and an endless red row of monkey attendants in gold braid wait to carry me up, ▶

> 66 All I would need to do was start at the beginning of June with high hopes and high-flying diction, and then work my way through the sex, drugs, and rock and roll to get to the oboes and bassoons of Labor Day weekend. 99

up, up, through the suites of moguls, of spies,
and of starlets; to rush me straight to the
zeppelin mooring at the art deco summit
where they keep the huge dirigible of August
tied up and bobbing in the high winds. On the
way to the shining needle at the top I will wear
a lot of neckties, I will buy five or six works of
genius on 45 rpm, and perhaps too many times
I will find myself looking at the snapped spine
of a lemon wedge at the bottom of a drink.

I went on in that vein for several paragraphs,
and some of what I wrote that first session
ended up, after much revision, at the end of
the novel, which I reached in the midwinter
of 1987, in the back bedroom of a little house
on Anade Avenue, on the Balboa Peninsula,
shortly before my twenty-fourth birthday.
At some point that first evening—as, with the
help of Ralph's ghost or of the muse who first
made her presence known to me, there, in
that room under the ground, with its smell of
earth and old valises, I invoked the spirit and
the feel and the groove of summers past—I
did something foolish: I started rocking in
my chair. Just a little bit, but it was too much.
I rocked backward, and fell off the trunk, and
hit my head on a steel shelf, and made a lot
of noise. There was so much racket that my
mother came to the top of the stairs and called
out to ask if I was all right, and anyway, what
I was doing down there?

I clambered back up from the floor,
palpating the tender knot on my skull where
the angel of writers, by way of warning
welcome or harsh blessing, had just given
me a mighty zetz. I hit the combination of
keys that meant *Save.*

"I'm writing a novel," I told her. ⌒

Have You **Read?**

The Final Solution

A BRILLIANT HOMAGE to the nineteenth-century detective story.

"On par with the best, most tightly written sections of Chabon's last novel, the marvelous *The Amazing Adventures of Kavalier & Clay....* Exceptional."

—*New York Times Book Review*

"At once an ingenious, fully imagined work, an expert piece of literary ventriloquism, and a mash note to the beloved boys' tales of Chabon's youth, *The Final Solution* is a major minor work that will come to be seen as a hinge piece in the development of Chabon's art.... A prose magician, Chabon is that rare literary anomaly: a gentle-spirited writer of boundless ambition. If *The Final Solution* finds him performing that beautiful trick all great artists do—growing while remaining recognizably the same—there's no getting around that title, which points the way to bigger novels, the call of history, and the twentieth century's black heart."

—*Village Voice*

"Chabon writes with plummy luxury... the language is luscious enough to lap up."

—*Washington Post*

"Deftly composed.... *The Final Solution* is a lovingly constructed tribute to a form."

—*Chicago Tribune*

"A profound pleasure."

—*New York* magazine

A Model World and Other Stories

ORIGINALLY PUBLISHED IN 1992, this collection of eleven stories ranks with the very best of John Cheever.

"Chabon manages to locate those fleeting moments that define a young man's initiation into the complexities of the grown-up world, and to memorialize those moments with such precision that they glow with the hard, radiant energy of one's own remembered past."

—*New York Times*

"Vignettes of life in the fast and facile lane, limned in a crisp, bright prose style shot through with quick-witted insights."

—*Wall Street Journal*

"Wonderfully wry . . . a lively, intelligent writer. . . . Chabon takes on the terrible twenties with a fine eye and an eloquent tongue."

—*Boston Globe*

Don't miss the next book by your favorite author. Sign up now for AuthorTracker by visiting www.AuthorTracker.com.